Also by J. Michael Straczynski and available from Titan Books

Together We Will Go

THE GLASS BOX

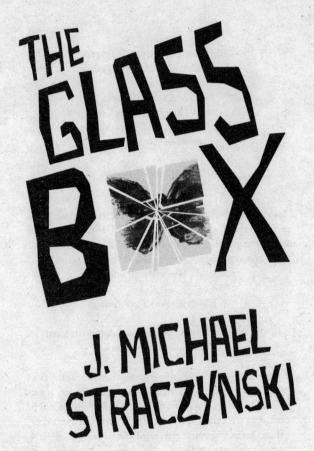

J. MICHAEL STRACZYNSKI

TITAN BOOKS

The Glass Box
Print edition ISBN: 9781803364223
E-book edition ISBN: 9781803367309

Published by Titan Books
A division of Titan Publishing Group Ltd
144 Southwark Street, London SE1 0UP
www.titanbooks.com

First edition: March 2024
10 9 8 7 6 5 4 3 2 1

A CIP catalogue record for this title is available from
the British Library.

Printed and bound by CPI Group (UK) Ltd,
Croydon CR0 4YY.

Dedicated to—
the troublemakers

The mass of men serve the state thus, not as men mainly, but as machines, with their bodies. They are the standing army, and the militia, jailers, constables, posse comitatus, etc. In most cases there is no free exercise whatever of the judgement or of the moral sense; but they put themselves on a level with wood and earth and stones; and wooden men can perhaps be manufactured that will serve the purpose as well. Such command no more respect than men of straw or a lump of dirt . . . Yet such as these even are commonly esteemed good citizens. Others—as most legislators, politicians, lawyers, ministers, and office-holders—serve the state chiefly with their heads; and, as they rarely make any moral distinctions, they are as likely to serve the devil, without intending it, as God.

Henry David Thoreau,
Civil Disobedience

Never run when you're right.

Frank Serpico

THE RULES OF ENGAGEMENT

Riley Diaz strapped kneepads over her jeans in preparation for the day's march, pulled on a heavy leather jacket, and checked her reflection: barely five feet six, slender but wiry. High-topped boots to keep her ankles from turning while running. *Check!* Fabric gloves, less likely to hold fingerprints. *Check!* Neck mask gaiter and scarf. *Check-check!* Backpack contents: first aid gear, loose cash, protein bars, nail clippers and file, cheap burner cell phone, air horn, visor, sunglasses, spare clothes, plastic raincoat, folding umbrella to defeat cameras, extra keys, tampons, water and baking soda to neutralize tear gas. *Checkety-check-check!*

Satisfied that she hadn't forgotten anything, Riley picked up the motorcycle helmet she'd adorned over the years with art and some magnificently rude comments, slid it down over her short black hair—her Cuban father's legacy—until it fit snug, then pulled up the gaiter and slapped down the faceplate. All that could be seen of her face were two blue eyes—her mother's legacy, first generation Irish American by way of Staten Island—bright enough that even the faceplate couldn't hide them. Then she grabbed the keys to the motorcycle and headed out.

Riley knew they would come for her sooner or later.

She knew it when everyone got used to seeing people penned in chain-link cages for the crime of walking from *somewhere over there* to *somewhere over here*. Then they started caging the same kind of people even though they were actual citizens of *over here*, which everyone said couldn't *possibly* happen because there were laws and guardrails against that sort of thing, except the laws got rewritten to make what was illegal yesterday legal today, and what was legal yesterday illegal today, and nobody—absolutely *nobody*—with the power to Do Something About It even blinked, and people got used to the idea and started calling it the New Normal, and once that train starts it doesn't stop until it comes right through the front door and *oh look, a pony!*

Ten thousand protesters packed downtown Seattle, a sea of voices, drumlines, banners, and rave-wear worn mostly by newbies who would zoom at the first notes of the rubber bullet symphony without understanding that their colorful clothes would just make it easier for the police to find them later. Even though the protest had been determinedly peaceful, cordons of tactical teams in helmets and Kevlar stood ready behind plexiglass shields at the other end of the street. Some held batons, while others cradled snub-nosed tear gas cannons that would be used to contain the crowd, a tactical strategy that could be augmented by automatic weapons if things went slantwise, which didn't usually happen, but that was a long goddamned way from saying it *never* happened or that it wouldn't happen *today*.

Yeah, Riley thought, *they've got weapons and tanks and shields, but we've got volume and enthusiasm on our side!*

Also, for some reason, an unusually high number of bunny ears.

Riley knew that sooner or later they would come for her when the new president rode into office on a wave of resentment after several city blocks went up in flames during the latest round of protests against urban squalor. The candidate, his spokespeople, and the TV Talking Heads Who Liked Him a Lot blamed the protesters, who had been marching in peaceful, orderly rows when the batons started falling, even though the actual footage showed Molotov cocktails thrown through windows by groups carrying the candidate's banner while yelling, "Burn it all down." But for some strange reason, the TV Talking Heads failed to mention that part of it, or the fact that all the places that *would* have been prime targets for the protesters—corporate headquarters, banks, and police stations—came through unscathed, while the low-rent housing projects that burned down were the very same buildings the protesters were trying to save, because that's where they *lived*—a remarkable irony that cleared the way for friends of the candidate to scoop up those lots cheap for redevelopment as shopping malls and hotels in the ultimate fire sale.

"This kind of criminal violence cannot be tolerated and will not be allowed to happen again," the new president said. His first official act was to revive an antiprotest program created back in 2020 that stitched together agents from the Justice Department, Homeland Security, the Bureau of Prisons, and US Immigration and Customs Enforcement into a tactical strike force answerable only to the president. A single executive order, barely noticed by the press, reassembled that coalition and created a new national police force that, after weeks of research and testing by focus groups to find the right name, was cunningly designated the National Police Force (NPF), which operated under the jurisdiction of the Department of Justice.

"This new policing system will coordinate national peacekeeping efforts, and supervise investigations across local and state jurisdictions in our ongoing effort to keep the country safe," the attorney general said, reassuring only the people who didn't fully understand what he'd just said.

In 2020, a twelve-year-old Riley had decided that she was old enough to ask her parents to bring her along to a protest. Her mother hesitated, then said, "Okay, we can start taking you along if we think it's safe, but only after we're sure you understand the Rules of Engagement."

Rule One: Never do anything illegal, remain peaceful, and never go looking for a fight. They want *you to break the law so they have a reason to come in swinging; gives 'em something to point to later as proof that we weren't peaceful protesters, we were lawbreakers and they had to step in to restore order.*

The NPF, on the other hand, was always eager to jump in, all rage and batons, dragging people into waiting vans even when nobody had broken the law. When videos surfaced later proving that the protests had been peaceful before the jump, reluctant apologies (totally insincere, but everything starts somewhere) were followed by settlements and a few badges, but that's where it ended because it's easier to boot out the *people* than change the *policies.*

Protesting isn't just about being mad at something, her mother had said, *it's about being right and true and honorable, and proving it.*

When people start getting picked up off the street for no reason, when they get disappeared or beaten, when the government falls into unethical hands and there's tyranny afoot—Riley loved that her mother used words like *tyranny* and *afoot* spoken in a voice that was 50 percent Irish lilt, 50 percent New York badass, and 100 percent do-not-fuck-with-me—*you have to do everything you can to gum up the works. You put sand in the engine to buy time for the people with law degrees and important positions to stop what's going on, hobble it, or if all else fails, show the world the truth of their intentions.*

That's why we protest. We put our boots on the ground and our bodies in the way of the Machine; we make noise, draw attention to what's happening, and force the bully boys and the tyrants to answer questions like, If what you're trying to do is so important, so right, then why are so many people upset about it, why did you hide it, and why are you lying about it now that you've been exposed, laddie boy?

Riley knew they would come for her sooner or later once the NPF started arresting protesters not because of anything they'd actually *done* but because somebody decided that they *might* do something *someday* or had the wrong attitude or deliberately chose to go outside while black or Hispanic. To *look* like trouble and *talk* like trouble was to *be* trouble, which was all the evidence the government needed anymore, and you got what was coming to you, but this just put more people in the street, because if they were going to arrest you for doing nothing, then you might as well do something. The protests grew in size and frequency—at first yearly, then seasonally, monthly, and weekly—until there were protests nearly every day over the latest government outrage.

Riley's mother had always taken great pride in the knowledge that her family had fought against the English occupation of Ireland for five generations, and that line still ran true in her. She believed in the value of protest. She believed in the Rules.

But the rules changed when the laws changed.

Masks fucked with facial recognition systems the police used to track protesters, so wearing masks at protests became illegal.

The police used rebreathers and face shields to protect themselves from tear gas, but they didn't want protesters to have the same advantage, so they made those illegal too.

Looking for a water kiosk where you can get a drink on a hot day or wash CS gas out of your eyes? Nope. Rebranded as operating an unlicensed food store, which was illegal, and *Bam! Take 'em away, bailiff!* Standby medics for when somebody gets a rubber bullet in the eye? Redefined as operating an unlicensed drug-supply store providing unauthorized medical services. Illegal. *Bam-bam!*

Meanwhile, the NPF were equipped with Armored Police Vehicles, tanks, and military-grade weapons (but strangely lacked nameplates or other identifiers on their uniforms) that let them do whatever they wanted to you, while making sure that there was nothing you could do to defend yourself, and if you tried, *ba-BAM!*

Just by showing up today, Riley had already broken at least six laws.

She glanced up as the NPF squads straightened at the same time, which only happened when orders came in through their headsets. Usually that meant somebody had just said, "Go get 'em!" but for the moment they remained in place. Sometimes they'd play it easy if there were too many cameras around or in hopes that the crowd would burn itself out as fatigue set in. But this time everyone knew that the situation had gone too far for fake-outs and compromise.

What did they just hear? she wondered. *What was the order? How long do we have?*

She didn't want to be here, would've given a kidney to be anywhere else. But the Ten-Plus ruling was too awful to ignore, even for those trying to lean into the middle, and lines were being drawn in simultaneous showdowns in dozens of cities across the country.

The Founding Fathers, being reasonably smart guys, had written that the right of the people to peaceably assemble will not be abridged. But even the brightest among them could never have anticipated the day a United States senator would stand up before his ninety-nine best pals ever and say, "It occurred to me the other day that the Bill of Rights doesn't actually mention how *many* people that right applies to in the same place at the same time."

When the NPF used this rationale to ban gatherings of any size, the case quickly landed in front of the Supreme Court—recently reconstituted to make it more politically malleable—where an attorney for the Justice Department laid out his argument.

QUESTION: Would the Court concede that an unregulated assembly of a million people in the middle of New York City would constitute an unacceptable risk to life and property?

ANSWER: Yes.

QUESTION: Does the Court also concede that the Amendment does not provide any guidance as to how many people should be allowed to assemble at the same time?

ANSWER: Yes.

QUESTION: Does the Court also acknowledge that at the time this document was written, travel was extremely difficult, making it hard for large groups of civilians to congregate in one place, further suggesting that the authors were likely thinking in terms of much smaller gatherings?

ANSWER: Yes.

QUESTION: And does the Court still agree with prior decisions made by this body concerning the Second Amendment, which stipulate that since it was written at a time when weapons were limited to muskets, it thus does not apply to some forms of heavy-duty armaments that only came along later?

ANSWER: I believe the majority still concur with those decisions and the proposition that the Founding Fathers could not have anticipated the social and technological changes that have arisen since the Bill of Rights was drafted. It has also been established, during the Coronavirus pandemic, that State and Federal Governments have the authority to limit the size and location of gatherings in the public interest, necessity, and convenience. That being the case, viewed from an originalist standpoint, what size of gathering does the Government feel was the intent of the First Amendment?

QUESTION: We're talking specifically about being outside, in open public spaces, yes?

ANSWER: Yes.

REPLY: Ten people.

Everybody assumed they'd get laughed out of court.

It passed 5 to 4.

The attorney had gone out of his way to stipulate that the new Ten-Plus restrictions only applied to outdoor settings to ensure that indoor gatherings at bars, restaurants, and country clubs were still considered legal. Baseball and football stadiums and outdoor concerts were also permitted, because money.

Within hours of the ruling, thousands of boots around the country hit the ground in opposition.

Riley was among them.

Because she knew.

They would come.

For her.

Sooner or later.

They would come.

To go outside was to risk everything.

But staying home was increasingly no safer.

Because *sooner or later.*

Fine. Bring it.

Today's protest marked week three, day four of the Ten-Plus Uprising.

Nine years, five months since her mother taught her the Rules of Engagement.

And four years, two months, and seven days since an eighteen-wheeler blew through a stoplight, T-boned their car, and tumble-dragged-pushed her parents down the street for a hundred yards before shuddering to a stop. The officer who gave Riley the news had always considered them "troublemakers" and took great pleasure in noting that there was barely enough of them left to put in a shoebox, which didn't go over well, and somehow a broom appeared in her hands and—

Riley glanced up as the police suddenly began checking their weapons and shields, and she knew that the order to advance had been given.

Rule Two, her mother had told her, *Never make the first move. Don't push them into a corner or force them to do something that there might still be a chance to avoid.*

"Here they come!" someone yelled from the front of the line.

Rule Three: Always make the second *move. That means you don't run away. Look after your people. Protect them where you can. Stand firm.*

Riley threw a fist in the air. "Boots on the ground! Bodies in the way!"

The crowd echoed the words, fists raised, closing ranks. "Boots on the ground! Bodies in the way!"

The moment when the police started to advance never failed to send a chill down her spine. Which was, of course, the intent. Uniforms, armor, horses, shields, and APVs all moving forward at the same time, perfectly synced, creating the overwhelming sense of a machine made of wheels and gears and teeth and blades that didn't give a shit what was in front of it.

Then the machine hit the front lines, and the crowd splashed and surged and pushed back, the police broke ranks and suddenly it was everyone for themselves, a roar of sirens and thousands of voices shouting at the same time, falling back or giving instructions, yelling and cursing as batons fell and flash-bang grenades flash-banged and there was blood everywhere as clouds of tear gas swirled through the crowd and the newbies ran or fell to their knees vomiting.

Somebody yelled, "Fall back!" and as the crowd pulsed south, Riley saw an old man facedown in the street, beaten and barely conscious, reaching for help, but no one was there—

Rule Four: Leave no one behind.

—and as more flash-bangs exploded, she ran to him, slung one arm over her shoulder, and began pulling him away, moving south, where there would be medics and water and they could regroup and—

Then something hit her from behind, the world kicked sideways, and she fell into the soft black.

INTERMEZZO

WASHINGTON (AP) — Dean Jurgens, the acting director of Homeland Security, announced the opening of 16 counseling centers in New York; San Francisco; Seattle; Miami; Portland, Oregon; and 10 other cities as part of the Safe Streets initiative.

"These clinics, designated American Renewal Centers (ARCs), are equipped with counselors, doctors and teaching staff dedicated to the cause of peace in our country," Jurgens said. "Many of those who take part in the mass disruptions we've seen recently are well intentioned but have allowed themselves to be used by anarchists, terrorists and agents working for foreign powers determined to tear down this country and everything it represents. These people have fallen victim to the virus of extremist propaganda designed to whip them into a frenzy of instability and convince them to walk away from family and friends, with only their paid handlers to tell them right from wrong. This programming makes them a danger to themselves and others.

"The intent of the ARC program is not to punish these people, but to free them from the influence of violent extremist propaganda so they can return to the world as functioning members of society. To that end, the DHS will assist families and local community leaders requesting preemptive interventions and give those who have been found guilty of protest-related offenses the option to avoid jail by attending these centers for six months of counseling under the guidance and supervision of dedicated, trained and caring professionals."

THE LANGUAGE
OF DOORS

Handcuffed and hard-strapped into the rear seat of an NPF police van, Riley craned her neck to peer out the window at the passing streets. The court paperwork said she was being sent to a facility in Ballard, in northwest Seattle. She'd never been to Ballard before, but so far it seemed to consist mainly of quiet, tree-lined streets dotted with restaurants and cute shops. She thought it'd be fun to stop for coffee but suspected the armed and armored cops sitting up front might have something to say about the idea.

West on Sixty-Fifth, then north on Twenty-Fourth, she mouthed silently, memorizing the streets with each new turn, less interested in knowing where they were going than being sure she could reverse the sequence to get back out again.

Because she had zero intention of staying put.

It's a hospital; assuming I can't just talk my way out, how hard could it be to slip away and get back into the fray? The first obligation of a prisoner is to escape!

Agreeing to spend six months in a mental health facility instead of the Mission Creek Corrections Center was a calculated risk. Jails were good at hurting you on the outside, but psychiatrists knew all the ways to hurt you on the inside. Some of her friends who had gone into mental hospitals for treatment came out stronger, but as for the rest, it seemed like every time they went in, a little less of them came back out again. She wanted no part of whatever *they* had in mind for *her* mind. She wanted only a wall low enough for her to climb over and get to the other side.

Four more turns brought them to a long, gated driveway beneath a sign depicting a bright ocean sunrise beside the words Westside Behavioral and Psychiatric Residences. A second sign just above it, newer and more hastily erected, read American Renewal Center #14.

They parked in front of a whitewashed three-story building labeled Inpatient Treatment. The upper-floor windows were covered in ornate wrought-iron designs: cats and dogs and giraffes and parrots woven into elaborate backgrounds of vines and branches. Bars designed not to *look* like bars to the people inside, even though that's exactly what they were. *Happy* barred windows.

They unstrapped her from the rear seat and led her through two sets of reinforced glass doors to the check-in station, where a receptionist in a bright green floral-print dress folded her hands and smiled in a calculated-to-the-kilowatt welcome.

As one of the officers handed over the paperwork, the other unlocked the handcuffs but kept a firm grip on Riley's arm in case she tried to run. The receptionist flipped through the pages and signed where required without making direct eye contact with her.

Screw that, Riley decided. Doctors, police, and serial killers had one thing in common: your odds of survival *absolutely* depended on making them see you as a human being.

"Hi!" she said, smiling broadly.

The receptionist glanced up, startled. "Hi," she said before she realized she'd done it, then quickly turned her attention back to the forms.

"Nice place."

The receptionist nodded but didn't reply, trained to avoid contact with new arrivals by remaining bureaucratically anonymous.

Okay, Riley thought. *Initiating the How Far Can I Push This Before You Realize I'm Fucking With You? program in five, four, three, two—*

"I don't want a room with a giraffe."

The receptionist paused, pen poised over the last line of the form. "Sorry?"

"The windows have animals on them, and giraffes freak me out. Something about the necks, you know? I get really nervous and scared and out of control, and I don't want to be any trouble. Can you check?"

Uncertain eyes flicked from Riley to the cops and back again. "I suppose . . . just a second."

A monitor flared to life, and with a few clicks she summoned up the details of Riley's assigned room. "It doesn't say. There's not a field for the window design."

"Can you find out?" Riley asked, still smiling.

The receptionist toggled a microphone on her desk. "This is Maria at the front desk. Could an orderly let me know what the window design is in room twenty-one forty-one?"

"Thanks, Maria," Riley said, enjoying the look on the receptionist's face when she realized that she'd not only acknowledged Riley's existence but had inadvertently provided her name.

The speaker buzzed back at her. "Parrot," a man's voice said.

"Parrot," the receptionist parroted.

"Perfect," Riley said, feigning relief.

The cop holding her arm shifted impatiently. "Can we get this over with?"

"Of course," the receptionist said, "sorry." She signed on the last dotted line, tore off the receipt at the bottom of the page, and handed it back. "All set."

She buzzed the intercom again, and a tall African American orderly came through a security door behind them.

"We're good to go," Maria said.

The orderly took Riley by the arm with 50 percent less pounds-per-square-inch of pressure, just enough to say *I've got you* without the subtext of *Does this hurt? Want to make something of it?*

As they passed into a long, puke-green hallway, Riley glanced at the nameplate pinned to his crisp white shirt: Henry.

"You know it's safe to let go of me, right, Henry?"

"Probably, yeah, but the rules say we have to maintain contact and control of all patients until they've been processed." His voice was firm but surprisingly gentle. "Just a little longer."

He led her through another set of doors—the door manufacturing business was apparently the place to be these days—to an administrative area, nodding and smiling at the support staff working in cubicles and small offices, the buzz of their voices low and efficient. At the end of the hall was an office with a brass nameplate that read Dr. Lee Kim, Chief Administrator.

Henry knocked on the open door. "The new patient's here, Dr. Kim."

"Bring her in."

Dr. Kim stood as she entered: late fifties, slender, Korean. The diplomas on the wall showed accomplishments and the photos on his desk showed a family man. "Please sit."

She sat in one of two straight-backed chairs as he settled behind his desk and checked her file on his desktop monitor. "You're here for observation under the ARC program," he said, trying to sound chipper about it. "Six months."

"Unless you want to leave the back door open and look away for a second."

He smiled thinly and glanced away. *He doesn't like this arrangement any more than I do*, she thought with a measure of hope.

"Since you're going to be with us for a while, would you like me to tell you a little about Westside?"

"Sure," she said. *Yes, let's change the subject to something more comfortable for one of us.*

"For twenty years, this was an assisted-living facility, then twelve years ago it was acquired by our parent company, upgraded, and turned into an inpatient mental health hospital offering round-the-clock treatment for acute psychiatric problems, drug addiction, anxiety, alcoholism, bipolar disorders, and depression. Our programs include individual counseling and group therapy sessions, therapeutic medications, and medical evaluation and management."

He continued to work through the list of protocols, as if stressing what the hospital *used* to do would let him avoid addressing what it was doing *now*.

"And now it's a prison," Riley said.

His face tightened. "We don't have prisoners here. We have patients."

"Well, both begin with the letter *P*, so there's that, I guess."

"Many of our patients check themselves in for treatment, but we've had a good history of working with the courts in situations where individuals are brought here because they represent a danger to themselves or others."

"So why am *I* here?"

"You came in through the courts, the usual channel."

"For the usual reasons?"

He shifted uncomfortably in his chair. "That decision is outside our jurisdiction. And technically, since you signed the transfer forms, this constitutes self-commitment."

"Then I'd like to self-uncommit."

"We can't do that."

"Why not?"

"It's not my place to discuss hospital policy—"

"But you're the administrator."

"Yes, but our license to operate requires cooperation with the state and federal agencies that regulate our industry, as well as law enforcement. The state board of health selected us to participate in the ARC program, and that's what we're doing."

"So you're as much a prisoner as I am."

He turned back to her file to avoid addressing the point. "Your records indicate that you have a bit of a temper."

"Cuban and Irish. Work it out."

"Also artistic, extremely bright, and can be very well spoken when necessary."

"Cuban. Irish."

He switched off the monitor and leaned back in his chair. "I'm going to be straight with you, Riley, because I think you're smart enough to know what's in your best interests. Under the new rules, I don't have direct authority over your treatment or the term of your stay here. All of that falls under the jurisdiction of Homeland Security and the ARC program, which, at this center, is run by Mr. Thomas McGann."

"Mister? So he's not a doctor?"

"No," Kim said, and he was grinding his teeth as he said it.

"Are all the patients here part of the ARC program?"

"No, most were here before the new mandate. So far, we have less than a dozen admissions like yourself, but I'm told that more are on the way. The original patients will eventually be moved to another hospital, but it's taking a while to find beds given how tight things were in the first place. For now, everyone shares the same facilities and common rooms. McGann has his own staff and his own priorities, which operate outside my authority. What I'm trying to say is that under the circumstances, the best thing you can do during your stay is to try to fit in."

"And if I don't?"

"I'll leave that to Mr. McGann to explain.

"One last thing," he said, lowering his voice as he buzzed for the orderly. "Our hospital is one of several that have filed a lawsuit protesting this arrangement with Homeland Security. The case will take time to make its way through the courts, possibly a long time, and there's no telling where things will end up when we finally *do* get in front of a judge. So my advice would be to avoid compromising your position while this case makes its way through the system. Don't give them anything they can use against you."

"For the next six months."

Kim raised his hands in a way that said *not my fault.* "That's the deal you signed," he said.

Then the door opened and Henry entered. "Ready when you are, Riley," he said, then smiled. "Ready Riley. From now on, that's your nickname."

Henry led her into an office new enough that it didn't have a nameplate. The man she assumed was McGann stood inside with his back to her, looking out the window. Once Henry had stepped out and shut the door, McGann turned to her, revealing a thin, severe face that was younger than Kim, probably late forties, but felt older, with hay colored hair and dark, unforgiving eyes. "Sit," he said, as though giving instructions to a dog.

She remained standing.

"I'll be brief," he said. "The waiver you signed that authorized psychiatric treatment in lieu of incarceration acknowledges that the violent tendencies you exhibited that led to you being arrested were the result of extremist influences and mental instability. The waiver stipulated your desire for corrective therapy, and ceded to us the legal authority to take whatever steps we deem necessary for your treatment, so there will be no debate on any of those subjects. During your stay, you will be evaluated on a points system. Constructive, cooperative behavior earns points. Uncooperative behavior subtracts them."

"If I get enough points, do I win a stuffed panda?"

"At the end of the six-month observation period, your accumulated points will be factored into our decision as to whether or not you have made sufficient progress to be released. If not, we have the option of extending your period of treatment for another six months. We cannot turn you loose on society if your violent tendencies remain unaltered. Should your condition remain unsatisfactory, we have the authority to prolong your stay for as long as is required to give you the help you need."

A hard knot formed in Riley's stomach as the implications sank in. Nobody had explained this part when she signed the paperwork. If she'd remained in jail, at least there would have been a clear release date. But if McGann was telling the truth, and the pleasure she saw behind his eyes left little doubt of that, there was no such thing as a statutory limit when it came to psychological disorders.

Her release would be subject to their *opinion* about her mental health, which was completely subjective.

McGann picked up a pen and notepad from his desk. "When you were arrested, several incriminating items were found in your possession, ranging from weapons—"

"It was a nail file."

"Which could have been used to gouge out an officer's eye or damage zip ties for the purpose of escape. There was also a burner phone which they managed to unlock—"

"By shoving it into my face."

"—but which did not contain contact information for the other protesters. I doubt you memorized all their phone numbers and email addresses, which means you're probably using a cloud-based text and voice-mail system. So, as a show of good faith, I want you to write down the URL for the system, your username, and password."

He held out the notepad. "And I want you to do it right now."

She took the notepad and began writing, then held up the page for him to see.

Cloud server: FUCKYOU.COM
Username: FUCKYOUTWICE
Password: ANDFURTHERMOREFUCKYOU

He tore off the page and slid it into a folder. "You've been here for less than an hour, and you're already down ten points."

"I've always been an overachiever."

He looked past her as though she no longer existed and pushed the intercom.

"So, how many points do I start with, and how many do I need to get out of here?"

"I'm afraid that's proprietary information."

How convenient, she thought, but for the moment, did not say.

The door opened and Henry reappeared. "All done?"

McGann nodded, then as Riley was led out, added, "We're here to help you. You may not understand that now, but you will in time. I believe that when this is over, you will thank us for intervening while there was still the opportunity to put you back on the straight and narrow."

"So, how're you holding up?" Henry asked once they were on the other side of the door.

"Swell," she said flatly.

He laughed at her tone. "Yeah, I hear you. Okay, just one more stop, then we'll get you to your room and you can catch your breath."

"So have you been here for a while, Henry, or are you part of the new crew?"

"Started here three years ago. It was a great place to work, lots of good people."

"And now?"

He shrugged. "Not my place to say."

He opened a door to an examining room. "Dr. Nakamura will be right in to do the admission examination. Medical gowns are on the shelf over there."

"Is this really necessary?"

"Afraid so. See you in a bit," he said, and shut the door.

As Riley shivered in the cold room, she thought about refusing to change into the thin gown but decided it wasn't worth the fight. There would almost certainly be bigger and better hills to die on later.

Once she finished changing, she sat on the examination table and waited for the doctor, growing sleepy with the silent, passing minutes.

Stress reaction. Haven't had much time by myself to process everything.
She pushed through the fatigue. *Don't give them an advantage.*

It was almost half an hour before Riley heard the rattle of paperwork in the wall folder outside the door. A moment later, the doctor—slender and dark-haired with a white coat over a deep-blue dress—stepped inside.

"Riley Diaz?" she asked with a slight British accent.

Riley nodded.

"Eleanor Nakamura." She settled onto a rolling chair near the table. "Sorry for the long wait, we were having an issue with one of the other patients. He's taking a bit of a nap now."

"So are you in charge of the ARC patients?"

"That would be Dr. Edward Kaminski. You'll meet him tomorrow, after you're settled in. I spend most of my time running individual counseling sessions in cognitive therapy, but pitch in to handle new patient admissions when the staff is busy with other things."

"Like whoever's taking a nap?"

"Exactly. So, how are you feeling?"

"I'm good."

"Excellent," she said, switching on a tablet. "I have a few questions so we can finish processing your admission for treatment, then a quick physical, and you'll be on your way. Are you having any issues with depression? Anxiety? Any suicidal thoughts?"

"Not until I got here."

The room abruptly dropped several degrees as Nakamura's gaze turned clinical, flicking from the screen to Riley.

Oh, hello, Skynet! Wondered when you were going to show up.

"We can do this quickly, or we can make a game of it," Nakamura said. "Your choice. I'm paid by the week."

"No, ma'am, no depression or any of the other stuff."

"Have you been treated previously for behavioral issues?"

"Nope."

"Any mental health issues in your family?"

"None."

Her eyes flicked up again. "You say that with a great deal of certainty."

"Never came up."

"People often avoid talking about any mental health problems they may be experiencing, but that doesn't mean those issues are invisible to family and friends. In response, we can become co-enablers, teaching ourselves not to see what we're seeing, in order to avoid confronting them with truths they don't want to hear about. So, regardless of what anyone did or didn't say, did you ever *see* anything in your family that might suggest psychological distress or instability?"

"My folks weren't crazy."

"Not what I asked you."

"Then no, I didn't see anything."

Nakamura swiped up to another screen. "Are you married or single?"

"Single."

"Boyfriend or girlfriend?"

"Not at the moment."

"What sort of work do you do?"

"Temp agency."

"Doing what?"

"Whatever they need me to do. Babysitter, assistant, cook, clearing out garages—"

"Would you say you're financially unstable?"

"These days, who isn't?"

"Do you find that stressful?"

"I get by."

"Yes or no, please."

"No."

Another screen.

"Any visible cold sores?"

"Can I borrow a mirror?"

Click! The look. *I'm a cybernetic organism, living tissue over a metal endoskeleton. Have you seen Sarah Connor?*

"No, ma'am."

"Any major traumas in your life?"

"Yes, and I don't want to talk about them right now."

"Later, then?"

"Probably not. Is there more, or can I go?"

Nakamura's fingers slid along the screen as she made a quick entry. "Do you use any recreational drugs?"

"Patient declines to answer."

Nakamura switched off the tablet. "That leaves just the physical exam, and we're done," she said, snapping on a pair of nitrile gloves. "Please lay back on the table, this will only take a moment."

"All set?" Henry asked.

Riley shrugged. Being poked and prodded by Nakamura made her feel like a piece of meat. Dismissive and as cold as the room itself. *At least the hard part's over,* she decided.

Wanna bet? another part of her fired back.

Three more puke-green hallways, four doors, and a passkey-activated elevator brought them to the second floor. Room 2141 contained a narrow bed, an empty bookshelf, one plastic chair beside a small table bolted to the floor, and a bathroom with a metal toilet and a metal mirror screwed into the wall above a sink. The few extra clothes she'd brought to the protest were spread out on the bed. Everything else had been confiscated.

"I thought we'd all be wearing hospital gowns or uniforms," she said as she picked through the clothes.

"Everyone assumes that, but no. Some patients spend years here, so the doctors want the hospital to feel as much like the outside world as possible. That way it's not too much of a shock when they leave. For the same reason, male and female patients are allowed to congregate in the common rooms under staff supervision, though for safety reasons you're not allowed to take other patients into your room unsupervised."

He began going down a series of bullet points on his clipboard. "The entire first floor is restricted to staff only. You can move around the common areas on the second and third floors as long as you don't interfere with the staff or upset the other patients. This floor has private rooms for examinations, medical treatment, individual therapy sessions, and a cafeteria. The women's shower is at the north end of the building, men's on the south. Third floor has larger rooms for group therapy sessions, an exercise room, and an arts and crafts room with music players and headphones along with some magazines, though somebody keeps tearing pages out of the damned things, so if you see who's doing it, let me know. There's a separate area on the third floor for staff members on shift that's also off-limits to patients.

"You're expected to be back in your room by ten p.m., with lights-out and lockdown at ten thirty. Rooms are unlocked at seven a.m., breakfast at eight, lunch at one, dinner at seven. Should you experience a medical emergency during the night or at any other time, there's a panic button by the bed that rings the on-duty nurse's station. If you're thinking about using it for laughs, don't—the ODNs have no sense of humor, and you'll lose a lot of points because it could take them away from someone in actual need.

"You'll get your therapy schedule tomorrow morning. If you have any nonmedical questions, you can ask me or any of the other orderlies. I know this is a lot to process on day one, but you'll be okay. I got a good feeling about you, Ready Riley. One day at a time, right?"

And then he was gone.

Riley sat on the bed, closed her eyes, and let out a long, slow breath, forcing calm. *You'll be okay. Like he said, one day at a time, right?*

When she opened her eyes again, the elongated shadow of the metal parrot in the window was stretched out on the bed beside her, cast by the fading afternoon light.

"Don't get too comfortable," she said to the shadow. "We're not staying. One way or another, we're getting out of here."

The parrot declined to comment.

ALGORITHMS
OF ADVICE

Having arrived too late for dinner, Riley decided to take a quick shower to wash off the jail and the road, then scope out the second floor in search of vulnerabilities and snacks.

She found neither. But she did run across a vending machine marked with a sign that read Staff and Authorized Patients Only. She peered through the plexiglass window at the rows of chips, pretzels, candy bars, and Life Savers. *Hello, little buddies, I missed you. Maybe I can come visit sometime.*

"Do you have change?"

She turned to see a man standing behind her, a few inches taller and a few years older than she was, with soft green eyes beneath a tangle of blond hair. "The machine only takes exact change."

"Fresh out," she said.

"You got anybody on the outside who can send you money?"

She hesitated.

Rule Five: If you get arrested, assume that anyone who approaches you on the inside is a plant gathering information to be used against you. Trust no one.

"No, nobody."

"Probably doesn't matter since you're not authorized." He dug into his pocket and pulled out a fistful of quarters. "What do you want?"

"Snickers."

As he carefully counted out eight quarters, Riley saw deep worry lines around his eyes. This was someone who felt he had to get everything right all the time.

He checked the amount again, then slid four quarters into the machine, pushed G7, and a Snickers bar tumbled into the pickup tray. More coins followed, and a bright-red Kit Kat was released from its spiral cage.

"Thanks," she said, unwrapping the Snickers. "So are you staff or an authorized patient?"

"Patient," he said.

"And how does a patient get authorized?"

"Well, you can either become the pet project for one of the doctors, or come from a family with a lot of money, and my family is *made* of money, going back six generations."

"And what are you made of?"

He pulled back a sleeve to reveal scars from deep cuts stretching up from his wrist. "Depression, apparently."

"Sorry. Didn't mean to pry."

"It's okay." He slid his sleeve back into place and began walking her down the hall. "There aren't a lot of secrets in this place when it comes to the patients. We hear each other's shit every day."

"So how did you end up here?"

"I self-committed six months ago. Well, sort of. My folks were embarrassed by me, and the scars, and my 'downer' attitude. They felt they couldn't have friends over, or parties, so they said if I didn't commit, they'd cut me out of their will. It was kind of unfair because I was already on meds and doing better, but honestly, they just wanted me gone. Out of sight and somebody else's problem. I never much cared about the money anyway, but when I told them to shove it, they switched tactics and threatened to disinherit my sister because she was always taking my side. I didn't want that to happen, so I said okay and checked in. It hasn't been too bad, really. Beats being around my folks, that's for sure. And some of the other patients, like Frankenstein, are completely fucking fascinating."

"Frankenstein?"

"You'll see," he said. "So what's your name?"

"Riley Diaz. You?"

"Steve Newman. Since the hospital's stopped taking regular cases, I'm guessing you're here because you pissed off somebody in authority."

"Yeah, I did that all right," she said.

He stepped into the arts and crafts room and started to arrange four chairs in two rows facing each other, creating a makeshift bench. "Can I give you some advice?"

"Sure."

"I saw you before you saw me, and from the way you were counting your steps, it looked like you were measuring the length of the hall. Whatever you're thinking of doing, don't. This place is solid."

"No idea what you're talking about."

"I thought you'd say that but figured I'd warn you anyway." Then he took a drop cloth from the front of the room, folded it into a pillow, laid down on the chairs, folded his arms across his chest, and closed his eyes.

Silence. A minute passed. More silence.

"Umm, okay, so, why?" she said.

"I can't sleep in my room. It never feels right. But this room . . . the smell of paints reminds me of grade school. I feel safe here. You should try it."

"Maybe another time."

"Okay," he said, and closed his eyes again.

She waited a little longer in case he had anything else to say, but when he began snoring, she walked quietly out of the room. A few steps further down the hall, she heard scraping noises coming from one of the meeting rooms. She peeked inside to see a young woman with long red hair arranging chairs into a circle as a heavyset man in his fifties looked on.

When he saw Riley in the doorway, he waved to her and grinned widely, revealing a missing canine tooth. "Come on in!" He had a slight Southern accent, a short gray beard, and wore an open plaid shirt over a T-shirt that announced Billy Joe Royal Tour, 1988.

"What's up?" Riley asked.

"Getting things ready for group tomorrow," the redhead said, blowing a stray hair out of her face. She looked a few years older than Riley, with a tight, pinched face and a heavily tatted left arm. "Callie Richardson. You just check in?"

"Riley Diaz. Yeah."

"Daniel Moss," the man said, extending a meaty paw. "Danny. Pleased to meet you."

She shook it then turned to Callie and the chairs. "Need a hand?"

"No, I'm good."

Danny laughed. "She doesn't like to share. You get extra points for helping out around the hospital, so if you jump in, she loses half the points."

"Then why aren't you helping? Don't you want the points?"

"Me? Not a chance. I'm just here for the comic relief."

"Fuck you, Danny," Callie said, flipping him off. "You can laugh all you want, but I'm getting out of this shithole."

"So you're both in for the ARC program?"

"Yep. Got here about six weeks ago," Danny said.

"Two months," Callie said, putting napkins and bottled water on the chair seats.

"But the news said they'd only started the program a few weeks ago."

"Yeah, well, they kind of had to," Callie said. "The way I hear it, they've been running this thing on the down-low for a while now. Then some reporter found out what was going on and Homeland Security offered him an exclusive on the story if he'd hold off long enough to let them announce the program like it was something they'd just come up with. I was the first one to get transferred here. Asshole over there was second."

"Were you arrested because of the protests?" Riley asked.

Danny looked at Callie and laughed. She turned bright red and threw a water bottle at him. *Guess I hit a sore spot.*

"It wasn't my goddamned fault!" Callie said. "My stupid fucking fuckface *boyfriend* was the one who jumped a cop when he already had two strikes against him which is why he told the judge it was all *my* fault so *he* got a reduced sentence and *I* got the book thrown at me which is bullshit. My folks were so pissed they wouldn't bail me out so I went for the program and now I'm stuck in a nuthouse so pardon the hell out of me if I'm really just about getting my ass out of here!"

Danny laughed so hard Riley thought he might fall off the chair. "That's what I came for," he said, offering heartfelt applause. "Drop a nickel in her and off she goes! Pure poetry!"

"Fuck you *twice*, Danny!"

"As for me, I didn't get picked up at a protest," Danny said. "I'm a preempt. They've got this mathematical model they use to predict behavior, I can never remember what they call it—"

"An algorithm?"

"Right! Algorithm! Anyway, there was gonna be this big protest in Raleigh, and I wasn't even sure I was gonna go, but a few days before, the police checked license plates and face IDs from the last one, dipped my file, saw I'd been busted at another protest for pissing on a statue of Rutherford B. Hayes—not because he was racist or anything, though he might've been, I never looked it up, but because I had a lot to drink and I needed to piss somewhere and I didn't like his look—so yeah, I got caught and fined, and from *that* they decided I was gonna go to the next protest, bust up some property or piss on stuff, and suddenly there's lights in my window at midnight, and they drag me out and arrest me to keep me from doing what they said I was gonna do even though I had no plans to even *go* to the protest, but that didn't bother the judge one bit 'cause he went along with the whole thing."

"Danny has problems with punctuation when he gets going," Callie called with her back to them.

"I don't see you embracing your inner period," Danny shot back.

"Yeah, well, none of us do, except pagans. Swear to Christ that's all they talk about: menstrual blood, star signs, and chamomile tea."

Danny laughed and slapped his hands together. "See? Just like I said. Anyway, yeah, it's true, I do get kinda riled up sometimes when I start talking. Hear tell it's quite a show. Oh, and I'm gonna preemptively answer the question I see on your face that you're too polite to ask out loud: yeah, I'm from South Carolina, and I like country music, and I'm a bit of a shit-kicker, but I've been on the front lines on the right side of history since I was eighteen, and there's more of us down there than you might think who still know right from wrong."

"Blah, blah, blah," Callie said as she maneuvered the last chair into a millimeter-perfect circle. "So how'd they get you, Riley?"

"Protest," she said, and left it there.

"Well, plenty of others here for that, with more coming all the time," Danny said, rising unsteadily. "I should probably head on back to my room, get in a little reading before they cut the lights."

He stretched, cocked his head from side to side to knock out the kinks, then said, "Want some advice?"

"May as well, everybody else seems to have something to say about what I should be doing. So what've you got?"

"Something my daddy once told me," he said, lowering his voice and looking around as if he were about to tell her the most important thing in the universe. "He said, 'Never eat anything bigger than your head, never eat food at a place called Mom's, never play cards against a guy with the same first name as a city, never get involved with anyone who's got more problems than you do, and the difference between horses and people is that they're not stupid enough to bet on what we're gonna do when somebody shoots off a gun next to us.'"

Laughing to himself, Danny headed out as Callie pulled on a sweater. "I'm going back to my room too. They take points if you're even a minute late. For what it's worth, I'm sorry you're here, sorry you had to put up with Danny, and sorry if I was kind of a bitch. This place gets to you after a while, you know? See you at group."

Once she was gone, Riley turned her attention back to the perfect circle of chairs in the middle of the room, a napkin and a bottle of water carefully centered on each seat.

Don't be a jerk, she told herself.

But because she had to do *something*, she moved one of the chairs a quarter inch to the right, then nodded contentedly at the result.

Now she could go to bed.

SEEKING SHELTER
IN METAPHORS

At 7:00 a.m. a loud electric buzz echoed through the ward as all the doors unlocked simultaneously. Exhausted and bleary eyed after a sleepless night, Riley smushed her face into the thin pillow, refusing to acknowledge the daylight. *Maybe they don't know I'm here, maybe I got lost in the admission system, maybe someone didn't get the update about which room I'm in, so if I don't move or say anything they won't know where to look for me and I can get just a little bit more sl—*

A nurse opened the door and knocked. "Riley Diaz?"

Another hope dashed. "Yeah," she said, and sat up, legs tangled in the sheets.

The nurse—tall, slender, nearly six feet, and probably middle forties—was dressed in a knee-length white uniform. A blue cap sat atop brown-gray hair pulled back in a bun so tight that Riley thought it might scream at any second.

"I'm Nurse Biedermann," she said, ticking a box on her tablet to confirm she'd found the expected patient in the expected room. "I'm in charge of all the patients on the ARC ward and your direct liaison with the rest of the staff. If you have any problems or concerns, bring them to me directly, not the doctors, unless you are in session. I will convey your issues to the appropriate staff members for follow-up. We try to keep nurse-patient interactions casual but structured, so during all conversations we stick to titles and surnames, and I expect you to do the same, Ms. Diaz."

"So do you answer to the doctors or to McGann?"

The nurse waited.

"—Nurse Biedermann," Riley finished.

"We don't discuss the administrative terms of our employment." Then another nurse entered carrying a tray of small paper cups. "This is my assistant nurse, Consuela Sanchez," Biedermann said, then checked the list of prescriptions on her tablet. "Number seven."

Consuela handed her one of the paper cups, which Biedermann then held out for Riley. "Take this, please."

"What is it?"

"Just something to calm your nerves a little. First days under observation can be difficult for some people."

"I'm fine, and I don't take anything unless I know what it is."

"Buspirone."

Riley nodded absently. She'd never heard of this one. "What's the dose?"

"You don't know what Buspirone is, do you?"

"Of course I know. Everyone knows what Busiperal—"

"Buspirone."

"—right, Buspirone is. What's the dose?"

"Ten milligrams. As I said, it's very light."

"And if I say no?"

"Are you *saying* no?"

"Yes."

Biedermann returned the paper cup to the tray then folded her hands in front of her. "Under the rules of the Washington State Medical Association, patients committed for observation who are not currently showing signs of violent behavior may decline to receive medication." From her tone she'd said this so many times that she knew the provision word for word. "However, I would remind you that this period of observation is to allow hospital staff to assess your readiness to return to society, which is at least partly determined by the degree to which you are willing to cooperate with hospital rules, regulations, and procedures. This includes your resistance to, or acceptance of, prescribed medications and other therapies necessary to your well-being and our ability to make a recommendation at the end of this period."

"Fine. It's still no."

Biedermann made another notation on the tablet, then reached into the pocket of her uniform and set a folded sheet of paper down on the table. "This is your schedule for the day. We kept it fairly easy given that this is your first day. You are expected to appear on time for all therapeutic sessions and appointments unless you have a signed exemption from one of the staff. Breakfast is offered in the cafeteria beginning at eight. Do you have any further questions, Ms. Diaz?"

"Not at this time, thanks."

Biedermann waited five seconds for her *Nurse Biedermann*. When it didn't come, she turned on her heel and padded down the hall to her next appointment.

The cafeteria was nearly full when Riley entered, drawn by the smell of eggs and toast. Danny, Callie, and most of the other patients ate silently by themselves, reading or staring out the window while others sat in small groups talking in low tones carefully modulated to avoid drawing the attention of the white-uniformed staffers stationed along the walls. Sterile-gloved servers manned a food station in front of the kitchen, where hot meals were prepared. Juice, cereal, fruit, and vegetables were available at an adjacent table.

Suddenly very hungry, Riley ordered waffles and juice. "Can I get coffee?"

"Not on the menu," the server said.

"How is that even possible? Coffee is nature's perfect food. I live *on* coffee, I live *with* coffee, I live *for* coffee."

"Caffeine interacts with some of the medications. But there are herbal teas over by the counter."

So far, not too bad, Riley thought, but she remained wary, fully aware that in every horror movie it's always that one person in the middle of the film who says, "Well, we're safe *now*," who gets a pitchfork through the heart a minute later.

As she picked up her breakfast tray and a cup of lemon tea, she saw Steve waving at her from a table where he was sitting with several other patients. "Riley, hey, over here."

"Shove over," he told the rest, pulling a chair from another table. Chairs scraped the floor noisily as they cleared a space for her. The orderlies glanced at the sound but didn't interfere.

As she took the empty seat beside Steve, an older, nervous-looking patient on his other side declined to make room as the other patients slid closer. Hispanic, with a tired, worn face that had never lost its baby fat, he began rubbing concentric circles over the surface of the table in front of him. "This is my spot," he said firmly. "This is where the wood grain makes a straight line."

The table was metal, painted green.

"This is my spot," he said again, looking at her with bright questioning eyes that were desperate for affirmation and promised tears if it didn't come. "Do you understand?"

"Don't question it; won't help," Steve said. "He's not seeing this table. Whatever he's seeing, it was a long time ago, am I right, Enrique?"

"Do you *understand*?" the man asked again.

"Yes, I understand," Riley said.

Enrique smiled and nodded happily, backhanding the just-in-case tears that had already formed.

"So did you meet Biedermann?" Steve asked.

Riley rolled her eyes. "Yeah, I did. Holy fuck. Whoever invented the term *resting bitch face* definitely had her in mind."

"Resting bitch face!" an older African American man at the end of the table repeated, then said it again, louder. "Resting bitch face!"

The orderlies positioned along the wall glanced in their direction.

"Let it go, Lester," Steve said, nodding ominously toward them.

Lester grinned with secret sin and went back to his grapefruit.

"I think I pissed her off when I asked which side she was working for," Riley said.

"Yeah, Biedermann doesn't like being questioned. She's been in charge of the general nursing staff since forever. When the ARC thing started, McGann poached her from Kim because she knows where all the levers are. Doctors may be the big shots, but it's the nurses who really run things. Handling the ARC patients is her main job now, but she still carries a lot of weight on this side of the aisle because she scares the shit out of the staff and they don't want to cross her."

"Resting bitch face," Lester whispered into his herbal tea.

"Lester's another self-commit," Steve said. "Walked in on your own power, right?"

"Yes, yes," Lester said eagerly. "I came here because I need help, and the staff have been very good to me. Very nice. I don't know if it'll do any good, because I've been here a while now and nothing's changed, but I have great hopes."

"How long?" Riley asked.

"Oh, golly, a few years, I guess. Problem is they know how to treat crazy people, and I'm not crazy. It's my insides that are the problem." He put his hand on his stomach. "It's all dead and rotten in there. I can feel it when I roll over in bed, cracking like dry wood. I tried drinking weed killer, thought that might help break it up a little, but it just made me really sick, which is why my niece told me about this place and said they could help."

"If your stomach doesn't work, why eat?"

"I can still taste," he said, his eyes sad and small and wistful. "I'm all dead inside, but I still get hungry, and I still taste, it's just there's no point to any of it. No point at all."

Then his face switched to a smile. "Resting bitch face," he whispered. "My guts may be dead, but nobody can say I have a resting bitch face."

Riley turned back to Steve. "So where's Frankenstein? I've been curious ever since you mentioned him."

"There was an incident with some of the orderlies yesterday, around the same time you got here. He goes a little out of control sometimes, so they've got him under restraint. Not straitjackety stuff, but leather-cuffed to his bed. The nurses check in on him once an hour to make sure he's okay and see if he's settled down enough to go back into the general population. Don't worry, you'll know him when you see him."

Then there was a burst of static from the PA system, and Biedermann's voice boomed through the cafeteria. "Group therapy for ARC patients begins in twenty minutes in room two seventeen. ARC patients will report to room two seventeen in twenty minutes."

"Looks like it's your turn in the barrel," Steve said. "Good luck."

Riley entered the room that Callie had straightened up the night before to find her, Danny, and five other ARC patients already seated. As she took an empty chair, a slender doctor with salt-and-pepper hair, dressed in a white coat, plaid shirt, and jeans came through the door and nudged it closed with his foot because he had a tablet in one hand and *a travel mug of coffee in the other!*

Just let me sniff it, Riley thought. *Just for a second. Hand over the mug and nobody gets hurt. Sweartagod.*

"Good morning everyone," he said, approaching the circle of chairs. "How are we doing today?"

A few of the others muttered *fine* or *good* while the rest shrugged or looked away.

"I see we have a new member of the group," he said, taking a seat on the opposite side of the circle. "Riley Diaz, am I pronouncing that correctly?"

"Yes," Riley said. "Rye-Lee."

"Good to meet you, Riley. I'm Doctor Edward Kaminski, Chief of Psychiatry. Since this is your first day, perhaps you can start off today's session by telling me and the rest of the group why you're here. Would you like to do that?"

"Not really."

Kaminski gestured toward the other patients. "All these people share your views and convictions. Why wouldn't you want to share your story with them?"

She shrugged. *Don't give them anything to work with.*

He turned to the rest of the group. "It seems Riley's shy. That's okay. Let's break the ice by having everyone else introduce themselves. Let's start with you, Becca."

A hollowed-out looking woman in her thirties, startled at being singled out, glanced up at him through a curtain of bottle-blond hair that had grown out to reveal long dark roots. "Could someone else go first?"

"I called *your* name, Becca," he said, as though addressing a child.

Riley immediately decided she didn't like him—a *lot*.

Becca looked down at her hands folded in her lap. "Um, hi, Riley, I'm Rebecca Thompson, but obviously, I go by Becca. I got here around the same time as Danny, so almost two months. I'm originally from Provo, Utah, but I moved to Portland when I separated from my husband."

"And . . . ?" Kaminski prodded.

She shifted uncomfortably in her seat. "I was arrested at a protest in Portland and given the same choice they gave you, and that's why I'm here."

"You were arrested because you made a *mistake*," he said, prompting her.

"Yes," she said, as if by rote. "I made a mistake. It was something I shouldn't have done. I fell in with the wrong people, and they got me to do things I knew were wrong. I'm glad to be here, and I know I'll come out the other side a better person."

"Very good, Becca." He said it as if she were a trained dolphin awaiting a snack. Riley wanted to put a fist through his face. "Who wants to go next? Callie?"

"We met Riley last night," Callie said. "Me and Danny."

"Ah! I see. Secret meetings."

"No," Callie said, a little too quickly. "I was fixing up the room and she wandered in."

"And what did you tell her?"

"That this was a good place, that you were a good doctor, and that if she followed the rules and dug in and worked hard, she'd come out of here better than she came in."

"Is that right, Riley?" he asked.

"Yeah."

"Good," he said, and looked to Danny. "And what did *you* say?"

"We just talked about how we got here, and I gave her some advice," he said and winked at Riley.

"About me?" Kaminski asked.

"Didn't come up," Riley said, taking Danny out of the firing line.

"Three full words," Kaminski said, and applauded. "That's the longest sentence you've spoken since we began. See? Ten minutes in, and you're already making progress."

She forced a smile so he wouldn't see her brain throwing up behind her eyes, thinking, *HateYouHateYouHateYouHateYouSOmuch*, over and over.

"Anyone else care to introduce yourself and tell Riley why you're here?" Kaminski asked.

The short, barrel-chested man to Riley's right crossed his heavily tatted arms without looking up. "Hector Ramirez, property damage." There was something about his face and voice that reminded her of an actor but she couldn't quite get there. *Who the hell is it?*

"You set a patrol car on fire while protesting outside an NPF station," Kaminski said.

Hector shrugged. "Well, yeah, that's how it got damaged."

Danny Trejo, Riley thought. *That's who he reminds me of, except not as scary.*

"Who wants to go next?" Kaminski asked.

"I'm Jim Sutton," said an African American man seated on the other side of Hector. He couldn't have been more than nineteen but he had the build of a football player. "Poli-sci major at University of Portland. Busted for defending myself against a police riot."

"For *assaulting* a police officer," Kaminski corrected.

"Matter of perspective," Jim said.

"A matter of *law*," Kaminski continued.

"Law's also a matter of perspective."

"Tell that to the courts."

"Tell *that* to George Washington, Rosa Parks, and Anne Edward."

Riley allowed a smile.

Kaminski sighed, made a notation on his tablet, then glanced up again. "Who's next? Lauren?"

A slender woman with auburn hair on the other side of the circle looked up and smiled. "Lauren Miller, 23, picked up during a protest in San Francisco. It was my third arrest, but the other two had nothing to do with protests. One was a DUI when I was in college, and the other was for shoplifting during a bad part of my life when I didn't have any money. With the whole three-strikes thing and all, I was looking at a long stay in County so I was one of the first to volunteer for the ARC program." She looked to Kaminski and the smile broadened. "Doctor Kaminski has been very helpful in getting me straightened out."

That's not the way a patient smiles at her doctor, Riley thought, and looked to Kaminski, then to Lauren, and back again.

Oh, shit . . .

Then: Don't judge. Anyone with three strikes against them would be tempted to do anything if it meant avoiding hardcore prison time.

Then: Maybe so, but I'm telling you, the eyes don't match the smile. Something's wrong.

Then: Cut it out. You could be wrong.

Then: I'm not, and you know I'm not.

Then: Yeah, I know.

By the time she turned her attention back to the room, she realized that she'd missed the last introductions and Kaminski had her back in his sights. "Everyone else is willing to talk about what brought them here, Riley. Won't you do the same?"

"Yeah, I can tell you what brought me here," Riley said. "A police van, two cops, and a pair of handcuffs."

Some of the group laughed.

Kaminski visibly darkened. *Note to self: he doesn't like having his authority challenged.*

"Then let me fill in some of the gaps," he said, "which may help you understand why *I'm* here." He fired up the tablet on his lap. "I always request a full history of a new patient's background: medical history, allergic reactions—sulfa drugs, in your case— and any other supplementary records that can help me to help them. And I was particularly struck by what I found in your background."

Riley leaned forward to see him scrolling through police records and files she'd never seen before, listing every place she'd lived, her family history, posts and photos from her social media accounts. "As I understand it, your parents started bringing you to protests when you were just twelve. That must have been terribly traumatic."

"It was my idea, I asked them to take me."

"Well, of course you did. They were your parents; you wanted to share in what they did. Since protesting mattered to *them*, it mattered to *you*. But no one at that age really understands what goes on at these things—the violence, the stress, the chaos, and the crowds. Your *parents*, on the other hand, knew exactly what they were bringing you into and should have known better, or at least waited until you were older before exposing you to this kind of psychological trauma, not to mention the risk of physical injury."

Riley bit her lip and said nothing. *He's just trying to get a rise out of you.*

"In every family, as we grow from childhood into adults, we either walk with the stream or against it. Your parents were anarchists who had been indoctrinated by extremist propaganda, so you floated downstream with their opinions, accepting their ideas without, I suspect, ever stopping to think, 'Why am I doing this, and does it make sense?'"

"I'm not here to talk about my parents."

"But that's what therapy is all about. So much of who we are begins and ends with our families. So when your parents were killed—"

"I *said*—"

"—just a few days after you turned eighteen, still in high school, it must have been terribly traumatic. An event like that can shatter a person's entire world. It's only natural to want to pick up where they left off, continuing the cycle of violent antisocial behavior, or to see the event itself as a kind of metaphor. They were killed by a truck carrying goods to market, so it follows that your subconscious would interpret that as a symbol of corporate America and want to strike back. You see that, don't you?"

You have no right to talk about my parents, she wanted to scream at him, *you didn't know them, you don't give a shit about them, you're just using them to get to me, so leave them the fuck alone.* But yelling would just give Kaminski something he could use to drill into her head, so she declined to answer and crossed her arms tightly, welcoming the pain of her nails digging into her flesh because it kept her focused on refusing to give him access to even an inch of her feelings.

"Humans are like trees, Riley," Kaminski continued. "We bend toward the nearest light source. Often we don't even realize we're doing it because that's how we were raised. My job, my *responsibility*, is to help you understand where you began to bend in the wrong direction, toward impulses that pose a danger to yourself and others.

"You're being given a second chance through this program because it's not your fault that you were misled and exploited by the very people you trusted most: organizers, fellow protesters, and yes, your parents. Most of them do it unintentionally, because they're playing out-of-date tapes in their heads, passing along old, debunked, second-generation misinformation. But for others, the subversion process is deliberate and dangerous, financed by foreign powers intent on tearing this country apart by encouraging extremist thought. They don't want you to ask questions or think for yourself. They want you scared and unstable, because that makes you vulnerable to their propaganda. So to answer the question I asked you a moment earlier, you're here because we want to help you return to a state of psychological stability, so you can become a productive member of society."

He leaned forward, tuning his voice to what he probably thought was a soothing frequency but which only creeped her out further. "It's very simple, Riley," he said. "You're here so I can *help* you."

She wanted to say, *Is that why Lauren's smiling at you like she's afraid of* not *smiling at you?* but there was always the chance of a misfire. She had six months ahead of her to figure this place out. No reason to blow up the world on day one.

"All right then," he said, leaning back in his chair. "Who else has something they'd like to share with the group?"

When the session was over, Riley made her way down the hall to a solarium that had been converted into a fake garden. Fake grass. Fake trees. Fake flowers.

Real tears.

She sat on a green metal bench, staring out into the harsh afternoon light, and angrily batted away tears. *Stop it*, she thought. *Not one more.*

During the session, she'd wanted to tear Kaminski's face off, but her mother's words kept playing through her head. *When people fuck with your mind*—though she'd pronounced it *fook*—*they do it because they want you to come at them right then and there, swinging wild, out of control, because they're ready for you, and that gives them the upper hand. That's why you have to wait. No matter how hard it is. Wait. Get the lay of the land. Find their strengths and weaknesses. Figure out who your allies are and who's looking to sell you out. Don't rush it. The time it takes is the time it takes. When you think you can't wait a second longer, wait some more. Wait until they decide you're not going to do anything about whatever they did to fook with you. Wait until they lower their guard and stop looking in your direction. That's when you come at them with everything you've got, hard and fast. And once you start, no matter what happens, you don't stop until you've absolutely and completely destroyed them.*

If you look up revenge *in the dictionary,* she'd said, *you won't find anyone's picture, just a really good description of what that word means. But if you look up who invented, patented, and trademarked revenge, it's the Irish. So trust me on this one.*

She was right. She was always right about that stuff.

But that didn't make it any easier.

"Is it all right if I sit?"

She looked up to see a white-coated doctor standing beside her: heavyset, probably close to three hundred pounds, with thin white hair and a matching beard that framed a wide, pale face.

"Sure," she said distantly, and started to stand. "I should go anyway—"

"I'd rather you didn't." Using a cane, he leveraged his massive frame onto the bench. "Julian Munroe, director of Inpatient Psychiatric Services," he said, extending his hand.

She didn't take it.

"Fair enough," he said, withdrawing the hand. "It's only noon and I imagine you've already had quite a day."

"You'd know," she threw back.

"Actually, I wouldn't. Oh, sure, in prior years nothing happened here without my knowing about it, and trust me, there were times when it involved petty interpersonal squabbles that I would've much preferred to be out of the proverbial loop. But ever since our staff was split by the ARC program, I don't hear much from the other side.

"I was sad to see it happen, you know. I was sure the others would refuse to take part in McGann's operation despite the state board's recommendation, because that would've forced him to go elsewhere. But there will always be people like Saruman, who'd rather lean into power than stand against it if the money's right or if it means being given unchecked authority over other people, which for some people can be even more attractive and considerably more addictive. 'Power corrupts, and absolute power corrupts absolutely.' Lord Acton said that, but honestly, it might just as well have been Gandalf."

Riley squinted against the sunlight to get a better look at his face. It was round and soft and there was a smile in the middle of it. *Okay, this is different.*

"Their willingness to lean into the dark side is what sets them apart from, say, the storm troopers in *Star Wars*," he continued, "who don't have much choice in which side of the Force they serve, they're just doing what's necessary to avoid getting shot or mind-choked by Vader. Which is what separates them from the Klingons, who do messy things to people because they like it."

Riley smiled despite herself. "Are you an *actual* doctor or just a patient who *thinks* he's a doctor?"

"Do you want to see some ID?"

"Yeah."

He pulled out a wallet, and the paperwork matched the allegation.

"So why are we talking like this?" she asked as he slid the wallet back into his jacket.

"It's my never-fails, always-works First Amendment free-speech methodology for talking about people in terms that everyone understands but won't get me dragged into a courtroom. No one has ever said to a judge, 'I'm suing because he called me a Klingon!' They'd be laughed right out of court."

He laced his fingers over the cane's silver handle and turned toward her. "In a reluctant nod to what remains of my position, McGann is required to brief me on new admissions to the hospital, and I still have the authority to speak with ARC patients and consult on cases when requested, but unfortunately, that's where my influence ends."

"So you *have* read my file."

"Nope."

"Why not?"

"Because as someone who took part in his fair share of protests when I was thirty years younger and fifty pounds lighter, it's my considered opinion that you have no business being here," he said, his voice surprisingly hard. "You *shouldn't* be here, because, as I have stated repeatedly to Mr. McGann, expressing an unpopular or controversial opinion is not a form of mental illness."

"So would he be Darth Vader?"

"No. Emperor Palpatine, maybe. This whole ARC business started off as his idea. He sold it to the head of Homeland Security, who sold it to the attorney general. They gave him money and a mandate to find someone on the mental health side to take his ideas and make them work. That led him to Kaminski, and the two of them partnered up to work out the details of the program. Once that was done, they took this place over as proof of concept, then added more facilities around the country as they fleshed out the program."

"You said, 'proof of concept.' What concept are they proving?"

Julian started to answer, then pulled back whatever he was about to say. "I have my suspicions about where this is all going, but for now that's all they are. The only thing I know for sure is that McGann and Kaminski are seriously invested in making this work, which is a pretty clear indication that there must be something bigger lined up down the road."

"If they're in charge of the ARC program, and it started here, why does the sign out front say ARC center number fourteen?"

"Moving the numbers around is how they obscure the chain of command. Everyone in Chicago is protesting ARC center number one because they think that's the epicenter for this wrongheaded conflation of civil protests and mental illness. Meanwhile, McGann gets to sit here in the middle of his web without anyone bothering him."

"So, Shelob the spider?"

"Yes. He wants to be Palpatine, but for now he's just a spider with a pituitary condition."

"Are you sure you're not worried, talking like this?"

He shrugged. "At my age there's not much they can do to me. Besides, they know that if they get too much in my face, it'll give Dr. Kim the grounds he needs to trigger all kinds of administrative reviews, and that's the last thing McGann wants."

"So are you Obi-Wan or Dumbledore in this story?"

He grinned. "I suppose we'll have to see how it ends."

"What about Biedermann? Who's she in all this?"

"I don't know," he said, and his voice grew soft. "She puzzles me. I know she's enthusiastic about her work, but beyond that . . . I don't know."

"And Kaminski? What story does he fit into?"

He leaned back against the bench, looking around for the first time to make sure no one was near enough to hear. "Seeing you leave his group therapy session looking distressed is why I sought you out. Some people get into psychiatry because they want to help people. Others do it because they enjoy climbing inside someone's head and taking it for a spin, even if that means driving it off a cliff. *Especially* if that's what it means. Kaminski enjoys having power over other people. He's good at what he does; he just has a disturbing tendency to do it the wrong way, for the wrong reasons, which is one of several reasons I was going to terminate his contract. But as it turned out, Kaminski's frivolous attitude toward ethical matters is the very reason McGann partnered up with him and gave him the keys to the kingdom.

"So to answer your question, I'd compare Kaminski to Snape for attitude, but that's where it ends, because as we know from the last *Harry Potter* book, Snape had something resembling a heart. If you look into Kaminski's eyes, all you see are little machines that can't wait to chew through your skull to whatever's on the other side. So be careful what you say around him, what you bring into the therapy room, and what you take with you when you leave. If you let him start crawling around inside your head, you'll never get him back out again.

"I'm telling you this for the same reason I told some of the others: you were brought here under unethical circumstances, and as far as I'm concerned, that supersedes any problems I might normally have when discussing certain issues and individuals. It's far more important to make sure you have the information needed to cope with what's going on here, because in a place like this, knowledge is power."

Looking suddenly tired, Julian glanced at his watch, sighed, then pulled himself to his feet slowly and with effort. "Gets a little harder every day," he said, red in the face. "I'd planned to retire this year, spend some time traveling, but I'm not about to leave while all this is going on."

He turned to face her, leaning on his cane. "As I said, I still have some privileges and minor influence here, which includes doing grand rounds in your ward every Friday afternoon. If you should find yourself in a bad place but not in a position to speak frankly when I come to see you, just say, 'Good morning, Dr. Munroe.' Just like that." Then he started toward the door.

"If you make your rounds on Friday afternoons, won't the other doctors think it's strange that I say good morning?"

He smiled over his shoulder at her. "It's a mental hospital," he said. "Work it out."

The wing of the building set aside for ARC patients was on the north side of the hospital, with the regular patients in the south and east wings. So Riley decided to loop through the south wing on her way back to her room from the solarium to continue familiarizing herself with the layout. The ARC rooms were pretty secure, but she hoped there might be vulnerabilities in the other wards she could exploit when the opportunity arose.

As she started down the hallway, which had been painted a soft robin's-egg blue, she stopped at the sound of a strange noise. It sounded like *hurrrrrrrr*. She assumed it was coming from the air conditioning building one floor down, but there was something not quite right about it, and she paused in case it came again.

Hurrrrrrrr.

Looking around to make sure she was alone, Riley followed the sound to the open door of one of the rooms and peeked inside. A man dressed in shapeless black pants and a worn black sweatshirt was lying flat on the bed, arms restrained by leather cuffs attached to metal guardrails on either side. His body was that of a young man, tall and massively built, but what she could see of his face was gaunt, his cheeks hollow, as though the skin had been stretched tight to cover his skull. He was staring straight up at the ceiling past a cascade of dark hair, and the light from the window cast such deep shadows over his sunken eyes that it took her a moment to realize he even had them.

Then he slowly turned his head, eyes lolling to the side until his gaze met her own.

"*Hurrrrrrrr . . .*"

Don't worry, you'll know him when you see him.

A lifetime ago, Riley had watched a documentary about mental patients who believed they were someone famous or important: the president, the queen of England, Christ, Sherlock Holmes, Michael Jackson, or in this case—

"*Hurrrrrrrrrrrrrrrrr . . .*"

—Frankenstein.

"You shouldn't be here."

Riley turned, startled to find a nurse standing behind her. "Common areas are shared by all patients, but the ward rooms on this side of the hospital are off-limits to ARC patients."

"Sorry," Riley said, backing away from the door to let her pass. "I got lost. First day here."

The nurse went to the figure in black, checked his temperature and blood pressure, and loosened the restraints. "We were just getting him calmed down," she said impatiently. "There's been a lot of construction going on outside, and the noise upsets him. Strangers also upset him, so if you don't mind, please head back to your wing before I call an orderly."

"Yes, ma'am," Riley said. As she started to turn away, she saw that his eyes were still locked on hers. Dark. Dead. But behind them, the slightest flicker of vulnerable curiosity.

"See you around," she called to him with a smile.

"*Hurrrrrrrrrrrrrrrr . . .*"

DEGREES OF
FUCKEDUPEDNESS

Day Two began the same as Day One.

At 7:00 a.m. the doors to the ward rooms buzzed open.

At 7:05 Nurse Biedermann entered, trailing Assistant Nurse Sanchez, a tray of medications, and a lifetime of resentment.

"Pass," Riley said, sitting on the hard bed.

Biedermann looked to the nurse. "Make an entry. Patient continues to resist medication."

"Patient *declines* medication," Riley corrected.

Biedermann regarded her with an expression as emotionless and implacable as an Easter Island megalith. "Second notation," she told the nurse, "patient resists analysis."

"Well, that's been true pretty much my whole life, so yeah, that's fair," Riley said, and flashed Biedermann a smile.

It was not returned.

Hurrrrrrrrrrrrr.

Fifty-five minutes later, Riley was having breakfast with Steve, Callie, and Danny, trying not to be too obvious as she watched a nervous orderly at a nearby table sliding small forkfuls of waffles past Frankenstein's lips, moving slowly and carefully in case the exposed teeth went for his hand.

"So you two met?" Steve asked, nodding to the ominous figure across the room.

"Yesterday. Just for a minute. We didn't exactly have a conversation."

"He doesn't talk to anyone," Danny said. "At least I've never seen it happen, but then I don't see a lot of him. Nobody does. Rumor is he found someplace where he can hide from the staff when he doesn't want to be found. It makes them crazy."

"What's wrong with him?"

"They used to call it *delusions of grandeur*, but not every delusion is grand, so they changed it to *expansive delusions*," Steve said. "At least that's what I heard one of the doctors say when they were talking about him, that it was some kind of psychosis, or schizophrenia—"

"No, I mean, what *happened* to him? Why is he like this?"

"No idea," Callie said, "and honestly, I don't care. He's weird, end of story—sorry, not sorry—and not interested in hearing more. As far as I'm concerned, the less I know and the sooner I get away from all the freaks in this place so I never have to think about it ever again, the better I'll like it."

"How about you, Steve? How much longer do you have to stay here?"

"Two months. By then my sister will come into her trust fund and I can go home."

Riley nodded at the scars on his wrists. "And once you're out, you won't do *that* again, right?"

"No idea. Depends. But I guess that applies to all of us, y'know?"

Riley nodded but didn't comment as a patient at the other end of the room took two bites of toast, got out of his chair, walked six paces up, six paces back, returned to the table, ate two more bites, then stood and did it all again.

"It's his routine for everything he eats," Steve said, catching her look. "If he gets interrupted, he starts screaming and has to begin all over again. Classic pattern behavior."

"You seem to know a lot about this stuff," Riley said.

"Self-defense," he said. "Know thy enemy."

"Did you know most patients in mental hospitals want to be psychiatrists when they get out?" Danny said. "Totally true. That tells you a lot about the patients, but it tells you even more about the doctors."

"So is there any way to make a call around here?" Riley asked. "Even in jail there was a pay phone."

"Phone privileges for ARC patients are based on the point system," Danny said. "In theory you can use the landline in McGann's office if you get enough points, but nobody's done it, because we figure it's hooked up to a recorder."

"Things are a little looser on this side for self-commits," Steve said. "If there's someone you want me to tell you're here, give me their name and number, and I'll see what I can do."

Riley hesitated. *You seem like a nice guy, but I'm gonna need to know you a lot better before I give you one of my contacts.*

Instead, she just nodded and said, "Okay, thanks, let me think about it." Then she glanced up as Jim tapped her on the shoulder from behind.

"Can I talk to you for a sec?" he asked.

"Sure."

Once they were out in the hallway, Jim leaned against the wall, his voice low. "I just wanted to say that was a great performance you gave in yesterday's session, but just so you know, we have a quarantine period for anybody new joining the group before we start to trust them. It's nothing personal. We just need to decide if you really are who you say you are or something else."

When you're incarcerated, everyone there before you will assume you're a plant or a snitch, her mother had told her, *and you'll assume the same about anyone coming in later. It's an evil logic, but a necessary one.*

"So you speak for the group?"

He shrugged away the question. "I'm just carrying the message," he said, and went back inside.

And how do I know that you're *not working for the other side and trying to hide the fact by throwing suspicion onto* me?

No, wait, let me save you the trouble.

I don't.

On Wednesday and Friday afternoons, the staff unlocked the exercise room from two to four. Riley was first in line when they opened the doors and grabbed an available treadmill, desperate to run the last two days out of her system. She needed to not think about therapy, who she could trust, who trusted her, where she was, or what she was going to do about it.

She had walked and slept and sat and paced for two days. Now she needed to pretend the walls weren't there, and just *run*.

She'd barely hit the 1K mark when Lauren stepped onto the treadmill to her right. Riley frowned but kept running. *She could've gone to any of the others, but no, she picked* this *one because she's gonna want to talk to me and I don't want to talk to her or anyone. I just want to run, can I please just run and not talk or be bothered for two minutes?*

"Can I talk to you?" Lauren said.

Right on schedule, Riley thought. "Sure," she said, but kept her eyes on the horizon that wasn't there.

"I saw the way you looked at me in session yesterday, and I don't know what you've heard but—"

"I don't know anything, I haven't heard anything, I was just—"

"—but I wanted to tell you myself, straight up: yes, I'm doing some things I probably shouldn't be doing, but—"

"Not judging, just running."

Lauren slowed, then stopped. "I have a three-year-old son," she said. "I divorced his father last year because he was always drunk or high, and frankly, I got tired of getting beat up all the time. When they arrested me, the court gave custody of Tommy to my ex. God only knows what kind of conditions he's living under, because I sure as hell don't, and nobody will tell me.

"I need to get out of here, Riley. I need to get my son away from that prick, and if the only way I can do that is to fuck every doctor, intern, and orderly in this goddamn place, then that's what I'll do. I'll do it *twice* if it gets me out of here and back with my little boy faster. So honestly, keep your judgments to yourself, okay?"

Riley sighed and stepped off the treadmill. "Lauren, nobody told me squat about your situation, and if that's really the reason you're doing it, I understand—"

"What do you mean, *if* it's the reason? I just told you—"

"I'm only saying that whether it's true is none of my business. I just want to put in my time and get out, same as you. So I apologize if my look offended you, or if you thought I was being judgy, and yeah, maybe I was a little, but now that I know your story, I won't be."

"It's not my *story*, it's the *truth*," Lauren shot back, as if looking for a reason to be offended. "So go fuck yourself, all right?" Then she stalked out of the gym, slamming the door behind her.

Riley stepped back onto the treadmill. *Fuck my life*, she thought angrily, and started running again.

Three p.m. twice weekly was set aside for Peer Group Counseling. Riley wasn't sure what that meant until she showed up and found only other ARC patients in the therapy room, no doctors or nurses.

"This is where we just talk among ourselves," Danny explained as he took an empty seat beside her.

"Talk about what?"

"Anything except what they want us to talk about. Big stuff, small stuff, personal stuff, sports, politics—it's all good as long as it doesn't get into, like Kaminski said, 'the things that brought us here.'"

"Good," Riley said, though she was no more inclined to participate here than she was in the other sessions. *The less anyone who's locked inside with you knows about you, the less they can use against you or trade to someone else for favors. Of course, the more you hold back, the harder it is for the others to trust you, but it also works the other way. If you give them your whole life story, it sounds like you're trying too hard to win their confidence, and that always bounces back the other way.*

There was no one in the entire hospital, including Steve, who she felt she could trust, and since nobody was willing to trust her, she'd decided to go her own way, keep her head down, and stay focused on getting out rather than making any new best buddies.

After the rest of the group had filed in and the door was shut, Danny started the session. Riley was surprised that the authority had fallen to him, but it soon became clear that everyone liked Danny. As much as he enjoyed hearing his own voice, he seemed genuinely interested in what the rest had to say, even Callie, despite their apparent antagonism. A joke Danny told about a farm that raised three legged chickens—"How do they taste? We don't know, we've never been able to catch any of them"—even managed to get a smile out of Lauren, giving her a momentary break from staring knives into Riley's face.

"So what's the one thing you're most looking forward to about getting out?" Danny asked. "And what do you miss the most? Aside from sex, obviously."

"Danny's only taking sex off the table because he hasn't had any since he was an altar boy," Callie said.

"I neither confirm nor deny. Jim? How about you? What do you miss?"

"Oh, man," Jim said, rubbing his high-boned cheeks, "Gaming. Especially VR. This past summer I bought a whole new VR system just so I could play *Star Horizon*. Got hooked when I was a kid, playing *Skyrim*, *Half-Life*, *No Man's Land*, *Superhot*—all of 'em. My dad did beta testing for one of the big gaming companies, which meant we always had everything first, so you can guess whose house everybody came to after school. As a black kid in a small town in Wisconsin that was ninety-nine point five percent white, that shit made all the difference when it came to making friends. Doesn't matter if you're the black kid, the Hispanic kid, the nerdy kid, the weird kid, or if you've got two heads, feathers, fangs, and fur, if you've got a game before it hits the stores, you're golden, and I liked that feeling a *lot*.

"Funnily enough, that's also what put me on the road to poli-sci. I'd play these games about exploring other worlds, and while everybody else was busy blowing shit up, I'd look at those places and wonder what sort of people lived there. What kind of clothes did they wear? What language did they speak? What form of government did they have? After a while I started making up whole civilizations, just to amuse myself. Then I found out that if you got a degree in poli-sci, you could actually make a living figuring that stuff out, so I was like, hell yeah, sign me up!"

A hand shot into the air, belonging to Angela Chao, one of the names Riley hadn't heard when she shut down the world during their earlier session. She had a broad face that never seemed to run short on smiles, even when she was sitting by herself. "Pizza!" she said. "I miss pizza! The frozen pizza we get here isn't the same as a fresh pizza with real cheese and sauce that somebody made with their own hands and pulled out of the oven two minutes ago."

"Pizza I can definitely get behind," Danny said.

"Lots of pizza up front too," Callie said.

The group laughed as Danny sucked in his gut. "I have no idea what you're talking about. This is a six-pack stomach, and I was pleased and proud to get it in a two-for-one sale."

"I miss my brother," said Hector, the only member of the group who seemed to say less than Riley. "We were tight, you know? Like two ends of the same thought. He was there with me the whole time I was in court, never even thought about walking away."

"Didn't you say he was going to talk to a new lawyer for you?" Angela asked.

"Off-limits," Danny said.

"No, it's okay," Hector said. "When I signed the papers, he said he knew a guy who'd take the case for free because it's a complete violation of my civil rights. Gonna file papers any time now, so we'll see how it goes. My bro, man, once he gets going, he never *ever* lets up."

"How about you, Riley?" Danny asked. "You got any relatives outside fighting the good fight?"

"Not really," Riley said, choosing her words carefully to avoid giving anything away. "My folks are dead, like Kaminski said, and they didn't have any other kids. I've been on my own for a while."

"Must be hard," Angela said. "I don't know what I'd do without my family being there for me through all this."

Riley shrugged. "I guess you get used to it after a while."

"What were they like?" Danny asked.

"They were okay," Riley said, trying to be casual despite the heat coming up behind her eyes. "They were, you know, my folks. We got along."

"She doesn't trust us," Lauren said, glaring at Riley from the other side of the circle. "Like we're gonna run to McGann and tell him what her parents were like when nobody gives a shit, when for all we know *she's* the one we need to worry about."

"C'mon, Lauren, go easy," Callie said. "This is just us, okay? Besides, I remember when you got here, you were the same way."

"Bullshit," Lauren said. "I was shy for a few days, that's all. I think when somebody comes into the group and doesn't say anything and just listens all the time, it's worth asking if she's doing all this listening for herself or somebody else."

"Go ahead and ask," Riley said, her cheeks flushing angrily. "If you've got something to say, say it, otherwise back it the fuck up."

Lauren feigned indifference. "Maybe later."

"Okay, I'm gonna call a ten-minute break," Danny said. "Give everybody a chance to cool down. Then let's come back and talk about other stuff, all right?"

"Sure thing," Lauren said, smiling broadly and fraudulently.

Riley closed her eyes and tried to make it all go away. *I've so got to get out of here.*

Patients were allowed two hours of unstructured time before dinner, and Riley used hers to continue scoping out the hospital for details she could add to the map she was drawing on construction paper she'd liberated from the art room, now carefully hidden in her room's air vent. As the sun began to set, she found herself back in the solarium. She left the lights off and approached one of the big windows that looked out over a residential area on the other side of the hospital's parking lot. Long shadows stretched across houses where dinner would be served soon, as kids lingered in front yards, calling for a hoped-for *Ten minutes more, Mom, c'mon!*

So near and yet so far.

The solarium was so dark and quiet that it took her a moment to realize she wasn't alone.

Turning her head slightly to the right, she saw a familiar figure dressed in black standing with his back to her as he gazed out a window at the other end of the room, his silhouette outlined by streetlamps. She didn't know if he'd been there the whole time or if she hadn't heard him come in; it was as if he'd simply materialized.

Rumor is he found someplace where he can hide from the staff when he doesn't want to be found, Danny had said.

Riley considered backing out quietly and leaving him to his carefully sought-after solitude, then pushed the thought down hard. *Then I'll be just like everybody else, walking around him or pretending he's not there.*

She gave it another minute to see what he'd do, then started moving slowly in his direction, gaze turned toward the street to avoid making direct eye contact or appearing threatening. *Like I could do anything to hurt him*, she thought, *he's twice as big as me.*

She stopped a few feet away, in case he made a grab for her, and remained there for several minutes, standing side by side in the shadows, staring out at absolutely nothing.

Screw this, she thought at last.

"You're doing this wrong, you know that, right?" she asked.

No response. Dead eyes piercing the night.

"Because here's the thing," she said. "My dad was a big horror fan. I mean, huge. You name the book or the movie, and if it's got monsters or demons or anything that wants to eat your brains, I guarantee he saw it or read it. When he was a kid he wanted to be a horror writer, like Poe or Lovecraft or Stephen King, but as he got older he could never quite get there because he was always busy working construction and chasing off-the-book jobs to fill in the gaps, so there wasn't time to learn the stuff that I guess you have to learn before you can start writing words that anybody's gonna want to read. But he never stopped loving horror, so by the time I was eleven I'd seen every George Romero movie ever made, and all the Universal horror movies about Dracula, the Mummy, the Werewolf— "

She paused. *You started the sentence, now finish it.*

"—and Frankenstein."

She looked over to gauge his reaction, finding only silence punctuated by the whisper of his breathing.

"Anyway, not only did I see all the movies, I read all the books, and that's why I said you're doing this all wrong. In the book, Frankenstein's creature . . . I don't call him a monster because when you really come down to it, Victor Frankenstein was more of a monster than what he made . . . the creature is *smart*. He reads a lot, and talks a lot, like a *lot* a lot. He knows Latin and poetry and mythology and philosophy . . . honestly, he would have done better in school than I did. Probably would've ended up giving the valedictorian speech."

A small voice in the back of her head said, *You've just used more of your words in the last thirty seconds than the whole time since you got here. And you never talk about your folks to strangers. So what's the diff?*

Maybe because unlike everybody else in this place he's not trying to pry it out of me, because he doesn't give a shit.

"My dad used to say that the Frankenstein in the book was the *real* one, and that the only reason the movie monster spent most of his time grunting at people was because nobody back then was really sure if Boris Karloff could act. He'd only done small parts before that, so they didn't want to risk giving him a lot of dialogue. They never really believed in him, which is why every time they made a new Frankenstein movie, it ended the same way: after the creature destroys whoever's trying to destroy him, he goes over a waterfall, gets burned alive in a windmill, or frozen in a lake. End of story, end of franchise, end of Boris, except the creature wouldn't stay dead, and neither would the movies. So after a while they finally let him talk a little, like in *The Bride of Frankenstein*, right before the castle blows up, when he tells the guy who made him, 'We belong dead.' Cool moment, long overdue."

He straightened a little at her words. *Okay, he's definitely seen that one for sure.*

"So in my opinion, which is totes subjective, if you *really* want to be Frankenstein, then you need to, y'know, *talk* to people, maybe read some books. That way we can sit around discussing poetry and philosophy and stuff like that. What do you think?"

He stared out at the night.

He stared out at the night.

He stared out at the night.

"Hurrrrrrrrr," he said at last.

"Okay, I'll take that as a *yes*," she said, and turned her attention to the world outside the window, allowing the soft safety of silence to sneak back into the room.

"I want to talk about rage," Kaminski said.

The group said nothing, waiting to see where this would go.

"We touched on the subject the other day, when Riley joined our merry band of misfits, but I want to do a deeper dive into the subject because I think that for many of you, this is the heart of the problem. Rage brought you here by making you vulnerable to people who could weaponize that anger for their own purposes."

"I'm not mad at anybody about anything," Jim said. "I'm the happiest man I know."

"People who are happy with their lives don't spend all their time joining angry crowds and telling the world how terrible things are."

"So you don't think people should get upset if their government is doing something wrong?"

"Of course they should. And there are civil, appropriate, *healthy* ways to address that. Rage is unhealthy, self-destructive, and almost always springs from something in our personal lives that has nothing to do with what we *say* we're upset about. The technical term for that is *transference*. You can't strike back at A, so instead you take it out on B. Like the guy whose boss is a jerk, but he can't quit or tell the guy off, so when he comes home his family inherits all that repressed anger through domestic abuse. We saw that sort of transference with Riley the other day. Her parents were killed in an accident with a shipping truck, but she can't take revenge against the driver, so she transfers that anger to the company and the system that sent it out on the road that day."

"Not true and leave me out of this," Riley bristled.

"All right," Kaminski said, "if you don't want to discuss it, then let's talk about Hector."

Hector straightened, surprised at being ricocheted into the conversation. "Don't know what you're talking about," he said. "I'm with Jim. Mister Quiet. Peace out, twenty-four seven."

"But is that really true, Hector? Are you sure there's nothing you'd like to share with the group?"

"Yeah, I'm sure."

Kaminski shook his head and sat back in the chair. "I'm disappointed in you, Hector, I truly am. I thought we were making real progress." He flicked through the screens on his tablet until he found what he was looking for. "Who is Domingo Ramirez?"

Hector stared down at the carpet.

"Tell the group who Domingo Ramirez is, Hector."

"My brother."

"Ever since you got here, you've been telling everyone that you and he are tight, and that he's working hard to get you out of here. Is that correct?"

"Yeah, so?"

"It's just that, as I understand the situation, you haven't been in contact with your brother for months."

Hector's face tightened, but he didn't respond.

Kaminski glanced down at the tablet. "According to this police report, a few days before the incident that brought you here, there was an altercation between you and your brother that sent him to the hospital. What was that about?"

"You don't have to tell him shit," someone said, and Riley was as startled as the rest to realize that it was her.

"Yes, you do," Kaminski said without looking at her, his voice low and firm. "Assuming you want to get out of here when your observation period expires."

"Yeah, we had a fight," Hector said at last. "He was pissed that I dropped out of college."

"Was he mad at you because you dropped out, or because you didn't tell him?"

"Because I didn't tell him."

"So you lied to him."

Hector shrugged, absently rubbing his fingers against the back of his left hand. "I guess. Yeah."

"Is it *I guess* or is it *yeah*?"

"Yeah. I lied to him, okay?"

"And when your brother confronted you, you became enraged—not because he was wrong, but because he was right."

"Yes."

"You lashed out at him because he caught you pretending to be something other than you actually were, because you didn't want to admit the truth, and because you're *afraid* of the truth, which is why you lied to the members of this group, people you consider friends, when you said your brother was still in your life."

"Yes," Hector said, and there was shame in his eyes.

Don't let him inside your head, Julian had warned Riley, and now she was beginning to understand why he didn't finish saying which movie Kaminski belonged to. *He didn't want to scare me by saying he's Hannibal Fucking Lecter.*

"And when your brother figured out that most of the money he'd loaned you for school was actually being spent on weed, beer, and parties, he tried to throw you out of the house where you had been living rent-free."

"Yes."

"And that's when you broke his arm."

"I didn't mean to—"

"Yes or no?"

"Yes."

"And what happened the day after you were thrown out of the house?"

"I went to a protest."

"And?"

"I got in a fight."

"You *picked* a fight. With the police. By torching a patrol car."

"Yes."

"Because?"

Soft wetness moved down his cheeks. "Because I was in a bad mood."

"You were angry."

"Yes."

"At your brother."

"Yes."

"Because he was right."

"Yes."

"And you took it out on the first badge you saw."

". . . yes."

"Yes."

Kaminski looked to the others. "This is how we achieve progress. We face our rage and insecurity, and acknowledge the ways it's ruined not just our lives but the lives of others.

"Hector's not the only one who's fallen victim to this kind of thinking. All of you have issues that put you into the street but have nothing to do with protests or police or whatever the government just said about something. You chose, consciously or otherwise, to go to war with the government over misdirected anger because that's easier than confronting the things that are *really* causing you pain. And that puts you in exactly the right place to be preyed upon by people who want to use *your* anger for *their* benefit."

He turned back to Hector. "If your brother were here right now, what would you tell him?"

Hector backhanded tears. "What do you think I'd do? I'd tell him I miss him. I'd tell him I'm sorry, and I didn't mean it, and I love him."

"Would you tell him you were wrong? Would you tell him all the ways he's been a good brother?"

"Yes, absolutely."

"And what if I could arrange that?"

Hector's mouth worked for a moment before managing, "Are you serious?"

"I don't have ultimate authority to make that decision, but it's definitely within my authority to make such a recommendation if I feel it would do you some good. Giving you closure in one area might give you room to address some of the others without letting old tapes and grudges get in the way. Would you like that?"

"Yeah, yeah, I would," Hector said, and Riley saw the light of hope in his eyes.

"What about the rest of you?" Kaminski asked. "There are people in your life who you've inadvertently hurt, friends or family you miss . . . would you support the possibility of having them come for a visit?"

The others smiled and nodded. A few cried.

Riley waited for the hammer. *I ate his liver with fava beans and a nice Chianti.*

"Okay, then let's do this thing." Kaminski reached into his briefcase and pulled out a clutch of pencils and blank pages. "Take one each and pass the rest along."

"Now here's what I want you to do," he said once everyone was settled. "On one side of the page, I want you to list all the things you love about the person you want to come for a visit, all the things you did that were wrong, where you were mistaken or acting out of misplaced anger, and how much you want to make things right. I'll make sure this gets filed and sent to your loved ones. If they're open to it, I'll do everything I can to get them in here for a visit."

Everyone grinned. Even the usually sedate Becca.

Around the circle, pencils touched paper.

"And on the other side of the page," Kaminski said—

Here it comes, Riley thought.

"—on the *other* side," he repeated for emphasis, "I want you to do the same thing for this administration."

"Sorry?" said Angela.

"All of you have said that you love this country, that there's a lot of good about it, that you're trying to save it. Well, here's your chance to tell us what some of those good things are. Does the mail come on time? Do the streetlights work? Are the schools still open? I'm not asking you to address the things you don't like, just acknowledge the things the government's doing that you *do* like, that are working.

"Once that's done, you can add anything about your participation in these protests that, in retrospect, were wrongly motivated because you were acting out of anger at something else entirely."

Bam, Riley thought. *There it is. The confession.*

"Just to be clear, you are absolutely within your rights not to fill out the other side, if that's your decision" Kaminski said, "but you have to understand that, just as every argument has two sides, every sheet of paper has two sides. It's impossible to turn in one side of a sheet of paper without turning in the other side, that's just physics, so if you choose not to turn in one side, then neither side can be turned in. So it seems to me that if you want us to read what *you* want on one side of the paper, then you have to write down what *we* want on the other. That seems fair, doesn't it? It's just words on paper. Where's the harm in that?

"So I leave the choice to you, and to how much you really care about seeing your loved ones."

Looks were exchanged around the circle, and slowly, one by one, they began writing, the sound of pencils scratching on paper the only noise in the room—

—until they looked up at the sound of Riley folding the sheet of paper in half, then carefully running a fingernail along the edge to create a perfect crease.

Moving with precision, she tore the paper in half along the crease, folded the two halves together, and repeated the process, the sheets becoming incrementally smaller. When they were the size of playing cards, she stacked them neatly in a pile.

"Done," she said, smiling her friendliest smile and looking to the others on the assumption that they would do the same.

They looked down at the pages and, one by one, continued writing.

Kaminski smiled and closed his eyes, listening to the scratching of pencils on paper as if it were the most beautiful music in all the world.

The Surrender Sonata.

———

"Exercise room," Jim said as they left the therapy room. "Meeting. Right now."

Two minutes later, Danny closed the door and leveraged his mass against it to make sure nobody walked in on them. The rest of the group stood back in a circle as Jim stalked up to Riley.

"Why did you do that?" he asked. "Why do you keep going out of your way to piss him off?"

"Because he's a user and we shouldn't just give him what he wants."

"What he wants isn't the issue, it's what *we* want, which is to get out of here. Are they *really* going to let us have visitors? Doubtful. Was that whole thing just a mind-fuck? Probably. But it doesn't matter. That's on them, that's what *they're* doing. What *we* have to do is show that we're willing to meet him halfway, and you pulling this kind of crap is just gonna make it harder for *all* of us."

"It won't do any good—"

"Yes it will. I may only be prelaw but I know this stuff, Riley. The laws covering commitment say they can't hold us past the observation period without cause. Those two words, *without cause*, are the whole ball game here. They can't hold us for our attitude, our politics, or what we don't like about the government or the doctors or anything else. The only way they can keep us here, and justify whatever this program costs, is to prove we're dangerous, crazy, or both. If we act out or behave irrationally, we give them the proof they need to say they were right to put us here, and *keep* us here. So the way out is to play it cool, individually and as a group. If we don't do anything they can hold against us, then every law on the books says they *have* to let us go."

"And what about those statements he asked us to sign?"

"They're not admissible in court, and even if they were, we could say we wrote them under duress. It doesn't matter."

"They can still use that point system against us," Becca started to say.

Jim cut her off. "We've already had this discussion. The point system is pure bullshit, there's no such thing under the law when it comes to mental health observation. The courts would never go along with it. They're just trying to intimidate us."

"You mean like you're doing right now?" Riley asked.

He started to fire off a response when he saw Becca's hurt expression and bit it back. "I'm just saying that the point system doesn't matter, because it doesn't exist under the law."

"Jim, if these people were focused on doing what's right under the law, none of us would even be here in the first place," Riley said. "Do you really think they're going through all the trouble and expense to drag us in here just so they can let us go in six months? Dr. Munroe said there's more going on—"

"I had the same conversation with him, Riley. We *all* did, and it's just more bullshit. Before McGann showed up, Munroe was the Big Dog on the floor. Now it's Kaminski, and that pisses him off. So he comes to us saying the only way he could've been cut out of the loop is if there's something big going on. Maybe he wanted Kaminski's job and he's just mad about not getting it. Who knows what really happened and why? I don't. Do you? For reals? Does anybody? No. So excuse me if I don't take Munroe's word for anygoddamnthing.

"The only endgame I can see is McGann using this program to make the case in the press that anybody who protests against the government is crazy. Yeah, well, good luck with that once the ACLU, the courts, and the American Fucking Medical Association land on their asses. I promise you, a year from now this program will be shut down and sued into oblivion.

"So look," he said, lowering his voice to a level that was 80 percent more constructive but 20 percent more patronizing, "I get it. You're angry at being here, and you don't want to play along with these guys, and I don't blame you. We all went through the same thing. But we talked it out, and everybody agreed that we'd do whatever it takes to get out of here. These people want to play games? Fine, we'll play them right back by bending this to *our* agenda, not theirs. That means we stick together, and we don't let anybody go rogue and make the rest of us look bad, and right now, that person is you, so you seriously need to knock it off."

Riley looked around at the others to see if there was a flicker of support for her position, but they were all busy trying to find something interesting to stare at on the carpet.

"Thanks, but no thanks," she said at last. "*You* think the right move is giving these people exactly what they wanted when they put us here. *I* think we have to fight them every step of the way. We don't agree, and that's okay. You do you, I'll do me, and we'll see who's right."

"You're being an asshole."

"Yeah, I get that a lot."

"Then don't look to us for help if you get in trouble. Fair warning: whatever happens, it's on you."

"Done deal. Can I go now?"

Jim looked like he wanted to argue the point further—*poli-sci students never know when to end an argument*—then nodded to Danny, who stepped away from the door.

I'm on my own, she thought, feeling their eyes on her as she walked out. *Not the first time, pretty sure it's not gonna be the last.*

It didn't make the long walk back to her room any less lonely.

ALIBIS IN THE AFTERNOON

Seven ten a.m. After Nurse Biedermann and her mouse-in-sensible-white-shoes left with Riley's latest medication refusal, but before she could head to breakfast, Henry knocked at her door. "Hey, Ready Riley!" the orderly said, grinning. "How goes the hardest convict in lockup?"

"I'm good, Henry. How're you?"

"Excellent. I'm *always* excellent. That way I have one less choice to make."

He dug in his clipboard and pulled out a sheet of paper. "Last minute change to your schedule. Individualized Cognitive Therapy with Dr. Eleanor Nakamura, tomorrow afternoon, room one fourteen, two o'clock."

She's baaaack. "Why the change?"

"Dr. Nakamura specializes in what the doctors like to call 'difficult patients.' Normally she doesn't see folks for ICT this early in the process—likes to let 'em settle in for a while—but I hear tell you've jumped to the front of the line on the 'difficult' part."

"Great," she said flatly, taking the revised schedule.

"I'll have somebody swing by tomorrow to bring you downstairs," he said, and started for the door.

"Hey, Henry?"

"Yeah?"

"Can we get books in here?"

"There's some in the cafeteria, the exercise room—"

"Yeah, and they're all stupid—self-help books, romance novels, books about how to catch fish in Montauk—"

"I *like* that book," he said ominously.

"Only because it's got lots of pictures."

"You trying to start something?" he asked, somehow managing to frown and smile at the same time.

"All I'm asking is, are those the only books we can get in here?"

"Yes and no. In theory we have a deal with a library down the street that lets us check out books requested by patients. It worked pretty well most of the time, except when the patients didn't give them back in the same condition they'd gotten 'em. Administration got tired of constantly having to pony up the cash to buy new books, so they hit pause for a while. Since then, all we get are magazines like *Home and Garden*, *Modern Bride*, *Family Attractions*, except some idiot keeps tearing out the pages until there's nothing left but shreds."

"Is the library program still on pause?"

"No idea. Nobody's mentioned it in a while. Probably avoiding the subject. Most of the newer orderlies probably don't even know about it. I can ask around, though. Why?"

"If I gave you a list of books, could you get them for me? Having something to read in here might make me less . . . what's a good word . . . *difficult*," she said, smiling as broadly as the edges of her face would allow.

Henry laughed so hard she worried for a moment that he might pass out. "Man, if I ever wondered what a shark looks like when it smiles, I never have to wonder again." he said. "Okay, I'll ask around, see what I can find out. Meanwhile, don't forget: two o'clock tomorrow. Be ready, Ready Riley."

"Roger dodger," she said.

Breakfast began uneventfully.

It didn't stay that way.

As the rest of the ARC group sat together at one end of the cafeteria, Riley sat alone at the other, finishing a bowl of cereal and her usual orange juice and tea, watching with amusement as the same nervous orderly as before maneuvered food between Frankenstein's lips. When the plate was empty, he returned the tray to the kitchen with the look of a man who had stared death in the face and survived.

When Riley looked back, she noticed that Frankenstein was doing something with his hands just beneath the edge of the table. It took her a moment to decipher the small, stiff movements and realize that he was unfolding a paper clip.

Then he shoved one end of the paper clip under his fingernail.

She shrieked before she even realized she'd done it.

Frankenstein didn't react, not to her, or to the hard metal clip as it dug deep beneath his fingernail. His face was blank, a tiny trickle of blood ribboning down his hand the only clue to what he was doing.

The orderly rushed back, drawn by her distress, and followed her gaze to the table. "Ah shit," he said, "not again."

Screwing up his courage, he returned to the table and held out his hand. "Hand it over. C'mon. Give."

Frankenstein kept doing what he was doing.

The orderly toggled his walkie. "Code green, Cafeteria. Need some help up here."

Several more orderlies quickly entered, followed by Kaminski. "I was on my way to my office when I heard the code green. What's the problem?"

When Frankenstein saw Kaminski, his eyes went from dead and empty to dark and dangerous, shadowed by rage. He pulled himself to his feet, the chair falling behind him, lips skinned back in a feral snarl.

"Deal with him," Kaminski told the orderlies in a way that sounded like he had given that order many times before.

Before they could move, Frankenstein launched himself at the orderlies, tearing wildly at them in a desperate attempt to get to Kaminski. Patients scrambled out of the way or stood back to watch the fight, except for Riley. She wasn't watching Frankenstein. She was watching Kaminski.

He was smiling.

There's history between them, she realized. *He's enjoying this. Fucking sadist. Bet he wishes he could be the one doing the beating but he's too much of a coward, so he just watches from the sidelines.*

"Stand back!" one of the orderlies yelled, and pulled a stun gun from his belt. He switched it on, electricity arcing between twin metallic poles, then zapped Frankenstein in the side.

He stiffened, arced back, and fell to the floor. The orderlies pinned his hands behind his back, slid zip ties over his wrists and ratcheted them closed.

Only now did Kaminski approach, reaching to an orderly for a syringe. "Hold tight," he told the others, "I've seen him shake off shocks before."

As they pushed Frankenstein's face into the floor, Kaminski pulled up his sleeve, found a vein, and pushed the needle deep. A moment later, the sedative reached the bright-red rage in his heart, and his eyes grew soft, then closed.

"Get him to his room," Kaminski said. "Full restraints. Twenty-four hours."

The orderlies slung him over their shoulders and dragged him out of the cafeteria toward a waiting stretcher.

When he was gone, Kaminski looked to the other patients as though inviting a challenge. *Anyone got something they'd like to say?*

No one spoke.

Didn't think so, his eyes seemed to say as he strolled out of the cafeteria.

Riley was walking to the exercise area, desperate to run off the events of the day, when she passed the art room and saw Steve sitting alone at a worktable, looking lost in thought.

She knocked on the door. "Hey. How's it going?"

"Okay. You?"

"It's been a day. Could I sponge some change off you for a Snickers? Honestly, the way this day is going, it's the only thing that's gonna help."

"Sure thing," he said, digging in his pocket for quarters.

"You weren't at breakfast this morning."

"Didn't feel like eating. I'm waiting for news about my sister. She was rear-ended at a traffic light last night by some asshole who was having an argument with his girlfriend and wasn't looking where he was going. Practically totaled the car. Just wanted to be by myself, you know?"

Yeah, I know what that feels like, she wanted to say, but this wasn't the time, the place, or the vibe. "I can go if you want the private time."

"I'm good. Just didn't want to be around a crowd is all."

"Is she going to be okay?"

"She got banged up pretty good, but my mom says she's awake and responding to the doctors. We'll know for sure once they finish the last of the MRIs. I'm supposed to have a supervised visit off campus with her in a few weeks, so with luck, this won't mess things up. I really think she needs to talk."

"Is this the sister your dad said he'd disinherit if you didn't check in for treatment?"

"Yep."

"Gotta say, that's pretty harsh. Totes nineteenth century."

He allowed a smile. "Money is what he uses to control people. I'm okay with fighting him because I can't stand the son of a bitch, and if I lose it all, then so be it. But I love my sister, she's always been there for me when I needed her, and he knows it, so he tries to hurt *her* to get to *me*, and I won't have it."

"What about your mom?"

"She doesn't get into it—like, *any* of it. As long as she's taken care of, so she can keep shopping at Barney's and have spa day once a week at the Four Seasons and do the golf thing with her friends, it doesn't matter what he does, she just pretends it's not happening and looks the other way."

"I'm sorry."

He shrugged. "It is what it is."

Then Riley heard something buzzing. She looked around for the source, when Steve held up a finger.

"One second," he said, and reached into his pocket and pulled out a cellphone.

"Yeah, hey Mom, what's the latest? . . . Okay, well, that's good . . . Yeah, muscles always hurt worse the next day, so that'll be fun. Are they still going to keep her overnight for a CAT scan? . . . Good, great, yeah, I'll give her a call when she gets home, make sure she's still doing okay . . . Yep . . . No, just sitting talking with a friend . . . Okay, chat later . . . Love you too."

He clicked off the phone and glanced up to see Riley staring at him, open-mouthed with astonishment. "What?"

"Why didn't you tell me you had a cellphone!"

"I said to let me know if there was anybody you needed me to contact."

Riley struggled for words. "I know, but there's a difference . . . I mean . . . I figured you were going to use one of the phones downstairs, and they're not safe and, and . . . and *why* didn't you tell me, and how the *hell* do you have a phone?"

"It's one of the benefits of being a self-commit, at least on this side of the hospital. They even let me use the Wi-Fi as long as there's no porn involved, and I turn the phone off during therapy sessions and overnight."

"Can I borrow it? Just for five minutes?"

"I'm not supposed to."

"Yeah, I figured. So can I?"

He frowned, thought about it for a moment, then started to hand over the phone.

"Under the table," she said, glancing to the open door. She didn't see any orderlies, but that didn't mean there weren't eyes or cameras on them. "Hand me the change for the Snickers with one hand and slide the phone to me under the table with the other."

"No problem, Double-oh-seven."

Okay, now what do I do? she thought as her hand closed over the phone, running names through her head until she found the only one she knew would be safe.

She turned her back to the door, opened the texting app, and typed in a number, followed by,

> Hey, it's Riley D. This isn't a secure number. Don't reply with your name. Just acknowledge if you get this.

A minute passed. Then:

> Where are you? Hospital still?

> Yes. Need to get out of here, let people know this place isn't the great deal they said it was. Can you help? This isn't my phone and may be my only chance to make contact.

> Maybe. Can you access Wi-Fi where you are?

> Yep. Sort of. For now. Why?

> How we can get you out will depend on what's in their files about you and how their operation is run. Once I'm inside I might be able to spoof a release-authorization email. Either

way I need access to the system. Will
send you an app that'll run in the
background of this phone, map out
IP connections, find helpful files and
addresses.

> I don't know. I don't want to get
> my friend in trouble.

He'll never know it's there. I'll only
use it long enough to piggyback into
the system, map out the network,
and update periodically in case any
of the IP addresses change. Once I
have that info I can cut my way in from
this side without using his phone so
even if they spot an intrusion there's
nothing that'll lead back to him.

> Okay. I don't know if you'll find
> much that can help, but it's good
> to know I have a fire alarm if
> needed.

Copy that. Sending a link to the app
and signing off. Delete these texts and
make sure this number isn't on your
friend's contact list. Take care, R.

> You too. Thanks.

"You about done?" Steve asked.

"One second," Riley said. Fingers flashing over the screen, she hit the link, downloaded the app, then quickly deleted the texts and the number.

"Thanks," she said, and was in the middle of handing back the phone under the table when Henry yelled her name, startling her so badly that she almost dropped it.

"Yo, Ready Riley!" he called from the doorway. "I looked into the library thing like I promised. I didn't talk to the staff or McGann about it to keep from putting it on their radar, 'cause I knew they'd say no, so I called the head librarian. Turns out the loan program is still up. So what books do you want me to get?"

She reached into her pocket and pulled out a list she'd written on the back of the previous day's schedule. "Is this okay?"

He ran a finger down the list. "Yeah, these should be fine—"

He stopped at the last entry. "You sure about this one?" he asked.

"Yeah. Honestly, if I had to pick one, that's the most important, so if you can get it, that'd be great."

"Okay," he said dubiously as he headed for the door, "no promises, but I'll see what I can do."

At 1:45 the next afternoon, an orderly appeared at Riley's door and led her to the second-floor elevators at the south end of the hospital. She watched carefully as he used a key card to open the elevator doors and punched in a code—41172—before descending to the first floor. *Good start, but I still need to figure out if the code is tied to his card or if it's for general use.*

When the doors opened, he led her down several familiar puke-green hallways toward the executive offices. Having paced out the upper floors several times, she was now able to triangulate their layout to the main floor, associating *this* window with *that* room directly above, *this* staircase with *that* fire door two stories up, and the location of offices and desktop computers.

Two more left turns brought them to room 114.

"Good to see you again," Dr. Nakamura said when the door closed. "I thought it might be more casual if we met here instead of the therapy rooms. Please have a seat."

"Couch or chair?"

"Whichever makes you more comfortable."

Riley took the chair facing the desk, then wondered if her choice carried any psychological meaning. *Aha! An uncomfortable chair person, not a fuzzy, happy couch person! Burn the witch!*

Shut up, she told herself. *We need to focus.*

"Riley?"

"What?"

"I asked how it's been going."

"Sorry. Sometimes the voices in my brain start ping-ponging back and forth and I tune out. But I'm not crazy."

"It's definitely not crazy," Nakamura said, smiling. "It's actually completely normal. We all have more than one voice in our head at all times, taking different sides or positions. You could say it's the inner *we* breaking apart to examine a question or a subject from a number of different perspectives in order to stress-test the truth or the question, and what we should say in response. Our understanding of this goes all the way back to Freud, who said there were three parts of the mind: the id, who wants things, the ego, which is our identity, who it is that wants those things, and the superego, which is the part of us that balances those desires against what we should or shouldn't do within the limits and rules of society. The modern term for it is *dissociative thinking*, which describes a process by which one part of the brain pulls away from the rest to assess information and emotions, then tells the rest of the brain how to respond. Any time you hear someone say, 'I was going to take that job, but at the last minute I went with my gut,' or 'I wanted to go on the trip, but some part of me kept pushing the other way,' that's dissociative thinking. Basically, it's the brain starting an argument with itself. In severe cases, this can lead to depersonalization, identity confusion—"

"Is that why some people think they hear voices?"

"Sometimes, yes. Trauma can lead people to interpret the voices in their heads as someone else speaking, which can be symptomatic of the personality beginning to fragment, creating new 'voices' with each break. But again, that only happens in extreme cases. For everyone else, it's natural to have ongoing inner debates. The field of psychiatry is all about humans *using* our brains to figure *out* our brains, which would be impossible without the distance provided by such cognitive processes."

She's being nice. Too nice. It's a trap. She's been upgraded by Skynet to a T-1000.

Will. You. Shut. UP?

"So, how *has* it been going? I imagine all this must still be a bit of a shock."

"It's fine."

"Everyone treating you all right, then?"

"*So* far." It was both an answer and a challenge.

"Good," Nakamura said, without acknowledging her tone. "The reason I wanted to see you is that Dr. Kaminski mentioned during our staff meeting yesterday that you've been having a hard time opening up in group therapy. I hope you understand that those sessions are intended for your benefit, and sometimes that means asking personal or painful questions, which can be even more difficult in a group setting. But the more you open up to the staff, the doctors, and other patients, the sooner you can heal, and the better we can evaluate the therapeutic process as we go forward.

"So I thought I'd see if I can help move that along a little by providing a safe space where the two of us can nonjudgmentally discuss anything you might not be comfortable sharing with a large group. My role here is to encourage, not to enforce, to listen rather than fill the room with my own ideas. This is about you talking out whatever is troubling you. I may sometimes lead the conversation in directions I think may prove constructive, but the rest of the time I'm happy to rabbit-trail into anything you'd prefer to talk about. I want you to think of my office as a place where you can speak freely."

Okay, let's test that. "So were you here before the ARC thing started?"

"Barely, yes. Just over six months. I received my formal training at St. George's University in London, then moved here to Seattle in search of opportunities outside the limited confines of the British mental health system. I was lucky enough to be hired by Dr. Munroe, who said that it might take time to work my way up through the roster because all the senior positions were filled. Then the ARC program started, and I was able to get in on the ground floor of something that would give me the opportunity to do some real good."

And having fewer senior doctors ahead of you meant a quicker road to advancement, Riley thought, remembering what Julian had said. *"There are always going to be people like Saruman, who prefer to bend with the wind than stand against it, especially if the money's right."*

Nakamura opened a file on her tablet. "In going over your paperwork, I was impressed by your high school records. Until your parents passed away, you were an A student. Then you quit school and started getting into trouble. The letters of support provided by your teachers the first time you were arrested said you were a brilliant student with a high IQ, interested in history, politics, literature . . . good verbal skills, convincing in debates . . . you even showed some talent as a writer before everything fell apart."

Riley shrugged. "I guess."

"No need to feel defensive about it. Anyone who suffered such a tragic loss at that age would have a hard time staying in school. You were angry at the world, and needed to do something with all that negative energy, so you started looking for a fight, a cause, anything that would fill the hole left behind by their passing. One of the ways people cope with extreme emotions is to externalize them. 'I can't punch my grief, but I can punch that thing over there.' That may be part of what led you to externalize your anger into protests, getting more and more involved until they practically became your entire life. Continuing your parents' participation in the protest movement may have been a way to help keep them alive in your heart. And that makes a rough kind of sense.

"But here's the part I can't quite work out, Riley. You're smart enough to understand how much you risk every time you take part in these things, you're living one of them right now, so why keep doing it?"

Riley clicked through half a dozen answers that would defer and deflect before deciding, *Let's tap on the goldfish bowl and see what we're up against.* "Because it's important to take a stand."

"Isn't that what elections and ballot boxes are for?"

"Everyone keeps saying that, but they don't work anymore."

"You think the process is rigged?"

"No. If it was rigged, that would be great, because then you could find out who's doing it and stop them. But that's not the problem."

"Then what is? Understand that I'm still fairly new to the ARC program, and I confess I've never actually been to a protest, so I genuinely want to get my arms around why this is so important, not just for you but the other patients as well."

Riley glanced out the window and frowned. *How do you explain water to a goldfish who's surrounded by it? It's everywhere but invisible, and she wouldn't want to see it even if she could, because that would introduce the concept of the fishbowl and the limits of being fed by a giant hand that only drops in food when doing so is useful to its agenda.*

"I can't speak for anybody other than myself," she said at last, "so if you're looking for someone to explain why everybody else is doing what they do—like, 'Speak for your generation'—that's not going to happen. So just speaking from my point of view, it seems like everybody running the government is on the take. Is one side worse than the other? Sure. But in the end they all work for the guys who have money and power and like to spread it around to their friends. Elections can't change that because the system itself has been corrupted.

"Once upon a time people voted for someone to represent their town who understood what needed to be done to make their lives better and he worked really hard to make that stuff happen before going back to his real job, planting or being a silversmith, or whatever. It was like doing jury duty. But that's not how it works anymore. As soon as they're elected they stop listening to anyone but the guys with the money and power, who help them get reelected forever in return for passing bills that give them even *more* money and power. They don't do squat for the people who actually voted for them because *that's not who they work for* anymore. You think the folks back home voted to destroy the environment? I never saw that on a ballot, did you? Nobody in charge ever asked for a vote about militarizing the police to where they look like an invading army, and there's never been a national public vote about health care and never will be, because the drug companies won't allow it.

"I read once that never in history have the people of one country decided to go to war with another. Not once. It's the *leaders*, the kings and the presidents and the parliaments, who make the call. *They* declare war and tell everyone to fight in it. They don't put it on a ballot so people can decide for themselves because they know what would happen. 'Do you want to die in a war or have your son or brother die so a bunch of people with money and land and crowns and titles can get even *more* money and land and crowns and titles? Pick A for *yes* and B for *no*.'

"Like I said, I can't speak for anybody else, but I don't show up for protests because it makes me feel closer to my folks, because they're always right here inside me. I don't do it because I enjoy it, or because it's fun. Nobody likes getting their head beaten in. But more and more lately it's like the only way we can get anything done or stopped is by taking to the streets and forcing the issue into the public eye, so the people in charge *have* to talk about it. *That's* our ballot box. *That's* where we vote. *That's* where we get heard.

"You said I was good at history, and you're right. As a kid I learned all about how the Founding Fathers threw British tea into the sea in a big protest. But the protest wasn't about the tea, it wasn't even about the taxes; it was about being taxed without a chance to *discuss* it and *vote* on it. 'No taxation without representation,' right? They could've just said, 'We're not gonna pay any more taxes' and stay home," but they didn't, because *that wasn't the point*. It was about not being given a voice in the process. That's where we are now. We don't have a voice or a choice anymore, because we're not being represented. As soon as the government starts doing what the people who can't afford to bribe them actually *want*, I'll hang up my boots and go back to school. Until then, I'm in the streets with everybody else."

"Not at the moment," Nakamura corrected. "Right now, you're here."

"True," Riley said, "but not to stay."

"One certainly hopes," Nakamura said.

And Riley didn't care at all for the way she said it.

"I can see why you also did well in debate, Riley, and I appreciate the emotions behind what you're saying. You're smart and you've clearly given this a great deal of thought, but you must know that no country can be run by mob rule."

"Don't recall suggesting that, but keep going."

"I'm not trying to antagonize you," she said. "And I'm not saying that you're entirely wrong. I'm just saying that there may be more constructive ways of dealing with our emotions. You said you want to get out of here. Did you really mean that?"

"Obviously."

"Then we have our first point of agreement. I want to see you leave here in six months, whole and healthy and ready to go back to your life. Whether you stop protesting afterward is outside my control. All I can do is to help you take the kind of practical steps that will show you're trying to get better."

"What kind of steps?"

Nakamura pulled a printed sheet of paper out of her desk drawer. "For instance, signing something like this would be a wonderful start. Give it a look and tell me what you think."

Riley took the form and began reading.

To Whom It May Concern:

I, _____, acknowledge and affirm that my participation in illegal protests, uncivil activities, and criminal actions against the Government of the United States was done at the bidding, encouragement, and facilitation of individuals acting on behalf of foreign powers hostile to American interests. I regret those actions and fully repudiate them. As an act of good faith, I hereby append the names and contact information of the following individuals who were engaged with me in these activities:

_____

_____

_____

_____

_____

_____

I am proud to be an American, supportive of this Administration, and thankful for the opportunity to address my past mistakes through the American Renewal Act. My treatment while in the ARC program was responsible, humane, and helpful.

I make this statement freely and of my own will, without duress of any kind.

Name (please spell) _____

Signature _____

Date _____

Several eternities passed before Riley raised her gaze from the page. "I can't sign this."

"Why not?"

"Because it's not true."

"It doesn't matter. It's just a piece of paper. You sign it, it goes in your file as a show of good faith, and that's that."

"Right, and later on, if I say I didn't mean it when I signed this, then I'm identifying myself as a liar, which puts me on the road to somebody saying, 'Okay, so if you were lying *then* how do we know you're not lying *now*, and why should we trust anything you have to say about anything—ever?'"

"Riley—"

"And what's this bullshit about giving up the names of my friends?"

"First, they're not your friends, they're using you. Second, you don't have to give any names that we don't already have. You could just give us the names of people who have already been convicted or arrested—"

"Which could be used against them when they come up for parole."

"I doubt it would make much of a difference. Most of these people already have long records."

"Well, I'm one of *these people*, and if I found out a friend turned on me, I'd never be able to trust them again, but that's the point, isn't it? To make it so we can't trust each other."

Nakamura sighed wearily and sat back. "Look, Riley, I'm going to be honest with you, and I hope you appreciate the risk I'm taking with that, all right? I don't agree with everything the government is doing. I thought the Ten-Plus ruling was a *terrible* mistake, and there's a lot about the ARC program that needs to be addressed.

We can either fight those things from the outside, which is what put you in here, or we can fight them from the inside. That's why I joined McGann's team, so I could give you and all the other patients the support and information you need to get out of here. If a stupid piece of paper means you can walk out the door when the time comes, I'm all for it, and you should be too, don't you think?"

See? I told you she'd been upgraded to a T-1000. She's trying really hard to look just like one of us, but every time she talks she goes all silver-faced on us.

Will you . . . Actually, that's pretty accurate.

THANK YOU.

"You don't want to know what I think," Riley said.

"Of course I do. This whole session is *about* you and *for* you."

"Okay, then here's what I think. I can't decide if you actually believe the horseshit you're shoveling, or if this is just what you say to convince people to sign that piece of paper. If it's number two, I can *almost* respect it, because that means you're really good at faking sincerity, and that's a gift. But if you've honestly convinced yourself that you're fighting McGann and Kaminski by making the machine work more efficiently, that's beyond fucked up. It's like you've created an entirely new level of fuckedupedness that I've never even *seen* before. That's the difference between you and Kaminski. He's totally on board with this nightmare. He doesn't pretend it's something else just so he can sleep nights.

"So you want to know what *I* think? I think I don't *like* you, and for sure I don't *trust* you.

"So, are there any *other* questions you'd like to discuss, Dr. Nakamura?"

Thirty-seven arctic minutes later, Riley emerged from Dr. Nakamura's office to find Henry waiting outside, cradling a heavy brown paper bag under one arm. "Hey, Ready Riley! What's shakin'?"

"Nothing," she growled.

"No, that's not it," he said. "When I say, 'What's shakin',' you're supposed to say, Ain't nothin' shakin' but the leaves on the trees."

"Ain't nothin' shakin' but the leaves on the trees."

"There you go. Much better."

He led her down a row of cubicles toward the elevator. "I just got back from running some errands, thought I'd swing by and take you back to your room. How'd it go with Dr. Nakamura?"

She shot him a glance that promised biblical degrees of pain and retribution if he pursued the question even an inch further.

He caught the look and laughed as the elevator doors opened. "You ought to trademark those glares," he said. "My aunt Rose used to call that one 'giving somebody the skunk-eye.' Said if you weren't careful, your face would freeze like that and you'd be skunk-eyed for life."

"So, you gonna ask what's in the bag?" he said once they were inside.

"If it's a meat cleaver, we need to head back downstairs for ten minutes."

"Nope, afraid not. It's better. And it's for you."

He pushed the Stop button. "Rather do this in private," he said, and handed her the bag. "I went by the library, and they had just about everything on your list."

Her mood improved instantly. "You're my hero," she said, flipping through the books until she hit the only one she'd really wanted. *Yes!*

He pushed the button and the elevator began to rise again. "The librarian told me to tell you that they have to go back in the same condition you got them in," he said. "So don't let 'em out of your sight, because if whoever keeps tearing up the magazines does the same here, it's coming out of my salary."

"I'll take care of them," she said. "Thanks."

"No problem. And if that book at the bottom of your list helps you understand our special guest, let me know, okay? Might be a raise in it for me. Maybe I can even pay off that Snickers habit of yours," he said with a wink.

Dr. Munroe's right. The staff sees everything, hears everything, knows everything.

Then she turned her attention back to the book cover.

FRANKENSTEIN
OR, THE MODERN PROMETHEUS
Mary Shelley

REAL POWER

As Riley sat on her bed, awaiting grand rounds and Dr. Munroe, the late afternoon sunlight streaming through the window scrunched the shadow of the wrought-iron parrot onto the narrow window ledge. It looked as if it had been pounded with a mallet.

I know the feeling, she thought.

Two weeks. I've only been in this place for two weeks and I feel like I've been here forever. How am I going to get through six months of this shit—or longer, depending on what they decide? I may not have been crazy when I got here, but if I have to stay here for six months I will definitely lose my mind.

She glanced up at a knock on the door as Dr. Munroe entered, followed by Biedermann, Kaminski, Nakamura, and two younger doctors Riley didn't recognize—probably members of the non-ARC staff tagging along for the ride.

"Good afternoon, Ms. Diaz," Julian said, then paused to see if she'd give the 'Good morning' distress call.

"Hey, Dr. Munroe," she said.

He drew closer, flipping through her file on his tablet. "And how are you feeling today?"

"Great. Couldn't be better."

He paused at an entry in her file. "It says here that you're declining medication."

"It's my right."

"Why, yes, it is at that," he said with a glance in Biedermann's direction. "Isn't it *amazing* that patients have that right?"

Biedermann nodded but said nothing.

Julian returned to the chart and began reading aloud. "'Patient shows resistance to authority'—yes, well, apparently that's why she's here in the first place—'and hostility to the staff.' Well, I'd say that covers most of the ARC patients on arrival, wouldn't you, Edward?"

Kaminski shrugged and looked away.

Julian skimmed further down, then frowned. "'Patient has exhibited signs of obsessive-compulsive behavior.' What's this about?"

"Some of the orderlies saw her pacing back and forth in the halls," Kaminski said, "like she was counting her steps, over and over."

Riley held her breath. She wasn't sure which was more dangerous: that Kaminski suspected she was measuring out the halls and wanted to send her a message or that he didn't have a clue about what she was doing but decided it was a good way to bolster his argument that she was crazy.

"Is this true, Ms. Diaz?" Julian asked.

"Yes."

"Can you tell me *why* you've been pacing the halls?"

"I'm having a really rough period. It's how I distract myself from the cramps."

"I thought there might be a simple explanation," he said, but as he glanced back at her, she saw behind his eyes the words, *Whatever you're doing, be careful; the staff see everything.*

"Riley is still reluctant to participate with the other patients in our group therapy sessions," Kaminski said, "but we're hoping she'll start to open up a little. It would certainly go a long way toward helping the other patients feel more comfortable talking in front of her."

"Chicken and the egg," Julian said. "Yes, if Ms. Diaz talks more, the others might be inclined to do the same, but by the same token, if *they* talk more, it might encourage Ms. Diaz to be more open. Whether or not a group session is productive is really the responsibility of the facilitator more than any single patient, wouldn't you agree?"

If Kaminski caught the underlying message—*Don't pressure her to do your job or try to blame her for impeding the other patients*—he didn't acknowledge it. He just continued staring at Riley in a way she didn't much care for.

"I see you had a cognitive therapy session with Dr. Nakamura. How was it from your side, Eleanor?" Julian asked.

Riley saw several possible answers scrolling behind Nakamura's eyes before she landed on, "Instructive."

"Unlike that reply," Julian said, only slightly under his breath.

He turned back to Riley. "Have you experienced any psychological issues since your arrival? Troublesome thoughts? Inclinations toward self-harm? Suicide? Any sense of depression?"

"Nope, I'm totally good."

"All right then, Ms. Diaz, we'll let you get on with your day," he said, then turned to the rest of the staff. "Shall we?"

Everyone except Biedermann followed him out the door. When they were gone, she went to the storage cabinet above the bathroom toilet and pulled out a still-sealed box of tampons.

She tapped the box against her palm. "Since you said you were on your period, I was going to have some more sent to your room, but it seems you don't need them."

Then she returned the box to the cabinet, closed the door, and left to catch up with the others.

By now the pecking order was clear to Riley: Nakamura was useless; Dr. Munroe was an ally but lacked the authority to directly confront Kaminski and could only resort to pointed asides; Kaminski was a pig, but a weak one.

The *real* power, and the real *danger*, was Biedermann.

On the other hand, her brain shot back, *maybe putting on that show was just her way of telling you to be more careful in setting up your alibis.*

Possible, she thought. *But honestly, what're the odds?*

Then she glanced at the clock. *Shit! I'm gonna be late!*

She reached under her bed, found the book hidden there, and hurried down the hall.

The ritual had begun several days earlier. When she realized that he could always be found in the solarium at four o'clock, eyes closed, standing silently before the window when the sun was at the right angle to warm his face, she began showing up at three thirty and taking her place on the bench. Once she saw his reflection appear in the window, standing behind her or off to the side, she would begin reading aloud, as if just for herself, without looking at him or inviting him to approach.

At first he seemed annoyed to find someone sharing his time alone with the sun, but the longer she read, day after day, the closer he came. Neither of them acknowledged the other until the day he sat on the bench beside her and she turned her head very slowly to risk a glance at his eyes.

And the mind behind them said, *Keep reading.*

And she did. Every day.

"All men hate the wretched; how then must I be hated, who am miserable beyond all living things! Yet you, my creator, detest and spurn me, thy creature, to whom thou art bound by ties only—"

She paused at the next word and looked to Frankenstein, seated beside her on the bench, body slumped slightly forward, hands dangling loosely between his knees, gaze fixed on a spot somewhere beyond the window to something only he could see. His expression, unrevealing as stone, gave no indication if he actually understood what she was reading, especially given some of the olde-school language.

But he wasn't walking away, either.

She took her best shot at the word. "—ties only *dissoluble* by the annihilation of one of us. You purpose to kill me. How dare you sport thus with life? Do your duty towards me, and I will do mine towards you and the rest of mankind. If you comply with my conditions, I will leave them and you at peace; but if you refuse, I will glut the maw of death, until it be satiated with the blood of your remaining friends.

"I was benevolent; my soul glowed with love and humanity: but am I not alone, miserably alone?"

She glanced over to see if the words were reaching their intended target, only to find him staring silently ahead, as if he'd heard none of it. But his reflection in the window showed a distant, locked-away gaze that hinted at hidden pain deep within.

"You, my creator, abhor me; what hope can I gather from your fellow-creatures, who owe me nothing? They spurn and hate me. The desert mountains and dreary glaciers are my refuge. I have wandered here many days; the caves of ice, which I only do not fear, are a dwelling to me, and the only one which man does not grudge. These bleak skies I hail, for they are kinder to me than your fellow-beings. If the multitude of mankind knew of my existence, they would do as you do, and arm themselves for my destruction. Shall I not then hate them who abhor me? I will keep no terms with my enemies. I am miserable, and they shall share my wretchedness.

"Yet it is in your power to recompense me, and deliver them from an evil which it only remains for you to make so great, that not only you and your family, but thousands of others, shall be swallowed up in the whirlwinds of its rage. Let your compassion be moved, and do not disdain me. Listen to my tale: when you have heard that, abandon or commiserate me, as you shall judge that I deserve. But hear me. The guilty are allowed, by human laws, bloody as they may be, to speak in their own defense before they are condemned. Listen to me, Frankenstein. You accuse me of murder; and yet you would, with a satisfied conscience, destroy your own creature. Oh, praise the eternal justice of man! Yet I ask you not to spare me: listen to me; and then, if you can, and if you will, destroy the work of your own hands."

She closed the book and joined him in watching the sun inch closer to the horizon.

"This is what I was trying to tell you," she said without turning from the view. "He's so smart, not like the movie creature at all. He's saying that if his creator, if the *world*, could understand what happened to make him the way he was, if he could just tell them his story, they'd feel compassion, and he wouldn't have to be the monster they all thought he was.

"I know you're in there. I know you can hear me or you would've stopped coming a long time ago. And since this is the part of the book where your namesake goes on to tell his story for the next ten thousand pages, I was thinking that maybe you could tell me a little bit of *your* story."

He said nothing, his gaze falling to the floor the way it always did just before he left.

"Okay," she said quickly, determined to hold his attention, "so how about I tell you my story first, and you can return the favor and tell me yours later. Fair deal?"

His gaze remained steady, but for the first time, his head moved slightly in an almost imperceptible nod.

"Done deal," she said, her voice softer than she normally allowed, then turned back to the shadows that had grown long outside the window. "It's actually kind of funny, because I was thinking last night about how you and I are alike in some ways. I think somebody in your life told you that you were a monster, and kept right on saying it until you started to believe it. And I know how that feels, because I did it to myself.

"I loved—"

She felt her voice catch, and paused, pushing her heart down until it reached a safe distance, then starting again. "I loved my mom and dad. They were like the best mom and dad in the history of really amazing moms and dads. I could talk to them about anything without feeling like I was being judged or shamed. They guided me but never tried to *control* me. My dad used to say that letting me go my own way was more about self-preservation on their part than being good parents. It was bullshit, obviously, but funny bullshit.

"He was just this rock-steady guy, the calm center between us and whatever trouble was coming our way. Everybody else on his side of the family was a mister-yelly-head, but I never heard him raise his voice. Maybe that's what made him his own guy in that crowd, y'know? He was a big man with a big face that was always so serious, especially when he was being funny, so you had to pay attention to see if he was actually saying something important or just messing with you. I see him in my head like one of those big trees in the middle of nowhere that have been around a long time, a *real* tree, with roots that go all the way down to the center of the earth. No matter how big the storm was, you knew that if you went under those branches you were safe, that he'd never, *ever* let anything happen to you.

"Back when the protests started going year-round, my mom used to invite people from her old college to come by for dinner: professors, students, writers . . . smart people. They'd talk all night about how much the Struggle mattered to them, but even as a kid I could tell that it was just talk for most of them. They liked to hear themselves speak, puffing up all brave and strong even though they'd never been in a protest when the tear gas guns came out. My dad would usually just nod and listen, never getting in their face about it, because that wasn't his style, but one night, after these guys had been going on a little too long about what they *believed* in and what they *stood* for, my dad finally just went off on them.

"'You know what?' he said. 'It doesn't *matter* what you stand for while you're sitting here all nice and safe in this living room. What matters is what you stand for when standing is the *hardest*. All the pretty words you keep firing off don't mean shit if you turn to smoke the first time somebody puts a boot on your neck or kicks down the door in the middle of the night. The only time you ever really know who you *are* is when somebody threatens to take away everything you *have*. Once you've had that moment, *then* you can come back and tell me about what you stand for.'

"They got really huffy about it and left feeling insulted, but you know what? When the antiprotest laws got passed later on, and the preempts started, and their jobs, scholarships, or publications were on the line, they were the first ones to take back everything they said, that it was all just a big misunderstanding."

She felt wetness on her cheek and batted it away with the back of her hand. "I miss him. Every day. I miss both of them so much."

Frankenstein said nothing.

Riley let out a long, slow breath, knowing what was coming next: all the stuff she never talked about to anyone, but which *had* to come next if she was going to make the point that she wanted, no *needed* to make, for both their sakes. *You can do this. Just take a deep breath, and as you let it out, say—*

"And it's kind of my fault my folks aren't here.

"I've always been what teachers call 'a discipline problem.' Big shock, right? It's not like I *want* to be a pain in the ass, but when someone expects me to do what I'm told, not because they're right but because they're wearing the Pointy Hat of Authority, I go the other way every time. If you want me to do something you think is important, then take two minutes to explain *why* it's important. I'm not stupid and I'm not arbitrary; if it's the right thing to do, then I'm absolutely on board *and* I'll back you up if anybody gives you shit about it. But for me to do something just because some entitled asshat orders me to do it? No. Not a chance.

"Anyway, one day my problem with authority figures blew up into a huge argument with one of my teachers. It wasn't the first time, and by now the vice-principle was pretty fed up with me, so she suspended me and told my folks I couldn't come back until they agreed to meet with her after hours to talk about my 'situation.' So they showed up and listened and nodded and tried to say all the right things, but after a while even my dad got tired of the bullshit, told her what she could do with her 'situation,' and walked out. On the way out, my mom called from the parking lot to say not to worry about it, they'd find a new school with fifty percent fewer assholes, and told me to get ready to go out for pizza.

"They were driving home through the worst part of rush-hour traffic, when one of those big eighteen-wheelers they use to deliver new cars blew through the stoplight and slammed into the car and . . ."

The tears returned. She left them alone. "And they were gone."

"I blamed myself for what happened because they wouldn't have been on *that* road at *that* moment if they hadn't been dealing with *my* shit. They would've been home, and we would've had pizza and maybe watched a movie and—"

She closed her eyes, pushing away all the yesterdays that would have happened had *that* yesterday not happened. "I went into a really dark place for a long time, and to be honest I wasn't sure I'd ever come back out again. I started acting out big-time. If something was illegal, I did it. If it was drugs, I did it twice. I was just angry, all the time. And *alone*. I didn't have many friends in the first place, because I was always the weird one, but when all this went down, poof, they disappeared.

"When I ran out of money, I started selling what little we had to make rent and buy more shit to slam into my veins. One of the last things left was my dad's laptop, but I didn't want to sell it with the hard drive still inside because that was *his*, you know? It was private. I've always been a bit of a computer nerd so I decided to pull the hard drive and pop in something cheap. But once I was inside, I got curious and fired up the drive to see what was there.

"You know what I found? No porn, if that's what you're thinking. Not even many emails or documents, mainly business invoices, receipts, shit like that. The rest was almost entirely pictures and videos of me, and my mom, and the three of us. I didn't even know he'd taken half of them because he was always so quiet about that stuff. Gigabyte after gigabyte of birthdays, late nights at Denny's, and the time we went to Disney World in Florida and my dad got sick on Cuban food and none of us ever let him forget it. And as I went through all that stuff, I knew my folks would want me to be more than what I was at that moment. They'd want me to fight my way out, to stand up, because like my dad said, it's only when standing is the hardest thing that you know who you really are.

"It took me over a year to crawl out of the hole I'd dug for myself," she said, suddenly feeling very tired, "and the road back led through some really bad places, but I made it. And now the only thing these asshole doctors want to talk about is my family, not because they give a shit but because they want to use what happened against me. But I won't let them. They don't own that pain, and I'll fucking die before I let them use my folks like that.

"I've always hated it when people say, *Oh, I know how you feel* about this or that, because most of the time they really don't. I don't know what you went through, so I can't say I know how you felt about any of it. But I do know what it feels like to look in the mirror and see a monster, because for a really long time that's all *I* could see, until I finally realized that I had a choice, that I didn't *have* to be that monster anymore. And neither do you.

"So anyway, that's my story. Like I said, I don't really talk about it much, but I guess it's good for me to talk about it to *somebody* once in a while, y'know? And telling you is safe, right? Because seriously, who are *you* gonna tell?"

And for just a second, she thought she caught the barest flicker of a smile.

It was getting dark as Riley started back to her room to stash the book before dinner only to find the hall blocked by orange safety cones. Further down the hall, orderlies with mops were scrubbing down the floor.

"What happened?"

"Patient puked up from here all the way down to the corner. It's Family Day Dinner for the regular patients, and sometimes they get a little too excited. Can't let you through until we finish cleaning, then disinfect."

"I have to get to my room before dinner."

"Then you gotta go around," he said, pointing to the corner.

"That's the staff area. Henry told me it's off-limits to patients."

He pulled the mop from the bucket and began soaking down the tiles. "Just go *around*," he said, frustrated.

Fine.

Dinnertime was end-of-shift for the doctors, nurses, and orderlies who worked days, so most of the offices were empty, dimly illuminated by desk lamps and the glow of password-locked monitors awaiting the arrival of the night shift. As she passed a conference room, she peeked in to see an orderly napping on a couch, barely visible in the pale white light of street lamps that filtered in through a window at the far end of the room.

Riley took two more steps forward, then abruptly stopped.

Did I just see what I thought I saw?

She backed up to the conference room and looked inside.

There were no bars on the window, animal-shaped or otherwise.

She kept going, glancing into each of the offices in turn.

None of the windows were barred.

Of course, she realized. *This is a hospital, it wasn't designed to be a prison. Yeah, that's what they're turning it into now, but that wasn't the original intent. Prison guards expect to spend most of their time in rooms with bars, but the doctors who were here before the ARC program probably liked their views, and why not? After all, if you tell most hospital patients, 'This area is off-limits,' they usually just go along with it.*

She glanced around to make sure no one was coming, then slipped into one of the empty offices to examine the window more closely. It was screened on the outside but could still be opened with a lockable handle on the inside. A narrow ledge beneath the window ran the length of the building before disappearing around the corner at the south end. Standing on tiptoes, she peered down a three-story drop to the parking lot, where trucks and heavy equipment were lined up next to racks containing rows of window-bars. White dust on the ground and the windows below showed signs of recent construction.

Must be working their way up floor by floor, making it more secure, she decided. *No wonder they didn't want patients roaming around this part of the hospital.* From the look of the worksite they were still locking down the first two floors. It would take time to get this high, but there was no way she could know how *much* time. She examined the window lock more closely, but couldn't find any signs of security wiring. *Makes sense, why bother putting in window sensors three stories up a sheer drop?*

Riley allowed an excited grin. There was a way out!

She was tempted to make a run for it right then and there, but pushed down the impulse. Getting out was only half the job; the other half was not getting caught and sent back. Now that she'd identified a weak spot, the next steps would have to be all about preparation, planning, and support, so she would be ready to move when the opportunity came.

Chance favors a prepared mind, her father liked to say. *That means you don't wait around for luck to happen. You put yourself in a position to take advantage of luck when it comes along.*

Then an electronic *beep!* chimed behind her and she froze, sure that she had been caught. She turned slowly, but there was no one in the doorway. *Get the hell out before someone finds you messing with the windows*, her brain yelled at her.

Once safely out of the room, she heard the telltale sound of a microwave oven being popped opened and closed again down the hall, and curiosity overcame caution. Edging closer to the source of the sound, she peered inside the open door of a break room to see Biedermann sitting at a small table, nibbling at the edges of a freshly toasted cheese sandwich. *Almost makes her look human*, Riley thought.

Keep moving, said the sensible part of her brain.

Naturally, she didn't.

"Hi."

Sandwich in hand, Biedermann looked silently to the door. Waiting.

"Hi, *Nurse Biedermann.*"

"Ms. Diaz. Is there something I can do for you?"

"No, they just sent me this way because the main hall's being cleaned up."

"Ah. I see."

She returned to her sandwich.

Are we going to move on now? the same part of her brain pleaded.

In a minute, she fired back.

"Can I ask you a question?"

Seeing that this was about to become a conversation, Biedermann resignedly set the remains of her sandwich down on a paper plate, brushed a few stray crumbs from her uniform, folded the napkin on her lap into a precise square, and set it down before looking back up at Riley. "I suppose that depends on the question."

"Do you enjoy what you do here?"

"Is it your assumption that I *shouldn't* enjoy my work?"

"Not judging, just asking."

"I like helping people who cannot help themselves. I like being part of a process that returns them whole and hale to the outside world."

"That's the job description, the kind of thing someone puts on a résumé. I was asking if you actually *enjoy* what you do?"

Biedermann's face showed not even a flicker of reaction. "That varies from moment to moment and patient to patient. The reason you were diverted this way—improperly diverted, I will add, and I will have words with someone about that— is because Nurse Sanchez was escorting one of the regular patients to a meeting with his family when he began projectile vomiting on his shoes, the floor, the doors, the walls, and not coincidentally, Nurse Sanchez. Do I think she enjoyed the experience? Almost certainly not. But that doesn't stop us from doing what needs to be done to help the patients."

"Smooth how you transitioned my question to Nurse Sanchez rather than talking about yourself."

Biedermann smiled without a trace of humor, then noticed the book in Riley's hand. "What's that?"

Oh, shit!

"Just a book."

"I can see it's a book. What sort of book?"

"Nothing, it's—"

"Bring it here, please."

Riley stepped forward and handed over the copy of *Frankenstein*.

Biedermann brushed dust off the cover that apparently only she could see. "I read this back in college," she said, her voice flat. "Led to a rather lively discussion about whether the book was pro-science or anti-science. What do *you* think, Ms. Diaz?"

Uh-oh! Trick question!

"Never really thought about it. I just like the story."

"Mmmm," Biedermann said as she riffled through the pages, glancing at random passages that caught her attention.

Can I just go now? You're starting to creep me out.

"I suppose what I'm asking," Bidermann continued—

Ohforchrisssakes.

—"is, do you consider Victor Frankenstein the *hero* of the story, the *victim* of the story, or the *villain* of the story?"

A parade of possible responses flicked through Riley's mind. At the head of the line was, *I don't know. From your perspective, as someone who will almost certainly have a house dropped on her by a tornado someday, what do* you *think?*

"Well, he says straight up that he wants to be like God, with the power of life and death. That sounds at least a *little* bit Doctor Doom–y, right?"

"Mmmm," she said again, then closed the book. "Let me come at the question a different way. Do you know when the first adult heart transplant was performed in the United States?"

Is this gonna be on the test?

Shut up before you get us both in trouble.

Both? Who do you think this is, *anyway?*

"No."

"December third, 1967. And do you know who was the most fervently opposed to the idea of heart transplants?"

Come on! Say it! Say "Is this gonna be on the test?" You know you want to!

"No, and what does this have to do with—"

"Religious groups were furious with the medical establishment for putting dead parts into living bodies, and frequently compared them to Frankenstein. They said these doctors were trying to take to themselves the power of God, to decide who lived, who died, and when. They believed that the heart was where the soul resided, so putting the heart of one person into another was the worst kind of sacrilege. But their complaints obscured a more important point. Any time a doctor saves someone's life, he is playing God, and most people are fine with that. They *want* someone who can play God just long enough to save them from cancer, heart failure, or the latest virus.

"Was Victor Frankenstein a monster because he wanted to play God? No. He was just being a doctor, same as every doctor in every hospital on the planet, and their actions spring from the same desire: to change the world, to make it a better place—a healthier, saner, and more rational place—by controlling disease, infirmity, and yes, even death.

"You asked if I enjoy what I do, so let me give you my answer: yes, I do, because I get to be part of something bigger than myself. Here, I make a difference. Here, I am in control. And control is everything, Ms. Diaz."

She folded her arms across the book. "My parents died when I was five. For the next twelve years I was shuttled back and forth between relatives who lacked the patience, the resources, and the will to look after me properly. I was a burden, an intrusion, an afterthought. My life was chaotic and outside my control, which made me susceptible to whim, to the casual cruelty of people who enjoyed seeing me helpless and in a box. In self-defense I learned to care for myself, cook my own food, wash my own clothes, and earn my own money. I did whatever was necessary to take control of my life and circumstances because having agency, authority, and control over oneself is the most important thing in all the world. It is the power to say, 'I will go this far and no farther.'

"You aren't who you think you are, Ms. Diaz; you are a subset of whoever you allow, consciously or otherwise, to control you. The worst of these are people who want everyone to line up behind *their* goal, *their* cause, *their* movement, *their* mission: users, losers, abusers, and the occasional martyr in search of a match and some oil. They get others to enlist in their cause, surrendering control and risking life and limb on their behalf, by spinning pretty words about what they're trying to achieve and the new society they're trying to build. But in the end it's really all about *them*, and it always ends badly.

"I do not enlist in causes or campaigns, follow martyrs over cliffs, or give anyone else agency over my life. No one owns me. No one controls me. I go my own way, make my own choices, and stick my neck out for no one.

"Which brings us to you, and this book," she said, holding it up. "You tried to hide it, then asked for it back, because you think it is yours. But this is your book only as long as I *allow* it to be your book. If I say no, if I take it away, if I say that as of this moment this is no longer your book, then it is no longer yours. Shall I do that, Ms. Diaz? Shall I, with a single word, take this away? After all, this is a horror novel, and we do not generally allow patients to have such books, because it can upset them. But you could ask me to allow it anyway."

"Yes, please."

"And by making that request, you tacitly admit that doing the things that brought you here had only one result: the loss of control. You have no voice and no choice. You have only what I choose to give you. Is that correct?"

Riley ground her teeth but didn't argue. "Yes."

Biedermann waited.

"Yes, Nurse Biedermann."

"Then I will give this back to you," she said, and handed Riley the book. "I hope you will take this as a teaching moment, because it's not intended to hurt or embarrass you. There's an old saying, *There is no shortage of love in the world, only of worthy vessels in which to put it.* You lost agency over your life because you invested yourself in unworthy vessels. If you want to regain that control, then you must begin to choose more wisely. Do you understand?"

"Yes, ma'am."

"Then you can go," Biedermann said, and went back to her sandwich.

Yes, ma'am? Riley's brain yelled at her as she stepped back into the hall. *Yes, ma'am? Why didn't you tell her to shove her 'teaching moment' up her ass?*

Because I need the book. Not for me, but for him.

Bullshit. You went all meek and mild because you know that in a place like this, the doctors can say whatever they want, but it's the nurses who get it done. Because you're afraid of her. Because she's the one with the real power here.

Yes.

Because she can hurt us.

Yes.

And because she may not be wrong.

I don't know . . . maybe . . . maybe . . .

The cafeteria was more packed than usual, with nearly every table taken up by non-ARC patients and their visiting families. Tray in hand, Riley was looking for an open chair when Steve waved her over to where he was sitting with Hector and Angela from the therapy group.

"Have a seat," Steve said, but as she approached, she saw the other two exchange a worried glance that said, *Maybe we should move.*

"Thanks, but I'm still on double-secret probation. I can go back to my room—"

"No, it's cool," Angela said, ignoring the look she got from Jim two tables over. "Sit, please.

"Did you hear about the puking-for-points incident?" she asked as Riley took her place at the table. "I saw the whole thing. It's always super crowded on Family Day, so I wanted to get here early and grab a seat, and it happened right in front of me. It was like someone shoved a firehose all the way up his ass and out the other end. Now I can't see anything else."

"That's Alex Lafferty," Steve said. "He's being treated for a ton of schizophrenic disorders including his trademark problem: cyclical vomiting syndrome. He loves his folks, but whenever they show up it's a break in his daily routine, and it totally stresses him out. Next thing you know, it's boom-splat all over the place."

"Do you know *everyone's* problems?" Riley asked, impressed.

"Let's just say I like to know who shouldn't be sitting across the table from me."

"Yeah, I know the feeling," Riley said, pretending she didn't mean what she meant.

"It was nothing personal," Hector said, absently rubbing the back of his left hand. "It's just a difficult situation, you know? Jim's just doing his best to make sure we keep our eye on the prize: getting out of here."

"Totally get it," Riley said, then to deflect the awkward conversation nodded to a small circular red mark on the back of his hand. "So what's that about?"

"What's what about?"

"I noticed you rubbing that earlier."

"Just something I do sometimes," he said, lowering his hands.

"Is that the start of a tattoo?"

He shook his head. "It's a burn mark. I was thirteen. I pissed off my old man one day, and before I know what's happening, he's got my hand down on the table, cigarette in hand. 'This'll make goddamned sure you never forget what you did wrong,' he said, then *bam*!"

"So what'd you do?" Steve asked.

"I don't remember," Hector said, smiling almost shyly as he rubbed at the mark. "I remember only the pain. Ironic, right?"

"Why didn't you tell us?" Angela asked.

"Never came up," he said, looking at Riley with an expression somewhere between *You know people have boundaries, right?* and *I think I'm glad you see enough to notice this stuff, but I'm still gonna need some time before I trust you.*

"I'm so sorry," Angela said.

"What about *your* father, Angela?" Riley asked.

"My dad doesn't believe I'm here."

"Well, sure, I'm sure it was a shock."

"No, he doesn't think *anything's* real. He believes in simulation theory, that what we call reality is just a big computer program and we don't know it."

"Sounds like your dad belongs on my side of the hospital," Steve said.

"He's one of those guys who lives way deep in his head, you know? Even as a kid, he was never entirely sure anything outside himself was real. So he got into simulation theory big-time. The way he explained it to me is that the number one problem for any species that figures out how to live forever is going to be boredom, because once you're immortal nothing's really at risk. The solution would be to create a computer environment where you forget who you are and become someone with a short lifespan, which lets you experience all the danger that goes with mortality until you 'die' and wake up in your *real* body. Then you're back to being bored until the next time you go in."

"So, basically like every serious gamer in the world," Steve said.

"Something like that. He says the only reason we sleep is so the guys who are in charge of running the program can debug the system and make sure everything's running properly."

"What about dreams?" Riley asked. "How do they fit in with all this?"

"Screensavers. Random thoughts to keep us occupied so we don't notice the upgrades. He says vivid dreamers can 'wake up' in the middle of their dreams and take over because the program is in neutral, like a car, so they can just gun it and go."

"What do *you* think?" Riley asked.

Angela pondered the question for a moment, then said, "*I* think my dad needs to get out more."

"And what does your mom say about all this?" Hector asked.

"No idea. She split when I was nine, got divorced, then married a really rich guy in Dubai. Haven't heard from her in years."

"I'm sorry," Riley said. "That must be hard."

"It's mostly okay. Ups and downs, you know? The hardest part was a couple of years ago when I realized I couldn't remember what her face looked like. I mean, yeah, I had pictures, but there's a difference between remembering what a picture looks like and remembering the person, you know? Living and breathing. I'd be in bed running all the moments we were together through my head instead of sleeping, and she just wasn't there.

"Before she walked out, she used to take me to the park and I'd play on the swings for what felt like forever. There was a little kiosk near the playground that served coffee and snacks, and she'd sit inside with a latte and a book and keep an eye on me until I was exhausted from swinging and swinging and swinging. I always knew it was time to go home when I saw her coming around the corner of the coffee shop. 'Had enough?' she'd say, then she'd take my hand and off we'd go.

"It bugged me that I could remember the moment but couldn't remember what she looked like, so about a year ago I went back to the park and sat on the same swing, trying to remember her. It wasn't crowded, but people looked at me like, *What's her deal?* But I stayed anyway, for one hour, then two. After a while everyone else left, and I was the only one still there. Sitting on that swing. Waiting for my mom.

"Then I looked up, and it was like I could see her coming around the corner of the coffee shop. She was wearing skinny jeans with dark-brown boots, with mud on them from the park, and an indigo blouse with little gold embroidered roses under a black leather jacket. Her hair was pulled back, and she was smiling at me—my mom was *smiling* at me—and she put out her hand and said, 'Had enough?'

"And if I close my eyes, right now, I can see her standing there as clear as I'm seeing you right now. Is that enough? Will that ever be enough? Probably not. But at least I can see my mom in my head, and for now I'm okay with that."

"Did she tell you why she left your dad?" Riley asked.

"No, but it's probably the same reason I haven't gone by to see him in a long time," Angela said, her voice soft and sad. "*You* try saying 'I love you' to someone who's pretty sure you don't actually exist."

"Maybe Kaminski's right," Hector said. "Maybe the road that put us in here really did start with our parents."

"You don't have to be crazy to have issues with your folks," Steve said. "You just have to be alive."

BALL SERVICE

By week six Kaminski's group therapy sessions had begun to blur into one another, repeatedly hitting the same notes, a tedious litany of "Do you admit that you were wrong?" and "You do see that you were being used by other people, right?" and "Do you really think that causing traffic jams is going to change the world?"

So Riley wasn't surprised when he began their next session by handing out questionnaires for the group to fill out. Most of the questions were straightforward and appropriate to a mental health facility: Do you feel nervous or depressed? Do you have suicidal thoughts? Do you have trouble sleeping? Do you sometimes hear voices when no one else is in the room? Do you want to get better?

And then there were these:

Do you think the government is evil?

Do you think people in the government are persecuting you?

Do you believe the United States Government is engaged in a conspiracy against you?

Do you blame the president of the United States for your incarceration?

Do you agree that preemptive compassionate arrests can be used to help people?

Do you feel you were led into your negative behavior by others?

Riley declined to answer any of the questions, but did find the form useful for its aerodynamics as she crafted it into a paper airplane and booped it across the room to a three-point landing under Kaminski's chair.

"Tell me something, Riley" Kaminski said, nodding to the airplane at his feet. "Would you have done that if it was just you and me in a room, without an audience to show how brave you are?"

She looked away, refusing to give him anything to work with.

He pressed on regardless. "Then let me ask the question a different way. What is more important to you: winning their approval or earning my disapproval?"

"If it helps you feel better," she said, her long-brewing irritation stepping firmly into the light, "—and I say this with great sincerity, from the bottom of my heart—absolutely *nothing* about you is important to me."

"So you don't care what people think about you?"

"Nope."

"So you're okay with the distance I've noticed between you and the rest of the group?"

Another trick question. If I say yes, the others will feel like I'm dismissing them; if I say I'm not okay with their distance, then I'm agreeing with him.

Exactly. So don't engage. Don't let him sink the hook.

I'm trying, but I'm tired, and he's seriously pissing me off.

"I don't want to talk about it."

"You sound angry."

"That's your opinion."

"And my opinion doesn't matter?"

Don't engage.

"Nope."

"Do the opinions of other people matter to you at *all*? Because that question is really at the heart of what we're trying to accomplish in these sessions. You're here because you fell under the influence of other people—"

"Nobody influences me, okay? I make my own decisions!"

Shit. You engaged . . . you cracked the door. Now he has something to work with.

"Really? That's an extraordinary thing to say, don't you think? At one time or another, aren't we all under the influence of other people? Our relationship to our parents—"

"Don't go there."

"—teachers, friends, and other family members shape us in a million ways. I'm a better person for the relationships I've had because they've helped me grow. Even casual relationships can affect us. When someone in the office is in a bad mood, pretty soon the whole place is on edge. We look to others to inspire us, to give us hope, to encourage us to be more than we think possible, to say to ourselves, 'I want to be like that.' Or the reverse happens, and we look at someone and realize that's not who we want to be. A negative influence is still an influence because everything we see and hear affects us. That's what it means to live in the world.

"But here you are, insisting that none of this happens to you. So what are we to make of that? Do we take you at your word, that you really are completely isolated from the rest of the human race, including friends, family, and loved ones? Because what you're describing is the textbook definition of acute psychological withdrawal. There are two outpatients and one inpatient suffering from exactly that disorder on the other side of the hospital. If you're telling the truth, then we need to begin treating you for this as soon as possible."

She looked to the others for support. No one looked back. Unwilling to dive into the line of fire.

Can you blame them? she thought.

"On the other hand," he continued, "maybe you're *not* telling the truth when you say none of us matter to you. Maybe you're lying, not just to me but to everyone in the group. You can treat me any way you like—I'm used to it—but why would you lie to the members of this group, your peers and, potentially, friends? What does that say about you? More to the point, what does it say about how you see *them*?

"But here's the thing: I don't think either of those possibilities are correct," he said, leaning forward, his voice low and intense. "I don't think you're telling us the truth, but I also don't think you're lying to us. I would suggest that you're telling us *your* truth, because you're lying to yourself. I offer that possibility because I believe in you."

"Totes moved by your belief."

Remember what Julian said. Don't let him inside your head. Fuck off. I've had it with this asshole.

"Which is why I *also* believe that you wouldn't be here if you hadn't been led astray by other people. Helping you to recognize and acknowledge that fact is going to be crucial to helping you get better."

"Not gonna happen."

"But isn't a decision not to get better ultimately self-destructive? Who do you think you're hurting? It's not me. I get to go home at night. You're the one who's stuck here, and the irony is that you're holding the key that opens the door. If you tell me that you're here because you were influenced by others, *used* by others, well, then it's really not your fault, is it? That provides a basis for you to go free. Everyone else in this room certainly understands that, which is why they're inching closer to release every day.

"But if the violent, subversive acts you committed outside were entirely your idea from start to finish, without any cause-and-effect relationship to what's being done by anyone in the outside world, well, that not only makes your actions arbitrary and unjustified, it's clear evidence of a pathological obsession, an irrational hatred for people who want only the best for you.

"You seem to think that I'm a bad person, that the government is evil. Which means you must be on the side of justice and righteousness. But is that really true? You say no one influences you, but we both know that's not true, so that's lie number one. You said you don't care what others think of you. But I've seen how the distance between you and the others hurts you, so we both know that's lie number two. I, on the other hand, have been absolutely honest with you from the start of this discussion. So which of us has the ethical high ground here, and which of us is being deceitful?"

Riley felt her cheeks flush with frustration at letting herself get outmaneuvered. *Idiot. My own fault. Walked right into it.*

"I'd very much like a response to my question, Riley."

"Okay, then here's my response," she said. "Go. Fuck. Yourself."

Kaminski sighed and looked to the rest. "I see we're about out of time. The rest of you can turn in your questionnaires now."

And every one of them did as he asked.

Every Friday was Barbeque Day, a welcome break from the usual diet of flavorless meatloaf, fish, or sliced chicken, overcooked vegetables, and any other foods that could be eaten with blunt plastic cutlery and chewed without expending the slightest energy. Barbeque Day was their sole respite from the barely edible horror of the rest of the week, offering up pork and beef ribs that were thick and chewy but soft enough to be eaten off the bone, along with catfish, Cajun cauliflower for the vegetarians, sweet potatoes, and beans and rice.

Barbeque Day also gave the cooking staff a break from having to wrestle with the massive and outdated oven that dominated the kitchen. Rather than struggling to coax it to life then keep it from sputtering out a minute later, they were able to cook over a grill in the parking lot, waving away the haze of tangy smoke as they flipped and braised and seasoned. "That stove's a damn beast," one of the cooks told Riley on the occasion of her first Barbeque Day. "Gotta know how to come at it just right or it'll bite you. It was part of the original installation, back when this was an assisted-living facility, and I hear it was trouble even then. Dr. Kim's been saying we're gonna get it fixed for almost a year now. Gonna see the Second Coming before that happens. But I'd come all the way from Heaven for these ribs, so who am I to complain?"

Patients sometimes skipped therapy sessions, or declined to use the exercise room, but *nobody* missed Barbeque Day, or as Danny put it, the happiest day of the week.

But in the aftermath of Riley's latest skirmish with Kaminski, 'the happiest day of the week' this most definitely was not.

"We told you before, you have to stop making trouble," Jim said. "All you're doing is making the group look bad."

"So what am I supposed to do? Just roll over and bark whenever he says so? I want to get out of here as much as you do, but I'm worried about what we're giving them on the way out. Signing papers that say we were wrong gives them ammunition they can use to go after the next bunch. If they want to call us crazy for protesting, fine, but that doesn't mean we have to go along with it. I refuse to sign a bunch of papers where I admit that I was crazy but that I'm *much* better now. If we were *sane* out there, if we were *right* out there, then we're sane and right in here, and we can't back away from that."

"Fighting them doesn't prove we're sane. That comes from being able to have a calm, reasoned conversation, so that's what we're doing, gaming the system to *beat* the system."

"What if they *want* us to think we're beating the system because otherwise we'd have no reason to cooperate and give them all this stuff."

"You're starting to sound paranoid," Becca said.

"If you're not paranoid in this place, you're not paying attention. I just can't shake the feeling that there's more to all this than what we're seeing. Something's wrong. There has to be some reason they're so intent on creating a paper trail—"

"It's easy to play the what-if game when you don't have to back it up with anything," Lauren said, eager to join in the fight now that Riley was being dogpiled. "If there's some scary reason behind why they want all this stuff, then what is it? Tell me, Riley. What's the big fucking conspiracy?"

"I don't know, because I can't see the play! But my gut keeps telling me there's more going on than they're saying."

"And what if you're wrong?" Hector asked. "Sooner or later you're gonna push Kaminski too far and he'll come back guns blazing, and the rest of us are gonna get caught in the crossfire."

"The sweet potatoes are especially good today," Angela said, trying to deflect the conflict before it could escalate further.

But Riley would not be deflected. "If I'm wrong, then it's my problem, not yours; I'm the one that'll get dinged, you can do what you want," she said, tired of the back-and-forth. Worse still, the ribs were getting cold. "Look, I understand that you don't want to inherit secondhand shit, and I'm already on the outs here. You gave me fair warning. If you want to stay out of the line of fire, fine; if you want to disown me or kick me to the curb if this goes bad, also fine. You do you, I'll do me, and we'll see where the pieces land."

"Suits me down to the ground," Jim said. "Anybody got a problem with that?"

No one at the table said no. But they didn't have to.

After a long silence punctuated only by the sound of plastic cutlery on plates, Danny looked up at Callie. "Angela's right. The sweet potatoes *are* really good today."

"Shall I respect man, when he condemns me?"

They were getting near the end of the book, and she still had no idea if the words were doing anything to encourage Frankenstein to start communicating in more than grunts, and abandon the monosyllabic movie monster he had bonded to for the more talkative one in the book. But he remained silent. Maybe it really was all for nothing. Maybe he was incurably what he was and would never change, and she was only providing a moment's distraction.

Then it's a distraction for both of us, she decided, and kept reading.

"Let him live with me in the interchange of kindness, and, instead of injury, I would bestow every benefit upon him with tears of gratitude at his acceptance. But that cannot be; the human senses are insurmountable barriers to our union. Yet mine shall not be the submission of abject slavery. I will revenge my injuries.

"If I cannot inspire love, I will cause fear."

She closed the book. "I think we all know how that feels," she said. "When people disappoint us, when the world hurts us, we want to hurt it right back, and pretty soon we're all about the anger because there isn't room for anything else. But here he's saying that he'll only cause fear if he can't inspire love. That means love came first, so despite all the shit he's been through, he still considers love a possibility, and that's amazing. All he's asking for is for someone to care for him, so he can care for them, to get love so he can give love back. He doesn't *want* to be a monster, he doesn't want to hurt *anyone*, he just—"

"Riley Diaz?"

One of the orderlies stood in the entrance.

Frankenstein turned, lips curled in a feral snarl at the interruption.

"You gotta come with me," he said, keeping a wary eye on Frankenstein.

"Why?"

"Above my pay grade. Someone says get so-and-so, I get so-and-so, and right now you're my so-and-so."

She looked to Frankenstein, who was becoming increasingly agitated. "It's okay," she said. "We'll pick this up later."

Accompanied by the orderly, she stopped by her room long enough to drop off the book before being taken to the first floor, passing cubicles until they reached Kaminski's office.

The orderly knocked, then opened the door. "Diaz," he said, and opened it wider.

Riley stepped inside. Kaminski was sitting behind his desk, filling out paperwork. "Thank you," he said without looking up. "That'll be all for now."

The orderly nodded and stepped out, closing the door behind him.

"Please sit," Kaminski said. "I'll just be a minute."

Riley took a seat on the other side of the desk and counted five minutes before he set down the pen and sat back in his chair.

"How's it going?" he asked.

"It *was* going great."

"How's your friend?"

"No idea what you're talking about."

"You can't help him, you know. I've dealt with expansive delusion cases before, and they're immune to talk therapy, especially if they've based their alternate personalities on fictional characters. If a patient thinks they're the president, or the queen of England, you can turn on the TV and show them the real thing, and sometimes that can make a dent. But it doesn't work if someone believes he's Don Quixote or Zorro or Superman or—"

"Were you his doctor before coming over to ARC?"

"One of them," he said, "and I have the scars to show for it. Then again, so does he, so I guess we can call it a draw."

Prick, Riley thought, and wondered what he'd done to Frankenstein to merit the word *scars*. *Topic for another time.*

"So what made him like he is?" she asked, trying to seem only casually interested.

"It's not important, and ultimately neither is he. He's not my problem anymore. I just hate to see you wasting your time on someone who clearly doesn't deserve it."

"It's my time to waste. It's not like I have anywhere else to be."

"That's the reason I wanted to see you. We're over a month into your treatment, and so far we haven't seen any improvement. You continue to resist every attempt to help you, even from Dr. Nakamura, who is just here to be your advocate."

Riley shrugged and said nothing. *Where is this going?*

He templed his fingers and tapped them against his chin. "I understand that you intend to keep fighting every effort to outgrow the behavior that brought you here because you're afraid that the government will use any act of compliance on your part against others."

On the outside, she held his gaze, determined not to give him any sense of her reaction.

On the inside, her brain raced through possibilities like an overclocked hard drive.

Option One: someone told him what I said, meaning there's at least one person in the group who can't be trusted.

Option Two: nobody told him anything, and he's making an educated guess. He's a shrink—that's what they're trained to do.

Option Three: the cafeteria is bugged.

"The problem with most people," he continued, "is that they tend to think in binary terms. The light is either on or off. Things are good or bad, fattening or healthy, positive or negative. But you and I know that's not true. There are all kind of gradients. People sometimes do the right things for the wrong reasons, the wrong things for the right reasons, and everything in between. Right or wrong isn't even the point. Living in the world is about being strong enough to do what it takes to achieve the result you're aiming for."

He stood and turned his back to her, looking out the window. "You're a bright young woman, Riley. That's evident in your records, your session with Dr. Nakamura, and the way you present yourself in group therapy. You volunteer nothing, watch everything, and say little when asked. But what you do say reveals a strategic thinker, and I admire that. Which brings me back to the fallacy of binary thinking."

He turned from the window and walked slowly to the other side of the desk. "One side of binary programming is, 'I have to fight everything and everyone, even if that means I get stuck here for the rest of my life.' Which is what you've been doing ever since you got here. The other extreme is, 'I have to cooperate with everything so I *don't* spend the rest of my life here.' Which is what the others are doing."

"That's their choice."

"Exactly," he said. "But as I said, both approaches are predicated on a binary assumption, which means it's a false choice. There are ways to get out of here that don't involve having to fill out forms the way some bureaucrat in DC wants them filled out. The government only cares about the final result: Is this person cured, or not?"

He stepped up to her chair. "I'm the one who gets to make that determination, Riley. I make that call. And there may be a *non*binary way to get out of here that you haven't considered."

His zipper was at mouth height when he said it.

And just in case she missed the message, he put his hand on top of her head, and left it there.

Okay, she thought, *here we go.*

She glanced up at him, because she knew they *liked* it when you looked up at them, and served up an obviously forced smile, because they *really* liked it when they felt they were making you do something you didn't want to do.

She pushed her left hand up his leg.

Glanced up again as she took firm hold of his belt buckle.

Then she brought up her right hand.

And punched him in the dick as hard as she could.

Twice.

He screamed and fell to the floor, clutching his groin as she jumped on him and got in a few more shots to his face before the door flew open and three orderlies rushed in. Two of them pinned her to the floor as the third dragged Kaminski out. "I was just walking past her, and she punched me in the goddamn nuts!" he yelled.

"Is that why you had your hand on the back of my head, asshole?" she yelled back, struggling with the orderlies.

"She's violently out of control!" he said. "I want her sedated! Right now!"

"No! He's lying! Let me go!"

A syringe flashed. A sliver of cold metal slid into her arm.

Then everything went soft as she fell backward through the floor and into the dark.

Riley floated through pools of darkness punctuated by fluorescent light.

Then: voices, distant and indistinct, giving and receiving instructions. She wondered if any of it had something to do with her but couldn't be sure because her eyes refused to open.

The elevator jostled and rose.

Cold. So cold.

For a moment she was seized by the sense that she had to be somewhere else, but let the impulse go when she couldn't figure out what happened to her feet. Maybe she'd left them in the other room.

Then: lifting and floating and lying flat again.

Heaviness on her arms. She tried to raise them. They wouldn't move.

She glanced up.

Biedermann.

There was a pinch of pain in the back of her hand as another needle found a vein.

Then with a sudden, precipitous crash, the world went far, far, very far away.

Slowly, gradually, Riley became aware of the whir of cool air moving through ducts, and conversations taking place at the other end of a thousand-yard hallway.

But she couldn't see anything.

She turned her head. Maybe that would help.

Nothing. Only darkness. She squinted harder. Still nothing.

Ohmygod, I can't see, she thought, and a part of her brain started screaming. *I can't see I can't see Ican'tsee—*

Then the part of her brain that wasn't screaming said, *Your eyelids are closed.*

Oh, the rest of her thought back. *Thanks.*

De nada.

She spent the next several centuries trying to remember how to open her eyelids, which now weighed about a thousand pounds each.

With one last effort she managed to open her left eye just enough to see that she was back in her room. Then it slammed shut again, exhausted by the effort. While her left eye took a well-deserved nap, the right eyelid skinned back a little but fell back before she could focus on anything useful.

Come on guys, she thought angrily, *let's get organized.*

She decided to sneak up on her eyelids by pulling her forehead upward. *They'll never see that one coming, lol.* She tugged and pulled and with a slight pop managed to open them both at the same time long enough to confirm that she was on her bed. She tried to turn her head for a better view of the room, but all of her available neurons were too busy trying to keep her eyes open to even *try* to deal with neck muscles.

Then a shadow fell over her as Biedermann's assistant, Nurse Sanchez, approached the bed. She checked Riley's vitals, then moved off for a moment before returning with a white paper cup. "Open."

Riley didn't.

"It's just ice," she said. "You're probably feeling pretty dehydrated."

Riley opened her mouth, and Sanchez fed in several slivers of ice. They felt good. She hadn't realized how dry her tongue felt until the ice began to melt.

Once the ice slivers were gone, Sanchez pulled a cell phone from her smock and walked out of the room.

Riley let her eyes slide shut again, saving them until there was something to look at.

I don't know what the hell they hit me with, but this is some pretty amazing shit. Somebody ought to package and sell this stuff.

Pretty sure that's how the pharmaceutical industry works, the logical part of her brain shot back.

When I want your opinion, I'll ask for it.

Fine!

Fine!

Her nose itched. She tried to scratch it, but nothing happened. She tried again and came to the drug-slowed realization that her arm was *trying* to accommodate her but kept bumping into something in the way.

She slitted her eyes open again and saw heavy cloth restraints pinning her arms to the bed rails. Her legs were also restrained.

Okay, this is officially bad.

The door opened and Sanchez returned, followed by Biedermann. And McGann.

He started in on her before he even reached her bedside. No greetings, no "So, how are you feeling," just, "Let me explain what you've done to yourself. You attacked one of our doctors."

"He tried to assault me," she said—though with her tongue numbed out and half-asleep, it came out as, "He tra da azult muh," but she was pretty clear he got the gist of it.

"Then why isn't there a single mark on you, except from where the orderlies had to subdue you, while Dr. Kaminski is upstairs being treated for penile trauma?"

She hadn't meant to laugh at *penile trauma*, but she did it anyway.

"Sorra," she slurred. "Izza meds."

"Get used to it. Until now you had the right to refuse medication on your own recognizance. But that right applied only as long as you obeyed the terms of the consent decree you signed when you were transferred to our care. By acknowledging that you were convicted of a violent crime, you waived your right to decline medication in the event of further violent acts. This incident confirms that you are a threat to the safety and well-being of everyone in this facility, which gives us the authority to administer medication *without* your consent.

"As a formality you will be given the opportunity to take those medications orally, but if you refuse, they will be administered intravenously. We also have the right to restrain you under staff supervision for up to twelve hours per day, during which time you will be catheterized to minimize the number of times the restraints will have to be removed and reapplied. This will continue for as long as we deem it necessary to moderate your violent impulses and guarantee the safety of the staff and patients."

Penile trauma! Penile comma! No! Penile Comma OwOwOwOwow!

"Do you understand me, Ms. Diaz?"

"Unnerstand. Peenee drama." She snickered despite herself.

Just a thought, but maybe we should be paying attention to what he's saying.

Shuddup. Peepee karma. Hah!

"The destructive behavior you engaged in outside these walls will not be permitted inside them," McGann said. "I regret the necessity of escalation, but you've left us no alternative." He turned on his heel and walked out, Biedermann following close behind.

Sanchez adjusted the restraints on Riley's arms, then rolled a stainless steel cart over to the bed, pulled aside a cloth to reveal a catheter, and began gloving up.

Don't think about it, Riley told herself, *people get this done all the time. They even did it to Dad after he had his appendix removed because they didn't want him pulling the stitches out. Focus on something else. Anything else.*

The phrase *penile trauma* rolled through her head again.

That could be a bit snappier. How about PTSD? Post-Traumatic Stress Dick?

"This will feel a little cold," Sanchez said, "but it won't hurt."

Riley nodded distantly, suddenly very tired.

Won't hurt.

Won't hurrrrt.

Hurrrrr.

Maybe that's what he was trying to say. Not hurrrrrr.

Hurrrrrrts.

Hurts. He hurts.

Then she closed her eyes, and the world went away again.

She was dreaming.

Again.

About the day it.

Happened.

In her dream instead of staying home she went with her parents to see the vice principal and was sitting in the back of the car for the ride home. Since it was Friday, her dad was trying to figure out which movie they should watch that weekend. He loved the movies, and when she was younger he would sometimes let her stay up past bedtime if they were in the middle of a good one.

Her mother was in the passenger seat, red hair cycloning in the breeze from the open window, arm thrown across the back of her dad's seat so she could gently stroke his neck as he drove. Feeling physically connected was important to her, and Riley loved the feel of her hand as it casually rested on her back or leg while they talked or watched TV.

But now they were driving home, and Riley was trying to remember something she wanted to tell them, or warn them about, something important, but she couldn't call it to mind. She checked her cell phone in case she'd written a note to herself about it but couldn't remember the unlock code, and for some reason it wasn't recognizing her face, so she put her face closer, but she couldn't see herself reflected in the glass, as if she wasn't there and—

—and her dad was talking about movies—

—and her mom was stroking his neck—

—and Riley remembered what she was supposed to tell them, what she was supposed to warn them about, but as she tried to form the words her mouth went numb and she screamed as loud as she could but nothing came out and they raced toward an intersection and she knew this street she knew this street she knew—

—and her mother turned just in time to see the truck blow through the stoplight, her eyes widening as the window shattered and—

Riley started awake, breathing hard. She could feel tears on her cheeks, but there was nothing she could do about them, her arms still restrained. To fight down the adrenaline and push the dream away, she tried focusing on every item in the room, but it was still half-dark and frankly, there wasn't much to work with. She couldn't tell if it was coming up on dawn or dusk, which only added to her disorientation, and she fought back a wave of panic.

Then suddenly there was a shadow, deeper than the darkness, and she realized she wasn't alone.

She turned her head as far as she could and saw a familiar silhouette standing silently beside the bed.

"Hey," she managed, remembering the moment she had wandered into Frankenstein's room to see him similarly restrained. "Guess we have more in common than I thought."

Silence.

Moving slowly, he raised his hand in front of his face, looking at it with eyes that were dark and dead, as if it belonged to someone else.

Then he reached toward her neck.

Oh shit, she thought, terrified. *Oh shit oh shit ohshit ohshitohshit—*

She was about to cry for help when he raised his hand slightly and, instead of going for her throat, stroked the tears on her cheek. Then he pulled back his hand, rubbing the wetness between his fingers with almost childlike wonder. His eyes, so lifeless a moment earlier, showed a strange, sad curiosity, as though he had never seen tears before and wasn't quite sure what they were for.

Then he glanced up, and his expression turned shy when he caught her watching him. Perhaps hoping to console her, but without knowing how such things were done, he put his hand on hers. His touch was cool, almost cold, but strangely, not unpleasant. With stiff outstretched fingers, he patted the back of her hand four times, watching himself do it each time, as though working hard to commit to memory a moment when he was gentle and capable of giving comfort, when he was not the monster he believed himself to be.

Then the moment passed, darkness returned to his eyes, and his hand fell loosely to his side, as though some part of him refused to allow even that simple human contact. *This is not for you. This can never be for you.*

His face lost to shadows, he walked out the door and down the hall, his footsteps gradually fading away in the distance.

What happened to you? she wondered, saddened by what she had glimpsed in his eyes. *Who or what made you into this?*

And why?

STARVED FOR
ATTENTION

Seven a.m. Biedermann entered, followed by Sanchez and her ubiquitous medical tray, and approached the bed where Riley was still restrained.

"Dr. Kaminski has recommended a treatment program of haloperidol twice a day," she said, her tone more formal than usual. "Unlike the broad-based sedative you received yesterday, which induces sleep, haloperidol is designed for daytime use on violent patients. It creates what's known as a state of conscious sedation. You will be awake and able to feed yourself, but for safety reasons you may require a wheelchair when moving around the facility. The medication can be administered orally, or by injection. Do you consent to take the haloperidol orally?"

"No," Riley said.

"Injection, then." Biedermann turned to Sanchez. "One five seven."

Sanchez opened a tray of prefilled syringes, labeled and cross-referenced by code to each patient. "One five seven," she repeated.

Biedermann uncapped the syringe, held it up to the light, tapped the side to ensure there were no air bubbles, then took Riley's restrained arm and slid the needle home.

"We'll check in on you when we finish morning rounds with the other patients to make sure the medication is working sufficiently and safely. If so, and if you seem properly relaxed and not aggressive, we can remove the restraints. Just remember that they can always go back on in the event of inappropriate or violent behavior.

"One last thing," she said on the way out. "Privileges are earned by constructive behavior; they are not automatic or freely given. Consequently, your library privileges have been revoked. We will, however, arrange for a television."

When the door closed, Riley looked to where her books, including *Frankenstein*, had been stacked the day before.

All gone.

Shit. Never even got to finish.

Biedermann and Sanchez returned an hour later, removed the restraints, slid out the catheter, and helped her into a wheelchair beside the small table. True to Bidermann's promise, the haloperidol let her remain conscious, but every move felt as if heavy weights had been attached to her body.

Riley glanced at the clock—9:30. "I'll miss breakfast," she said, her voice slow and slurred. Her stomach had awakened before the rest of her, cramped with annoyance at having missed dinner the day before.

"You are confined to your room for the next forty-eight hours for purposes of observation, so you will be taking your meals here," Biedermann said.

Sanchez set a bowl down on the table, containing milk and cereal that barely came a quarter of the way to the top.

"Is this all?" Riley asked.

"Dr. Kaminski recommended a reduced caloric intake while you adjust to the medication. Haloperidol can sometimes induce nausea, and he wants to be sure your system can handle it. It's for your own good."

Translation: he's getting even with me for shoving his dick all the way up to his tonsils. She reached for the spoon, but her first attempt went onto the table because her hand was shaking from the meds, so she used them both for the next salvo. When she was done, Sanchez collected the bowl and trotted out.

"We won't lock the door for safety reasons, but if you're seen outside your room in the next forty-eight hours you will be returned and restrained. Is that clear?"

"Yes," Riley said.

Biedermann waited.

"Yes, Nurse Biedermann."

She shook her head. "For what it's worth, I *did* try to warn you, Ms. Diaz, but you refused to listen. And now here you are, with less control over your life than you had even a few days ago. I'm very, very disappointed in you."

And with that, she was gone.

At 10:00 a.m., an orderly brought in a small television and hung it in a corner of her room before tuning it to a children's streaming network.

"Can I watch something else?"

"Sorry, no can do," he said. "This is the only channel allowed in the rooms because news programs or shows with too much action can agitate the patients." Then he tucked the remote into his pocket and headed out.

She turned her attention to the television, where a cartoon horse-drawn stagecoach was talking to a group of children about how roads are built, and why. After ten minutes of this, even the horses looked ready to shoot themselves.

At 12:30, Sanchez returned with lunch: half a tuna sandwich and a glass of water.

On the screen, a bear was very sad because he didn't have any friends.

Riley was transfixed. Haloperidol had its benefits.

She closed her eyes for what felt like only a moment, but when she opened them again, the sun was nearer the horizon and the shadow of the parrot was stretched across her bed. *Good idea*, she thought. *You get some rest, I'll take first watch.*

On the TV, a pair of inch-high teachers dressed in the height of 1920s fashion appeared in a puff of smoke at the base of a huge blackboard and began to explain why some letters, like *C* and *K*, may sometimes *sound* the same, but are really very, *very* different.

They continued to explain this for half an hour.

C stands for Catch, Riley thought at the television. K *stands for* Kill. *Would you like to hear me use both words in the same sentence with a* U *after each one?*

I didn't think so.

Six o'clock: Biedermann, Sanchez, and haloperidol—round two.

"Do you consent?"

"No."

"One five seven."

Uncap.

Tap-tap.

Push.

Dinner was a starter-sized green salad with lemon juice, four cherry tomatoes, and croutons. She picked out the croutons and hid them in her pocket for later. They would give her the illusion of having something to eat when the hunger set in, a plan carefully crafted to distract her from the knowledge that the hunger had set in several hours earlier.

Shortly before lights-out, she wheeled herself into the bathroom to pee for the first time since they'd removed the catheter. It hurt but she was pleased at being able to do it on her own.

Morning, Day Two.

"Do you consent?"

"No."

"One five seven."

Uncap.

Tap-tap.

Push.

One-quarter bowl of cereal.

Television.

"Tell the boys and girls watching at home why they should never ever look straight into the sun, Sailor Bob!"

Half a tuna sandwich for lunch. From the flavor, she wondered if it was the other half of the sandwich from the day before.

"How many kinds of birds can you think of," a matronly woman on-screen asked a crowd of young children. "Call out the names!"

"Parrot!" Riley said, then wondered guiltily if looking to the wrought-iron figure in the window counted as cheating.

Don't ask me, it said in her thoughts. *I just work here.*

The hours bled into one another. Sometimes she dozed. The rest of the time she stared at the TV without thinking about anything, letting the sounds and images wash over her.

Then a memory drifted up out of nowhere, an echo from the first time Riley went on a dinner date with a boy.

During a silent moment as they ate, she'd glanced over to see him staring into the distance for what seemed like a long time.

"What are you thinking about?" she asked, eager to share in the deep ideas that, from his thoughtful expression, must surely have been gliding through the caverns of his mind.

"Nothing," he said with a shrug, and kept eating.

She'd always resented that answer, believing it dismissive at best, duplicitous at worst. Her brain was constantly processing what she was doing, what people would think about what she was doing, how she planned to *react* to what they thought of what she was doing, what *she* thought about what she was doing, what her plans were for after she was done doing what she was doing, what she'd done the day before, and how it all tied together in a thousand myriad ways. How could someone think about *nothing*? For *hours*?

Now she knew.

Men are gooned on haloperidol twenty-four seven—it's the only thing that can explain them.

Her pride at this discovery lit up whatever parts of her brain were still reporting for duty, and she smiled in anticipation of a congratulatory phone call from the Nobel Committee.

Six p.m.

"Do you consent?"

"No."

"One five seven."

Sanchez reached for the syringe.

"I was thinking about not thinking," Riley said, her right arm back in its restraint for the injection, "and I remembered what you said a while back. That no one owns you, no one controls you."

Uncap.

"You seem to think that being in control is all about what other people can or can't do to you. But I'm not sure that's right. I think the part you're missing, the part *you're* not thinking about, is that we have no control *at all* over what other people do to us. The only thing we can control, the only real choice we have, is how we react when they do those things. Do we bend, break, or fight? You're doing this because Kaminski wrote a prescription and a treatment plan, then gave you the order. You're doing this because you *have* to. I'm saying no because I *choose* to. So which of us really has control here?"

Tap-tap.

"You said no one owns you. No one controls you. How's that working out for you, right about now?"

Push.

Sanchez looked away.

But Biederman's eyes were as cold as the tip of the needle.

As the warmth of the drug traveled up her arm, Riley shook her head and said, "I'm very, *very* disappointed in you, Nurse Biedermann."

Solitude.

Television.

Green salad. Lemon juice. Four cherry tomatoes. (Were they literally counting them?) Croutons for later.

Solitude.

Television.

Pee. Poo.

Lights out.

Sleep.

Morning, Day Three.

"Do you consent?"

"No."

"One five seven."

As Sanchez carried out the tray, Biedermann stepped up to Riley. "Your forty-eight-hour observation period has now expired. Since there have been no subsequent violent incidents, you are free to leave your room and move about the facility. Bear in mind, however, that this permission can be immediately revoked if there are any further disruptions. Finally, per your treatment plan, we will continue to administer haloperidol twice a day until instructed otherwise by Dr. Kaminski. Do you understand?"

"Yes, Nurse Biedermann," Riley said, and immediately began planning what she would have for breakfast: *waffles with fruit and whipped cream, eggs, and toast—and oh, yeah, bacon, lots and lots of bacon.*

An orderly appeared at the doorway with a wheelchair. "You can escort her to the cafeteria," Biedermann said.

The orderly helped Riley into the wheelchair—she kept hoping she'd adjust to the haloperidol, but she was still having a hard time walking without falling over—and rolled her to the cafeteria where the other ARC patients were sitting together at the same table. Some of them waved to her as she approached, but the rest appeared oddly subdued. Something seemed different about them, but she couldn't figure out what it was.

The orderly rolled her toward the one spot at the table that was open, pushed the wheelchair into the gap, and locked the wheels.

On the table in front of her, *waiting* for her, was a bowl of cereal, one-quarter filled.

She looked up at the orderly, her eyes asking, *What the fuck?*

"Doctor's orders," he replied in a tone that said, *It's not my fault, I gotta do this or it's my job.*

Riley reached for the lock on the wheelchair.

"Not allowed," he said. "Kaminski gave instructions that the wheelchair is to stay locked during meals for your own safety, but that if you felt strong enough to walk to the serving counter, we shouldn't stop you."

The distance from the table to the counter at the far end of the cafeteria seemed as long as a football field. Wobbly from meds and lack of food, she knew she'd never make it all the way without falling.

He wants to see me weak.

Then she looked around the table and finally realized what was different. The other ARC patients never had breakfast all together at the same table, preferring instead to break up into groups of twos and threes. So why were they all sitting together *now*, at the same table, waiting for her, with an open spot reserved for her with a bowl of cereal already in place? And why were none of them making eye contact with her, not even Danny?

I'm wrong, she thought. *It's not that Kaminski wants to see me weak. He wants* them *to see me weak. To make an example of me.*

So what am I going to do about it?

She knew she could never make the long walk to the serving counter, and unlocking the wheelchair against Kaminski's orders would almost certainly result in getting confined to her room again. And she wasn't about to give him the satisfaction of pleading with the orderly for more cereal.

There was only one acceptable response. *But are we up to this? No idea. Let's find out.*

As the others looked on, she picked out a single corn flake, put it on her tongue, then pushed the bowl away and laid her head on her arms.

"No, no, really," she said as the room spun around her, "I'm *so* full, I couldn't *possibly* eat another bite. You go on ahead."

The others looked from their full plates to Riley and back again, hesitated, then silently began eating, stealing little glimpses at her as she pushed the bowl farther away.

Game on, she thought.

Dr. Nakamura sat in for Kaminski at their next group therapy session, explaining that he was still "a little bit under the weather," but that he was resting at home and would be back in action in time for their next meeting.

"I thought we'd start today's session talking about violence," she said, and to no one's surprise looked at Riley as she said it. "I think we can all agree that violence never solves anything."

Riley started to ask *What about World War Two*, but Danny got there first.

"Worked against the Nazis," he said. "The first bunch, anyway."

"That's war, and war isn't the same as violence."

"Tell that to my grandfather," Hector said, and Riley could see that he was getting his back up over it. "Well, actually, you can't, because he's in a cemetery in France."

"Wars are authorized under prevailing laws, and waged by one government against another," Nakamura said. "Violence is something that happens between individuals that's not authorized and is thus illegal."

"Being legal doesn't make it right," Angela said. "As I recall, during World War Two, the laws of Japan made it legal for *your* ancestors to rape and kill *my* ancestors in China."

Go Angela! Riley thought, grinning, then tucked the smile away when Nakamura saw it.

"I'm not going to relitigate World War Two, Vietnam, the Mideast or any other war," Nakamura said. "This is about what happened three days ago, when Riley attacked Dr. Kaminski without provocation."

"He tried to make me suck his dick."

"That's your interpretation—"

"You weren't there."

"—there's not a shred of proof—"

"Because the doctors don't have cameras in their offices."

"—and Dr. Kaminski would never do anything like that. Am I right, Lauren?"

Lauren's head shot up, startled at being pulled into this.

Riley's cheeks flushed red in anger. *Nakamura knows! Or at least suspects! That's why she picked the only person in the room who'll say exactly what she's supposed to say!*

"Yes, you're right," Lauren said quietly, turning her gaze to the floor. "He'd never do something like that."

Riley closed her eyes, projecting fatigue as a cover while she blocked out the session with an image of hitting Nakamura in the face with a snow shovel, really hard, over and over, a lot.

Violence solves noth—

WHAM!

She opened her eyes again when she heard the session grinding to an end, unlocked the wheelchair, and rolled out of the room as fast as she could.

"Riley?" Lauren called from behind her.

Riley turned to see her near tears. "I'm sorry, I had to say that."

"I know, it's okay," Riley said, not wanting to get into it.

"It's just . . . you did what I couldn't, and God, I wish I could've seen it. But I can't do anything, can't *say* anything, until I get out of here. I promise, once I go home and get my son away from his asshole father, I'll—"

"Once you're out of here you won't do shit, because you'll be too busy trying to forget you were ever here," Riley snapped, then yanked back her anger. *This isn't her fault. He's using her the way he tried to use you. She's not the bad guy. You're mad at him, don't take it out on her.*

"I apologize," she said, "that was out of line."

"No, actually, it wasn't," Lauren said, wiping away tears, "and I'm sorry you're going through all this."

"I'll be okay," Riley said, though she knew Kaminski wasn't finished with her yet. "How does he keep getting away with it? Why doesn't someone on staff do something about it?"

"I think some of them want to, but they're afraid he'll hurt their careers. Sometimes, when I was . . . *with* him, he'd laugh at how nobody will say anything against him as long as he has McGann on his side, because that puts him inside Homeland Security, and they're not accountable to anyone. It was like he couldn't be touched."

"Not anymore," Riley said.

And that finally got a smile out of Lauren.

Lunch: the same half-of-a-tuna-sandwich served at the same table for the same audience with full plates before them.

"Gosh, I'd love to, but I'm still full from breakfast," Riley said, pushing away the plate. "Anyone else want it? No way can I fit this in."

Callie leaned in close. "Riley, stop it, we know what you're doing, but you have to eat."

Riley shook her head. If they weren't going to feed her properly, then she wouldn't eat at all. *Nothing like a little hunger strike to see who runs out of patience first.* But Callie wasn't wrong; between the haloperidol and being half-starved, she was hurting and pretty spaced out.

"I'll be fine," she said, putting her head on the table. "Just need to rest a bit."

Six p.m.

"Do you consent?"

"No."

"One five seven."

"I understand you're not eating," Biedermann said as she searched for a vein; the one she'd been using for the last several days didn't want to come out and play.

"Not hungry."

Biedermann held her gaze. "I hope you realize, Ms. Diaz, that there are steps we can take to make sure you get proper nutrition."

"Well, you can *try*," Riley said. "There's nothing you can do to force-feed me that a finger down my throat five minutes later can't undo."

"I wouldn't count on that," Biedermann said.

Green salad. Lemon juice. Four cherry tomatoes. Croutons.

Riley pushed the bowl away, but surreptitiously slipped out one of the croutons.

Later, after the ward was locked down for the night, she took the crouton out of her pocket and let it slowly dissolve in her mouth, savoring the saltiness and crunchy texture.

Just got to hold on for another two days, she thought. *Friday afternoon is grand rounds. Friday is Dr. Munroe. He'll come in, I'll say, "Good morning," and he'll fix this.*

She closed her eyes but did not sleep, her mind focused entirely on food and Friday.

Seven a.m.

"Do you consent?"

". . . no."

"Sorry, I couldn't hear you."

"No."

"One five seven."

She did not eat at breakfast.

She did not eat at lunch.

Six p.m.

"Do you consent?"

". . . . ."

"I'm sorry, I didn't hear that, Ms. Diaz. Do you consent?"

"No."

"One five seven."

She did not eat at dinner.

She did not sleep.

Seven a.m.

"Do you consent?"

"No."

"One five seven."

Riley rolled slowly down the hall toward the cafeteria, barely able to push the wheelchair, and took her place at the table. As before, the other ARC patients sat behind trays bearing eggs and toast and juice. She looked at the quarter bowl of cereal in front of her. She was so hungry, so starved, that the bowl was all she could see.

You can have one bowl. Just for now. You can pick up the strike later.

No, she thought, and looked away.

"Fuck this," Danny said angrily, and took the plate of eggs from his tray and slid it to Riley.

Callie was next, and a cold glass of orange juice appeared.

One of the orderlies, seeing what was happening, moved to stop them.

Danny, Hector, and Angela formed a defensive line between them.

Jim hesitated, then joined the others blocking the orderly. "I wouldn't butt into this if I were you."

"Yeah, what he said," Angela said.

The orderly trotted off, reaching for his cell phone.

"Go ahead, Riley," Becca said, "take your time. We've got your back."

Hands shaking from hunger, Riley sliced off a piece of fried egg and lifted it to her mouth.

It. Was. Magnificent.

The insurrection, small as it was, put the staff in a difficult position. There were no rules against sharing food unless it contained contraindicated nutrition, which wasn't the case here. But Kaminski had made his instructions concerning Riley very clear, and no one under him had the authority to countermand those instructions. Responding aggressively against the other ARC patients would only escalate the situation, leading to further insurrections, but they couldn't just ignore the situation.

The countermove came at lunch, when Riley and the others arrived to find that all the regular patients had been served an hour earlier. The service counter was closed, the door to the kitchen locked.

On the table were eight individual plates containing one-half of a tuna salad sandwich. The message was simple: *You want everyone to have the same meals, great, but understand that it works both ways.*

The sandwiches went into the trash, followed by the plates they came on, the plastic cutlery beside them, the napkins, and one of the chairs, just in case the point wasn't sufficiently clear.

Six p.m.

"Do you consent?"

"No."

"One five seven."

Dinner.

Eight plates. Eight green salads with lemon juice, four cherry tomatoes, and croutons.

They all went in the trash. Even the croutons. Also another chair.

They didn't talk about their decision, not even to each other, because nobody knew if the cafeteria or the halls or the other rooms were bugged. Besides, there was nothing to talk about. A line had been drawn. Now they had to stand behind it. And not move.

Boots on the ground! Bodies in the way!

Lights out. Doors locked.

Riley lay in bed, shaking with hunger. Two days of *virtually* no food had been followed by two days of *literally* no food. She felt bad that the others were now going through the same thing she was enduring, but she was also proud of them, and angry, and in for the fight.

Seven a.m.

"Do you consent?"

"No."

"One five seven."

One-quarter-filled bowls.

In the trash.

Then back to their rooms for grand rounds. *Finally*, Riley thought. *Dr. Munroe will fix this.*

When she heard his voice down the hall, she pushed hard on the arms of the wheelchair, forcing herself to stand. She didn't want him to see her on the *outside* the way she felt on the *inside*: ready to pass out from malnutrition and the drugs.

She looked at the clock, sweat pooling in the small of her back. It was taking him longer than usual to get to her room. Her knees wobbled and threatened to buckle under her. She locked them in place. *We're defined by what we stand for when standing is the hardest.*

So stand, goddamnit.

Stand!

After another five minutes, Dr. Munroe came through the door, followed by Biedermann, Sanchez, Nakamura . . . and Kaminski, who regarded her silently but angrily.

"Good afternoon, Ms. Diaz," Julian said.

"Good *morning*," she replied.

He nodded, silently acknowledging the reply. "How are we feeling today?"

"Couldn't be better," she said, staring pointedly at Kaminski. *Don't say anything they can use to put you back under restraints. Save the truth for when we're alone.*

"Any issues or problems?"

"Nothing I can't handle."

"I understand there was a bit of trouble between the staff, yourself, and the other ARC patients."

"Yeah, but we're working it out."

"Still declining oral medication?"

"Yes."

"Even though it's now a requirement?"

"Yes."

"Agreeing to take it would be simpler."

"Yes, it would."

"It took us a bit longer than usual to get to you because apparently everyone has chosen to be singularly uncooperative. Do you know anything about this?"

"Of course she does, she's the ringleader," Kaminski snapped.

"Ms. Diaz?" Julian said, ignoring the outburst.

"We haven't discussed anything. If we had, I'm sure someone, somewhere, would have heard it. Or recorded it. Isn't that right, Nurse Biedermann?"

Biedermann said nothing.

"All I know," Riley said, "is that apparently Dr. Kaminski decided to weaponize the food supplies, and I'm pretty sure it's against the law to deliberately starve patients to punish them or force them to do what you want."

"It's a bit more complicated than that," Julian said, "but in principle, yes, that's correct."

Then he made a notation on his tablet, nodded, and turned to the rest. "On to the next patient," he said, then paused as they started for the door. "Actually, you go on ahead, I forgot a couple more questions I need to ask."

Kaminski bristled. "We're supposed to do this together—"

"Yes, we are, and I imagine Mr. McGann would be the one to talk to about my decision, but by the time you call downstairs and request intercession, I'll be done here. So you and the rest continue on to the next room, and I'll be with you in just a tick."

They didn't like it, but technically Julian still outranked them, so they left.

"You've caused quite a stir," Julian said when the door was closed.

"Kaminski made the first move."

"So say the rumor mills," he said ruefully. "There's no evidence, of course, which reduces the situation to he-said/she-said, so I doubt anything will be done about it, but for what it's worth, I absolutely believe what you said about the encounter. Before the ARC program moved in, there were stories going around about Kaminski taking liberties with some of the patients. We were about to investigate when he flipped to McGann, who claimed jurisdiction over the inquiry and strangled it. Just one more way that he and McGann are linked at the hip."

Which is about what I figured, except worse, she thought, then caught her knees starting to buckle again.

"Please sit," Julian said.

"I'm okay," she said, though they both knew she was lying. "I'm guessing that if I file a complaint about the food situation, it won't go anywhere because McGann is protecting him, so is there anything *you* can do to stop him? Putting all of us on a starvation diet has to be illegal. I appreciate that the others are with me on this, but I don't want to see them get hurt."

"My authority was cut back significantly after McGann took over, and he's been whittling away at it ever since. It was he, by the way, who authorized the dietary changes recommended by Kaminski. As an administrator, not a doctor, McGann has more wriggle room than a physician when it comes to this sort of thing. The AMA probably wouldn't recognize the distinction, but that would require a full administrative review, which McGann could block through Homeland Security. The best I can do is threaten to open an inquiry of my own into what's going on. Stopping such an inquiry once it gets started is a lot harder than making the accommodations necessary to keep it from getting that far, so I suspect they'd blink. The question, of course, is what comes afterward. It's the doctrine of unexpected consequences; if I do X, they might do Y, and I don't know what Y would mean for me, or for you.

"But it has to be done," he continued. "This can't go on. If I don't speak up, then I'm complicit, and that's simply not an option. I can justify getting them to back off on the food issue on the grounds that it will defuse the tension and let things get back to normal. But the situation is more complicated when it comes to the meds. Once a physician prescribes a program of treatment based on his formal appraisal that it's best for the patient, it's hard for third parties, even me, to change that program without getting lawyers involved or getting three staff doctors to support an appeal, and I don't think we'll find any willing to stand up to McGann."

"So I'm stuck being Nurse Biedermann's pincushion?"

"I'm afraid so, but she's . . ."

Then he caught himself, and tucked away whatever he had been about to say.

What was that *about*? she wondered.

"There's an old saying, Riley: 'Keep your friends close, and your enemies closer.' If I were in your position, I'd keep close to Biedermann."

He started toward the door.

"Can I ask you something?" she said.

"They're waiting for me."

"I know, but this is important." She hesitated, trying to find a way to ask her question delicately before deciding, *I don't have time to be polite.* "It's about Frankenstein."

He allowed a thin smile. "I heard that you'd more or less adopted him. His lead therapist, Dr. Morris, wanted to intervene because some patients don't respond well to unsupervised contact, but I said let's see where this goes. What do you want to know?"

"Why is he the way he is? What happened to him?"

He frowned. "Under the rules of patient confidentiality, physicians don't generally discuss case histories with anyone other than family members or authorized guardians, but there simply aren't any. He's been a ward of the state since he was fourteen. Besides, his story was covered extensively, and quite luridly, in the press, so there aren't a lot of secrets left. Even so, I can only ethically discuss what's in the public record.

"From the age of three onward, he was abused by his parents. Beaten regularly, fed table scraps, locked in the basement and forced to sleep in his own waste. He used to hide in a corner that was his special place, where he convinced himself they couldn't find him or hurt him, but of course they always did. They never sent him to school or allowed anyone inside the house. Neighbors didn't even know they *had* a child.

"For children to develop normally, they need two things starting from about age four. The first is access to their peer group, other children their own age, who can help them learn how to socialize. More importantly, there must be someone in their life, a parent or authority figure, to whom they can bond as a protector. They need the security of knowing that there's at least one adult they can call out to for help if they're hurt, someone they can look to as a role model. But if there are no other children to teach them how to form friendships, and if the only authority figures in their lives are vengeful, violent, and emotionally abusive, they grow up incapable of forming normal relationships, unable to show compassion, affection, or vulnerability, because they know that expressing those emotions will result in retribution and further abuse.

"To drown out any cries he might have made, they put a TV in the basement behind wire mesh, tuned to a local cable channel that showed old movies that didn't cost much to license. One of the movies that regularly popped up in rotation was *Frankenstein*, and in that movie he found a reflection of his own situation: someone who was caged, beaten, reviled, and hated by those who had given him life. The difference was that the monster never seemed to feel the pain of the whip. No matter what they did to him, he just kept on coming.

"When we are in pain, we will grab on to anything that will let us survive. Lacking friends, genuine family or anyone he could look to as a role model, he bonded to Frankenstein, and learned to shut down the pain impulse, a not uncommon survival mechanism in cases of severe trauma. No matter how badly his parents beat him, he wouldn't scream or cry out. His defiance enraged them further, so they began switching up their methods, becoming even more extreme to elicit the pain they needed to see in his eyes. The more he adjusted to the latest form of abuse by cutting off the pain of being alive, the more his personality shut down, until there was very little of him left.

"One night, after his parents had been drinking heavily and beating him to within an inch of his life, they neglected to return him to the basement, and passed out in the living room, leaving him chained to the floor by his ankle. It wasn't the first time this had happened, but now, courtesy of what he had seen in the Frankenstein movies, he had a plan: he would burn down the 'castle,' with all of them inside, ending the nightmare once and for all. According to the medical report, he fought so hard to reach his father's cigarette lighter that he tore away most of the flesh at his ankle, exposing the bones underneath. I can't begin to imagine the agony he must have felt, but he kept going until he reached his goal and set the house ablaze.

"When the firefighters broke in, his parents were already dead of smoke inhalation, and he was nearly dead himself. Once the physical evidence found in the basement revealed the ugly truth of what had been going on, psychiatrists were brought in to try and salvage what was left of him, but their efforts proved unsuccessful. All he'd ever known was pain and rage, and with the death of his parents he no longer had a target for that anger, so he began acting out, attacking anyone who got close to him. During his first year in treatment, he put two orderlies in the hospital."

"So he's never getting out?"

"I'm afraid not. Given the horrors he was forced to endure, his actions on that day are understandable, but they still constitute premeditated murder. The judge allowed a very generous period to evaluate his condition in the hope that something could be done to help him, but after years of no progress he was ruled criminally insane and sentenced to a lifetime in psychiatric custody. He is never ever leaving here.

"So I advise you to be *very* careful around him. Just last year he broke the arm of an orderly who made the mistake of getting too close. He would've killed the man if other staff hadn't intervened. He's dangerous, Riley. Seriously dangerous. Be careful."

His phone blipped with a text. "The others want to know what's taking me so long. So I should get going."

"One last question," Riley said. "Everyone calls him Frankenstein, and maybe that's who he is now, but that's not how he started. What's his real name?"

"Doesn't matter," Julian said as he headed for the door. "Whatever that name was, and whoever he was before the nightmare began, he's not there anymore. The vulnerability of that child stood between him and freedom from pain, so it had to be eliminated. In a way, his earlier self was Frankenstein's first victim, murdered in order for the monster to survive.

"And now the monster is all that remains."

CONSEQUENCES
AND CIRCUMSTANCES
OF RAGE

Saturday. Seven a.m.

"Do you consent?"

"No."

"One five seven."

Exhausted from lack of food and sleep, Riley rolled into the cafeteria to find the serving counter back in operation. She turned to see the other ARC patients sitting behind trays loaded up with toast and eggs and waffles and orange juice. When they saw her, they came to their feet, cheering, whistling, and applauding.

She forced herself to stand, throwing a fist in the air. "Yes!" she yelled back. "*Yes!*"

For the next half hour, if it wasn't nailed down, she ate it; and if she could pry it up, then it wasn't nailed down.

Over breakfast, she learned that after Munroe filed his complaint, Kaminski had withdrawn the dietary changes, and canceled all therapy sessions for the next two days, presumably so he and McGann could figure out their next steps. *They know they have to think twice about going too far now that someone in authority, someone who's not afraid of them, is watching them.*

Even better, she seemed to be adjusting to the haloperidol. Usually all she wanted after getting a shot was to take a nap. But today she was feeling a little more energy than before, and a lot less dizzy. *I can probably start getting by without using the wheelchair, but I shouldn't go much beyond that. If they see I'm adjusting to the meds they'll increase the dose.*

After breakfast she rolled back to her room and was just coming out of the bathroom when she heard the outer door shut.

Kaminski stood with his back to the closed door.

Her heart slammed against her chest. *I don't know if I'm strong enough to fight him if he starts something.*

He took a step toward her, his face red with rage. "You think you've won," he said in a voice that was low and sick and dangerous. "You haven't. All you've done is hurt yourself and the others in ways you don't even understand yet. But trust me, you will.

"Munroe suggested we return you to jail. Did you know that? He said that if I thought you were violent, then you should be returned to serve out your sentence. I said no. I told him that you needed help, and patience, and compassion, and that I wasn't about to turn my back on you just because of one incident. Got to give it to the old fuck, he did everything he could to pry you away from me, but you're. Not. Going. *Anywhere.*"

He lowered his face until it was inches from her own. "I am going to fuck with you in ways you can't even imagine. I am going to hurt you in ways that are *disgusting*. Because I *own* you, and—"

He stopped at the sound of a knock as Biedermann entered. "Ms. Diaz, you know the rules about keeping the door open—" She stopped when she saw Kaminski.

"I'm sorry, Doctor, I didn't know you were in here. Patients aren't allowed to close their doors during ward hours, so—"

"Not a problem," Kaminski said. "I was just checking on our patient. Door must've closed when I came in. We're done now.

"See you later, Riley," he said, and winked at her before walking out with Biedermann.

See you later. It was a promise and a threat, but for the moment there was nothing Riley could do about it. He'd just deny he said any of it, the whole thing would turn into another he-said/she-said war, and there wasn't much doubt who'd come out the winner.

Dr. Munroe will want to know, though, and as long as he's there, Kaminski can't go too far, no matter what he says.

That afternoon she returned to the solarium for the first time in over a week and looked out at the city, the sun warm on her face as she let go of the stress of the preceding days.

She felt him in the room before she saw him, having emerged from whatever hiding place he used to disappear from the world.

He put two orderlies in the hospital.

She glanced over her shoulder to see him silhouetted against the open door.

He broke the arm of another orderly who made the mistake of getting too close.

Moving slowly and stiffly, he shuffled across the room and sat heavily on the bench beside her.

His actions still constituted premeditated murder.

"Hey," she said.

He looked at her with dark, dead eyes.

"Pretty day," she added.

He turned his face to the sun, and she wondered if the brain-block that kept him from feeling pain also prevented him from feeling its warmth.

"I'm sorry, but I can't read to you anymore," she said. "They took away my books."

He didn't react, as if he was having a hard time processing her words, and she felt a pang of guilt at having let him down. Then he pushed against the bench, rose to his full height, and started to walk away. But instead of leaving the room, he crossed to a fake topiary in the corner of the room, reached behind the planter with long, searching fingers—and pulled out the copy of *Frankenstein*, which he had apparently liberated before the staff could confiscate it.

He returned to the bench, sitting hard enough to rock the seat, and stroked the cover with obvious satisfaction. Then he turned to her with a broken smile that was almost but not quite right. Conspirators sharing a secret.

Then his mouth moved, and she realized he was struggling to speak, forcing his lips to shape the sounds. *I was right! You were listening! Come on, you can do it!*

"If," he managed at last, pleased at his achievement.

She threw her arms up in the air. "Yes! That's it! Keep going!"

He struggled again, taking almost two full minutes to get to, "I."

He paused at the next word, a two-syllable Everest. "Can . . . can*not*."

The one to come was harder still. He looked down at the book, touching the cover as he fought to get the word out.

"Inspire," he managed, followed quickly, and tellingly, by, "Love."

And she realized what line he was quoting.

"Then."

"I."

He paused to catch his breath, exhausted from the effort this was requiring.

"Will."

"C-cause," he said, visibly angry at having muffed the consonant.

Then he raised his head, and his gaze met hers in a look that was deeper and more profound than anything she had ever experienced.

"*Terror*," he said, in the voice of someone who knew exactly what that felt like, and how to make others feel it.

He could've said anything, Riley thought, subdued. *"I like puppies." Anything. Even from the book. But he chose the one line where he declares war against the whole human race.*

Remember what Julian said. He's dangerous. Seriously dangerous. Be careful.

Then again, that probably describes me as much as it does him.

"You and me both, my friend," she said, putting a hand on his arm.

He let it stay, the darkness leaving his face as he heard her say the word he remembered from the movies.

"Friend." He put his fingers to his lips to feel the sound of the word as it passed over them, as if he'd never said it before to anyone.

"Yes," she said, blinking away tears. "Friend."

He nodded slowly then looked away, his eyes moist in the sunlight. "Friend," he said again, and she heard the catch in his voice when he said it.

She took the book, opened it to where they had left off, and continued reading.

———————

As the days passed, Riley felt her thoughts becoming increasingly clear despite the injections, and a slow realization began to grow.

Someone's cutting back the dosage.

The numbered syringes in the medication tray were always prefilled with the required dose, making it impossible for anyone without proper authorization to tamper with them. The only person other than Biedermann with access to the syringes was Sanchez, who maintained custody of the tray during all the room visits.

It's Nurse Sanchez, Riley thought with a thrill of realization. *I have another ally on the inside! With Julian, that's two!*

Then she remembered Frankenstein saying, *Friend*, and thought: *No, not two allies*

Three.

Sanchez would get in trouble if Biedermann found out what was going on, so it was even more essential for Riley to downplay her condition whenever she was around the rest of the staff. So even though she was feeling better, every day Riley dutifully shuffled down the hall to meals, the solarium, and her room, head down, shoulders slumped, eyes distant.

One afternoon, Frankenstein came up alongside her for the long walk to the solarium, where the book remained safely concealed. As they padded down the hall side by side, almost in the same slow, lumbering gait, one of the orderlies sweeping the floor saw them and nudged the other.

"Yo, check it . . . Bride of Frankenstein."

Hurrrrr.

———————

After lunch, as the other ARC patients scattered to enjoy their free time, Steve came over from the *okay-fine-we're-crazy-so-what?* side of the room and joined Riley at her table. "So how's it going? Haven't had a chance to catch up with you in a bit."

"It's been kind of crazy."

"Yeah, so I hear," he said, trying without success to tuck away some unexplained annoyance.

"What's wrong?"

"I'm not stupid, you know."

"Never said or thought otherwise."

"Yeah, but you *did* otherwise." He held up his cell phone. "You planted an app and didn't tell me. That's not something a friend does."

She let out a long breath, then nodded. "You're right. I was desperate, there wasn't time to think about it, so yes, I did it, and I apologize."

"Well, that sucks."

"I know, and like I said, I'm sorry, I—"

"Not that part," he said. "I thought you might try to deny it, so I came armed with a whole bunch of evidence to show it was *there*, and that it had to be *you* because it started logging into the system right after I loaned you my phone. I built up this big head of steam, ready to go to war. I wasn't counting on you just saying, 'Yeah, it was me,' and now all that steam has nowhere to go, and that's not fair."

"We could pretend to argue. I could even let you win."

"Not the same," he said, grudgingly letting the Pinched Face of Annoyance fade a little.

"So how did you find out?"

"I had a hunch something was weird with my phone because it started running down faster than usual, which meant there was increased battery usage going on. I'd started doing some diagnostics.

Then last night *this* popped up in my notifications." Making sure no one was around to see, he unlocked the phone then slid it to her under the table. "See for yourself."

A text message was up on the screen.

> NEED TO TALK. IF THE PERSON I'M
> LOOKING FOR READS THIS, WHAT'S
> THE NAME OF MY DOG?

"Go ahead," he said resignedly when she glanced up at him, seeking permission to reply. "And for the record, if you'd just asked me if you could plant the app so nobody else could find it, I would've said sure. Remember that for the future, okay?"

"I will, and thank you," Riley said, then glanced down at the phone in her lap.

> Bowser. What's up? Were you able
> to get inside?

> Yeah. Hit some firewalls but was
> able to go in through the wifi air
> temperature control system, they
> never think to firewall that stuff. From
> there I got to the front desk system &
> out to individual cubicles.

> You are a Jedi.

> Not yet. Some IPs still out of reach.
> Started searching for your name. Don't

know any nice way to say this so I'll
just say it: they filed a motion with
the court to extend your observation
period for six more months based
on an "incident of violence." Court
agreed. So you're looking at a full year
minimum.

Riley's skin went cold, and she fought the urge to throw up. *This
must be what it feels like when the doctor says, "We got back the test
results, and it's cancer."*

Who signed the paperwork?

Form submitted by Edward Kaminski,
approved by Thomas McGann. You
okay?

Yeah. Figured it might happen,
just kind of hits hard, you
know?

Copy that. I'm sorry. Can you handle
something else? Has to do with those
two names. Or we could do this
another time.

No. I'm good. Don't want to risk
losing the connection. What's
what?

Most of the firewalls I ran into were
standard duty, so no problem. But
I can't get into K&M's files because
they're using military-grade
encryption/security put in by serious
people who know what they're doing.
Both computers are totally isolated
from the rest of the system.

> Military grade? Is that unusual?
> Are you sure you can't get in?

Yes, very yes, and not a chance. I can
see metadata from emails between
K&M & Homeland Security but
can't get past the headers. Found
something that might be important.
Need to get hard access to confirm.
Any chance you can get in physically?
I can send you a link to a keylogger.

> Offices are locked away from
> patients, floor is keycard access only.

Shit.

> Yeah. Why the heat?

Too long for text. Short version:
from the emails it looks like ARC is

just phase one of a larger program.
Homeland Security & DOJ definitely
involved. Maybe more, maybe
higher-up.

Remembering Julian's words, she typed back, "Proof of concept?"

No idea. Maybe. But proof of what?
And if this is phase one, what's
phase two? Only thing I have is a
reference number in one of the
email headers: PL 92-98 85/Stat347
18/4001(c). That mean anything
to you?

Nope. Maybe something in the
patient records?

Not so far. Still looking. You find a
way out yet?

Maybe. If so can you have
someone waiting?

Will need at least a few days' notice.
ETA?

Not sure yet. Still scoping things
out. Need to be careful because I

> only have one shot at this, don't
> want to blow it.

> Okay. Will let you go. Remember to delete
> this. Be careful. These people have teeth.

Riley deleted the texts and handed the phone back to Steve.

"You okay?" he asked.

"Yeah, why?"

"It's just that I've always heard that line about how somebody went pale as a ghost, but I've never seen it actually happen until about thirty seconds ago."

"Got some bad news."

"You want to talk about it?"

She shook her head, pushing down the emotions that were fighting it out inside her. "Safer for you if I don't."

Then she heard Biedermann's voice on the PA system: "Peer group counseling for ARC patients will begin in ten minutes in therapy room one."

In the nearly two months since her arrival, Riley had begun to look forward to the peer counseling sessions, mainly because there wasn't much actual peer counseling going on, just bullshitting, fart jokes, histories of unlikely incidents, improbable relationships, and a ton of laughter. The hunger strike had pulled them together, and now that Riley no longer felt like she was on the outside looking in, the sessions were an opportunity to relax and blow off steam. And the knowledge that her hospitalization had been extended left her in serious need of distraction.

Callie had won the day's competition for *What was the worst situation when you didn't make it to the bathroom in time?* with a detailed description of her first trip to the opera after a long day spent with her aunt shopping for the right dress, followed by a heavy meal that turned upside down in her stomach. Midway through the first act, everything inside clenched and she hurried down the row, stepping on the feet of anyone unlucky enough to be between her and the aisle. As microfarts blipped out tiny bits of diarrhea, she raced into the bathroom, slammed the stall door, lifted her dress, and dropped her panties, but in the instant before she could actually sit down, "everything I'd ever eaten in my entire life came shooting out of my ass, covering the toilet seat so I couldn't sit down. I'd heard of projectile vomiting but nobody warned me about projectile diarrhea and I was doubled over spray-painting my legs and the floor and the stall like a goddamn shit-comet and when it finally stopped I saw there were only four squares of toilet paper on the bottom roll and the top roll wouldn't come down so I spent twenty minutes using my bra and slip to clean it up the best I could with one hand, holding up my dress with the other so I wouldn't get shit all over it, and just as I got back to my seat the act ends and I feel this lurch as my stomach turns upside down and it happens *again* and I race all the way back but now there's a huge line at the bathroom so I run outside and shit beside a dumpster, just blasting like a firehose, and a cat runs out covered in awfulness and all I wanted was to die, right then and there, in front of God and everyone."

It took almost five minutes for the applause and screams of horror to subside. Finally Danny wiped away laugh tears and said, "Okay, new topic? Anyone?"

"Well, it's not bathroom humor," Angela said, side-eyeing Danny, who had brought the messy subject up in the first place, "but I was wondering . . . Who was your one great love? The one that got away?"

"Haven't had one yet," Callie said, claiming immunity from the question. "But if that changes, I promise you'll be the first to know."

"Same here," Jim said. "I've had a lot of swipe-right hookups, but nothing that made me say, 'Okay, this is the one.'"

"How many is a lot?" Danny asked.

"A gentleman never tells."

"Yeah, well, that's why I'm asking *you*."

"Fuck you," Jim shot back, trying to look pissed but laughing along with the rest.

"I got one," Hector said. "But it's kind of a long story."

"Not like we have anyplace else to go," Lauren said.

Hector leaned back to compose his thoughts, draping his arm across the empty chair beside him in a way that made Riley think, *Whoever it is, she's still there, sitting next to him, even if he doesn't realize it.*

"Her name was Kathy. We met in community college, before I screwed up that part of my life. Now, I come from a very conservative family—prayers at dinner, church every Sunday—so I won't lie, I was kind of a stiff. But Kathy was wild, funny, and *good* crazy. Curly red hair, green eyes, just ridiculously, unfairly beautiful. She loved books, music, movies, and she loved to fuck like nobody I've ever met before or since. Completely spun my head around.

"She was barely getting by, washing dishes at the on-campus cafeteria, and I had a part-time job working the cash register at a coffee shop, so neither of us was flush. Then one day she called and said she wanted to go out for dinner. I said I didn't have any money, so could we do another day, after my next check? But she had a real hunger for Indian food and said she'd cover it. When the check came, she pulled out a fistful of twenties, and a part of my brain started whispering to the rest of me that something wasn't right. I guess I must've shut down or gotten quiet, because when we walked out into the parking lot she asked if I was okay.

"I said that a few days earlier she told me she was tapped out, couldn't even afford to put gas in her car. So where'd all that money come from?

"She took this deep breath and said she'd been tricking on the side for the last couple of years to make ends meet. Then she hit me with what I said for a long time afterward was the best line I've ever gotten from somebody. She said, 'They have my body, but you have my heart.'

"And instead of just talking to her about it, all that conservative Bible stuff that I thought never mattered to me bubbled up inside, and I got all self-righteous and pissed and the door in my heart slammed shut so hard the hinges came off. Broke up with her right then and there. She tried to call a few times after that, but I straight-up ghosted her. Finally I blocked her number, and the calls stopped.

"In short, I was an asshole," he said, and his eyes were soft. "We were just six months into the relationship, and that's not the kind of thing you just talk to someone about until you've known them enough to trust them. And that's the awful part, because she'd finally come to a point where she felt she *could* trust me with the truth because she loved me, and I loved her just as deep. We could've worked it out. Instead I got all huffy and proud and walked away from the most amazing woman I've ever known. And there's not a day passes that I don't regret it."

"So why don't you call her?" Rebecca asked.

"Because there are some things you say that can't ever be called back. Besides, I heard from a mutual friend that she got married about a year ago. She's happy. And you know what? I'll bet she told him the truth, because that's how she was, and he was strong enough to handle it. I wasn't. So yeah, for me, that's the one that got away."

"How about you, Angela?" Danny asked to break the silence that followed. "After all, it was your question."

"Cameron Taylor," she said. "Senior year of high school. Tall, good looking, and super smart. We went out every weekend for most of the semester, but never hooked up, even though I made it pretty clear I was good to bash the cherry. When prom came along, I was sure this would be it, but in the car, afterward, he told me he was gay. He didn't want his family to know until he was out of the house at college, too far away for them to give him shit about it. He said he liked me a lot, but it just wasn't to be. I'm over it, but I still stalk his social media without telling him."

"Don't really have a story," Rebecca said with a crooked smile. "Guess I need to get out more."

"Same-same," Danny said. "Not a lot of guys in my part of the south who are openly gay, so I didn't have a lot of options. How about you, Lauren?"

"I don't want to go into details," she said. "Let's just say that I blew it when I had an argument with my boyfriend and I was so pissed off I slept with his best friend. Unfortunately, the kind of guy who would sleep with his best friend's girl probably isn't the kind who'll notice when the condom tears—assuming he didn't tear it himself so he could enjoy the ride more—and I ended up pregnant. He got stuck with me, I got stuck with him, and now I'm stuck in here and he's got my kid. Next?"

Riley realized that *next* was also *last*, was also *her*, since everybody else had spoken up. "Not much to say."

"That's okay, we're used to boredom," Danny said, and Callie slugged him in the shoulder.

"It's just not much of a story, that's all." She began lining up what she could and couldn't say in case there were microphones or snitches. "I've only been in a few relationships"—*actually only one real relationship, but saying there were more will throw off anyone trying to figure out who's who*—"and most of them were pretty brief. Not swipe-right brief like Jim, we just weren't what either of us were looking for. Anyway, about a year ago"—*two years, in case anyone's listening*—"I met this guy, and I liked him right off." *And no, I'm not saying where we met.* "Crazy smart, super ethical, a little on the short side"—*dude is six three*—"and very funny.

"We had a lot in common, but we never connected in the emotions department. Getting him to talk about his feelings was like trying to shove a marshmallow through a wall. The first time I texted him, 'I love you, you know that, right?' he texted back, 'Copy that,' which is how he always acknowledged stuff, but that was *so* not what I needed to hear at that moment. So yeah, that didn't work out."

"Still friends?" Angela asked.

"Sort of, but I haven't heard from him in ages."

Not counting the texts earlier today.

Tuesday. Seven a.m.

"Good morning, Ms. Diaz."

Riley waited for a moment, then said, "Aren't you going to ask if I consent?"

"No," Biedermann said. "The first mandatory medication period has concluded without further incident, so rather than issuing a second prescription, Dr. Munroe's latest guidance to Dr. Kaminski is that he can forgo the haloperidol."

"That's great!"

"For the time being."

"Of course."

Steely gray eyes and a silence vast as space.

"Of course, *Nurse Biedermann*."

After a few formalities—a schedule change in hours for the exercise room and a pointed reminder, after several Snickers wrappers were found in Riley's trash, that the vending machines were for staff and approved patients only—Biedermann headed out, nodding for Sanchez to follow.

As Sanchez finished packing up the Box of Infinite Needles, Riley leaned in and said very quietly, "Thank you."

"Sorry?"

"For what you did. For helping me. I just wanted you to know I appreciate it."

"Well, that's why I'm here, why we're *all* here, to help the patients," Sanchez said, looking more than a little flustered by the conversation. "I'm just glad you're making progress."

Then she snapped the case closed, tucked her clipboard under her arm, and hurried out to catch up with Biedermann.

Maybe she didn't want to acknowledge lowering the dose in case Biedermann came back and heard the exchange, Riley thought.

And maybe she didn't have any idea what we were talking about, a small part of her brain whispered back.

No, it has to be her, she decided.

Because if it wasn't Sanchez lowering the haloperidol dosage, then who the hell was it?

"Before we get started," Kaminski said once everyone was assembled for the day's group therapy session, "I'm afraid I have some difficult news to deliver.

"Lauren?"

Her head shot up, startled to hear her name called. "Yes?"

"I received a call late last night from a Dr. Alfonso Espinoza in Atlanta. He said that your boyfriend was walking upstairs, carrying your son, when he tripped and fell, breaking his neck. Your son was also badly injured."

Lauren's hand shot to her mouth. "Ohgod . . . How bad? . . . What did they say?"

"Cranial damage. The skull is still very soft at that age. They're fighting blood clots in and around the brain caused by subarachnoid hemorrhaging. At the moment, he's in a coma—"

"Is he going to make it?"

"They say they're doing everything they can, but it could go either way."

"And you knew this last night?"

"Late, yes, but—"

"Why didn't you tell me when you found out!"

"Patients are not to be disturbed after lights-out. Besides, there's nothing you can do at the moment, so I thought it would be better to talk about it here, where you have support—"

"Fuck you and your support!" she screamed. "Was his father drinking when it happened?"

"It's not really my place to—"

"Was he drinking!"

"According to the police report, there were apparently substance issues, but Dr. Espinoza didn't go into detail except to say that he's unconscious but stable."

"I have to get to my son."

"I'm afraid that's not possible."

"I have the right!" she said, sobbing now, "I know the rules, I have the right to see him!"

"I'm afraid that's not correct, Lauren," he said, his voice infuriatingly calm and patronizing. "ARC patients are subject to the criminal codes under which they were convicted. Those rules stipulate that in the event of sickness or death in the family, a patient can be escorted to off-site locations *provided* they are within state lines. The accident happened in Atlanta. My hands are tied."

"Yeah, well, you'd know a lot about *that*, wouldn't you?" she shot back.

"Calm down, Lauren. You don't want to burn any bridges."

"Fuck you and your bridges! I want to see my son!"

Kaminski folded his arms. "I'm sorry, there's nothing I can do. But if you'd like to talk about it—"

"Fuck you!" she screamed again, and ran out the door.

Riley glanced back at Kaminski and caught a look in his eyes that brought a chill to her skin. *He's enjoying this . . . enjoying how he used her, enjoying hurting her.*

"The other reason I wanted to bring this up when everyone was assembled," he said to the rest, as though it were an ordinary session, "was to use this incident to reinforce the negative consequences of your actions. If Lauren had stayed out of trouble, she would never have been sent here, would have been home last night, and none of this would have happened."

Riley stood and headed for the door. "You know what? Lauren's right. Fuck you."

"If you leave therapy midsession, you'll be docked additional points," he called after her.

She wanted to fire back, *What're you gonna do, extend me by six months?* but that would raise questions about how she knew about the extension, so she settled for slamming the door as hard as she could.

She found Lauren curled up into a ball in a corner of the exercise room, head down, crying and shaking.

"I'm sorry," Riley said, sliding down the wall to sit beside her.

"Don't say you're sorry!" Lauren snapped back. "People say that when someone dies! He's not dead! He's hurt, and I need to get to him! If I can get there, I can fix this."

"How?"

"I don't know! Maybe I can find another doctor or a better hospital—something! But I can't do anything while I'm stuck in here! I can't even—"

Riley saw the rest of the sentence in her eyes. *—say goodbye, if it comes to that.*

"There are people you can call," Riley said. "Lawyers, civil rights organizations, family support groups. They can go to the courts and—"

"There's no time! That could take weeks! He's in a coma right now!"

Lauren wiped away tears with her sleeve. "He's all I have, Riley, the only decent part of my whole shitty, stupid life. Take that away, and there's nothing left. And it'll be my fault that I wasn't there when it happened, when he needed me to protect him! Now he's in a coma and I'm *still* not there for him! How the fuck do I even live with that?"

Riley shook her head and said nothing. For some questions there are no answers.

Then Lauren got quiet for a moment, as if considering something dangerous before finally turning back to Riley. "You could get me out of here."

"How?"

"I've been watching you. We all have. You're looking for a way out."

"I haven't found anything."

"Bullshit. You're lying. I can see it in your eyes."

"Even if I did find something, we'd need time to scope out the situation so we don't screw something up, then arrange to have someone parked down the street so we can get clear before the police show up. We're talking at least a few days."

"I don't *have* a few days! *He* doesn't have a few days! I'll take my chances."

"It's not just you on the line here," Riley said, dropping the pretense. "If you go, I'll have to go too because this is the only soft spot I've found, and the second it gets used they'll seal it up for sure."

"Fine. Whatever. Then we'll both go. Once we're outside, we can split up, make it harder to find us—better odds for both of us." She took Riley's hand. "I've never begged anyone for anything in my whole life, but I'm begging you now. My son is in a coma, and maybe there's something I can do to help him and maybe there isn't, but if he dies and I'm not there, I won't be able to live with myself, so I have to try, even if the odds are shitty. I need your help, Riley. Please!"

Riley cast her memory back to see if there was anything her parents might have said that would give her guidance in a situation like this but found nothing. There was only the grief and rage that Riley understood all too well at never having had the chance to say goodbye to her folks. *Can I really let the same thing happen to someone else?*

No, she decided, though she hated herself for it, *I can't.*

NOTHIN' SHAKIN'
BUT THE LEAVES
ON THE TREES

Midnight.

Riley stared at the ceiling, furious. Furious at Lauren for putting her in this situation. At herself for agreeing. At the world and the hospital and Kaminski and what she knew would happen if they got caught, hating herself for being rushed and not having time to plan things out properly, and it would be so much easier if she was going alone, and even though she knew why she agreed to it, and her heart still said it was the right thing to do, her brain was calling her heart an asshole, and—

Two a.m.

—so we just need to be quick and quiet and we can do this, the street going west is on the left side of the hospital, will take us close to the shore and there will be tons of tourists and shops where we can hide or we can go down to the beach because cop cars have a hard time on sand so it'll just be a few bicycle cops, and let's go over the steps in sequence one more time to make sure I haven't missed anything or—

Three thirty a.m.

Riley stared at the ceiling.

Four twenty a.m.

"Fuck."

Six fifteen a.m.

Maybe if I close my eyes and tell myself I'm just going to rest I'll fall asleep because I won't be trying to fall asleep, no pressure, I'll just turn my back on sleep and let it sneak up on me like the fox in The Little Prince *because that never fails and—*

Six fifty-seven a.m.

Fuck.

Seven a.m.

The doors on the ward unlocked. Riley sat up at the sound of sensible shoes on tile.

"You look tired, Ms. Diaz," Biedermann said.

"Didn't sleep much."

"Probably a reaction to stopping the haloperidol. You should be back on a normal sleep-wake schedule in a few days."

"Good to know, thanks."

While everyone else went to breakfast, Riley headed for the women's showers, where she and Lauren had agreed to meet. Most of the patients hit breakfast as soon as the doors opened, so with luck they'd have twenty minutes before anyone else came in. She didn't *think* there were microphones in the showers, because that would be seriously against the law, but *most* of what was being done under the ARC program was pretty sketchy, so she turned on all the showers to muffle the sound as soon as Lauren hurried inside.

"When are we going?" she asked before Riley could get a word out. "We have to go today!"

"We are."

"How?"

And for just a moment, Riley hesitated.

What if this whole thing is a setup? There's no way for me to know if any of this is real. It's all between Lauren and Kaminski. If he suspects I've been scoping out the place, he could've cooked up this whole thing to find out what I'm up to and convinced her to help out. On the other hand, maybe this whole thing about her son is true and she made a deal with Kaminski to get out in exchange for selling me down the river.

Wow. Paranoid much?

I'm just saying it's possible.

You saw the tears.

I've been fooled by tears before.

She's not that good an actor.

You willing to bet a prison term on that?

Okay, maybe it wouldn't hurt to hedge our bets a little. See what she does when the moment comes.

"The less you know ahead of time, the less you can tell anyone if you get caught," Riley said. "Meet me at six fifteen by the entrance to the third-floor staff offices. That's after the day shift leaves but before the night crew shows up, so nobody should be around. Then do exactly what I say when I say to do it."

"What should I bring?"

"Do you have any money?"

"No."

"Then leave everything where it is. If you take any clothes, the orderlies might notice, figure out something's up, and start looking where they shouldn't. This is strictly come-as-you-are, okay?"

"Okay."

"Six fifteen *sharp*, Lauren."

"Don't worry, I'll be there."

There wasn't much time to arrange for ground support, but she had to try. She'd gone looking for Steve when the shit hit the fan with Lauren, but nobody seemed to know where he was. So after scrounging up a hardboiled egg and cold toast in the cafeteria, Riley made her way to the regular-patient wing of the hospital, walking casually from room to room. But Steve wasn't at any of his usual spots, and his room was locked.

She turned a corner to see Henry carrying a load of blankets down the hall. "Hey, Henry."

"Ready Riley," he said and smiled. "What's shakin'?"

"Nothin' but the leaves on the trees."

"There you go," he said, laughing as he passed her.

"Do you know where Steve is? Steve Newman?"

"He's out."

"Out? As in *out* out? Discharged?"

"Left last night on a supervised visit with his sister. Should be back later tonight. Why, you need a Snickers?"

"No, I'm good," she said as he continued down the hall, "just wondering."

Changes nothing, she told herself, pushing down the first tremors of panic. *We went into this knowing that in the worst-case scenario we'd be on our own, and we are, and that's that, and here we fucking go.*

For the next nine hours Riley did everything possible not to draw attention to herself without *looking* like she was trying to avoid attention. She nodded but not too much and talked but not too loud and smiled but definitely not too big because she wasn't known for being a smiler, not that any of it mattered because she didn't hear any of the things she was smiling or nodding about because 99 percent of her brain was screaming.

Lunch lasted a day and a half.

Four o'clock came.

Two years later, five o'clock finally showed up.

Nerves on edge, in desperate need of silence but too agitated to go back to her room, Riley walked to the solarium, where a big clock adorned the wall opposite the windows. She kept glancing to the clock, certain at times that it had stopped ticking. *Just breathe*, she told herself. *We can do this. Just breathe.*

Five fifteen.

Five twenty-one.

She looked up as Frankenstein sat beside her on the bench, his eyes eager for the day's reading.

"I can't," she said. "Not today. I'm . . . there's a lot going on and . . . this isn't a good time."

He took a moment to process what she said, his expression turning soft and lost when the words finally lined up.

I can't do this with him here. I need to focus.

"Why don't you head on back to your room and get some rest?" she said. "We can do this tomorrow."

She knew it was a lie, that with just a little luck she'd be far away by tomorrow, and from the hurt look in his eyes, he knew it too. *I'm such a terrible liar*, she thought. *I should probably work on that.*

He stayed where he was.

"Fine, I'll go," she said, and started to stand.

He took hold of her by the wrist. Not enough to hurt, just enough to say, *Don't go.*

She remembered the day he launched himself at an orderly trying to feed him, and knew that *don't go* could turn into something far more dangerous in a second.

"Let go," she said, her voice low but firm.

He searched her eyes.

"Let. Go."

His lips thinned, fighting some inner instinct to lash out, and for a moment Riley thought this could go either way. Then he let go, his arm falling limply to his side as he turned away, gaze fixed on the fading daylight beyond the window.

"I'm sorry," she said, then hurried out of the solarium.

Five fifty-seven.

Let's go.

As she approached the final turn that led to the third-floor offices, Riley felt herself shaking and wasn't sure if it was fear or adrenaline. *Doesn't matter, I'll take either one as long as it helps me get the job done.*

She stopped at what sounded like footsteps behind her, and glanced back. The hall was empty. She started walking again. The sound returned.

I was right. She sold me out. That's Kaminski or an orderly or Henry, and he'll be so disappointed, or—

Riley allowed a sigh of relief as Lauren turned the corner behind her. She held up a hand—*no talking*—and started walking several paces ahead of Lauren, so it would look like they just happened to be in the same hall. At the next intersection, Riley made sure no one was watching, then quickly sidestepped around the corner and waited, back to the wall as Lauren followed. The office wing was off-limits to patients, and this time she wouldn't have an excuse for trespassing, so if anyone saw them, it would all be over.

As they made the final turn into the office hallway, Riley stopped at a sight that sent her heart straight up into her throat.

All of the doors that had been open during her first visit were now shut.

Shut doesn't mean locked, she told herself, fighting panic.

The first door was unlocked, but she knew from her previous expedition that it was too far from the outside ledge to be of use, just a straight three-story drop.

The second door was locked.

Door three—locked.

Door four—locked.

Door five. Last chance.

She turned the knob.

Unlocked.

She hurried inside, waved Lauren in after her, then shut the door and ran to the window. From here it was a four-foot drop to the narrow, ivy-covered ledge. It was awkward but doable as long as they didn't slip and fall and smash their spines on the concrete. *Easy peasy, right?*

Lauren reached for the window lock.

"No, wait!" Riley said. "Check for sensors first!"

Lauren ran her fingers along the left edge of the window as Riley examined the right.

"Anything?" Riley asked.

"Not here. You?"

"No. We're good." *Maybe. Only one way to find out.*

Riley took a deep breath and cracked the window open. Nothing happened. She moved it a little further. When no alarms sounded, she slid it open the rest of the way. Cool air blew through into the office.

She checked the screen in case it was wired, found nothing, and tugged hard. It refused to budge. "Give me a hand," she said. "Hold the bottom while I push up at the top, so it doesn't fall outside."

They rocked the screen back and forth until it popped out of the frame, then eased it back inside and set it on the floor.

"Okay, here's what we do," Riley said. "That ledge goes all the way to the end of the building, then turns left and goes around back. If I've paced this out right, once you turn the corner there should be a short drop from the ledge to the roof of the air conditioning building. From there we can climb down to the parking lot. Once we hit the ground, do not run, you'll draw attention. Just walk out like you parked around the corner while you were visiting someone inside, turn right, then go left at the first street. That'll take you west, toward the water. After that we split up. Got it?"

"Yeah, I'm good."

"Okay. You go first."

"Why not you? It's your idea."

Which is just the sort of question she'd ask if Kaminski wanted me to go out alone so they can grab me.

"Someone has to push the screen back into place so the room will look normal if anyone comes by," Riley said. "I'm taller, so I should be able to reach it from the ledge."

"All right. Thank you."

"We're not clear yet, so get your ass outside."

Lauren pulled a chair to the window, climbed on, and balanced precariously on the edge, legs swinging out into space. "It looks slippery. Give me your hand."

Riley took hold as Lauren swung the rest of her body out the window, stretching down until her toes reached the ledge. "You got it?"

"Yeah, I think so," Lauren said, and risked letting go. "Okay, I'm good."

"Start moving, I'll be right behind you."

Fingers pressed to the outside wall for balance, Lauren inched her way along the ledge as Riley reached for the screen, then looked outside one last time to make sure no one was around.

Here we go, she thought as she leaned out the window and—

Powerful arms grabbed her from behind, pinning her arms to her side. She tried to cry out, but a hand covered her mouth. She kicked against the wall, trying to throw them both to the floor, but he held on tight, carrying her back through the door. She thrashed and elbowed him as hard as she could, biting at his hand, but the skin was too tight to get a grip and he wouldn't feel it anyway because now she knew, even before she saw their reflection in the window that it wasn't Kaminski, it was *him*, dragging her down the hall as—

Alarms shrieked all around them. He pressed his back to the wall, hugging the shadows as orderlies raced down an intersecting hallway. Once they were gone he started moving forward again, dragging her with him to an empty room outside the office area. He pulled her inside, kicked the door closed, and let go.

"Why did you do that?" she yelled. "I was almost out!" She slammed a fist into his chest, but he didn't move, didn't react, as if she was beating dead flesh, so she hit him again. "What the fuck is *wrong* with you?"

He said nothing but didn't move or try to stop her from hitting him. When she finally slid to the floor, exhausted and spent, he studied her for a moment, then turned, opened the door, and stepped back out into the hall. As he walked away, she recognized the sound of his footsteps and realized that he was the one who had been following her earlier.

She wiped away tears of rage. *Goddamnit! Fucking asshole! Was he mad that I didn't read to him? Is that why he didn't want me to leave? Selfish prick!*

McGann would find the hole now, and they would plug it, and her only way out was gone, just like that—gone and fucking gone!

*Sonofa*BITCH*!*

Once the alarms were turned off, the ARC patients were ordered back to their rooms, and the ward was put into lockdown overnight. Unable to sleep, Riley rocked back and forth on the narrow bed. She didn't know if Lauren had gotten away or if she'd been caught, and the uncertainty was eating her alive. Attempted escape from a prison program was a felony offense, and they'd want to know if there was anyone else involved. Riley had been willing to roll the dice when it was just her because she had at least the illusion of being in control of her own fate, always able to find some angle to play, but she had no idea what Lauren was doing or saying, or if she was making a deal to give up Riley to save her own skin.

She closed her eyes, feeling as if she couldn't breathe, wishing she could tear her skin off or sink into the earth, where no one could find her.

Seven a.m.

The door didn't open. Biedermann did not appear.

They know, she decided. *They're not opening the door so they can keep me locked up until the badges show up.*

Then she realized that she hadn't heard the buzz of *any* of the doors being unlocked. *Something's up*, she thought. *Maybe Lauren got away.*

Holding tight to that fragment of hope, she threw an arm over her eyes and finally dozed until being startled awake when the doors buzzed unlocked at a quarter past eight.

Biedermann's voice echoed on the PA system. "All ARC patients report at once to therapy room one. All ARC patients to therapy room one."

Riley stepped into the hallway as the others came out of their rooms. "Does anyone know what's going on?" Danny asked the group.

"No idea," Jim said, glancing at Riley. "You?"

Riley shook her head, too tired to lie.

Then Hector looked around and said, "Where's Lauren?"

"I heard one of the orderlies say she tried to escape," Angela said. "Wasn't sure if it was true or not, but I guess maybe it was."

As they waited in therapy room 1, Riley leaned forward in her seat, stomach knotted so tight that she had to fight the urge to throw up.

"You okay?" Callie asked.

Riley shook her head no but didn't answer. Couldn't reply.

Not knowing is the worst. Can we just get this over with so I know how badly I'm fucked?

After another twenty minutes, the door opened and McGann and Kaminski entered, followed by Lauren, her arms held firmly by Henry on one side, and an orderly on the other. Her eyes were red from crying, and when Riley caught her gaze she looked away.

She told them, Riley thought as the rest of her stomach fell away. *They know. It's over.*

McGann stepped to the front of the room and turned to face the group. "As some of you may already know, we had an attempted escape last night. This is a serious incident because while this is a hospital, the ARC program operates under the jurisdiction of the criminal judicial system under which you were convicted, and incidents like this are punishable to the full extent of the law. In this case that means a penalty of between three and ten years in state prison."

Riley closed her eyes, fighting panic.

"After we're done here, Lauren will be taken to the Washington Corrections Center for Women to await additional sentencing based on this latest offense. However, as an act of charity we told her that we will ask for a shorter sentence if she gives us the name of anyone else who was involved in this incident."

Here we go.

"We brought you here because if that person will step forward and voluntarily confess to their actions, we will be inclined to make a similar recommendation. If not, we will recommend the maximum available penalty."

It's over. You lost. Take what's coming to you, she thought, and shifted her weight to her feet.

"*I told you there wasn't anybody else!*" Lauren said, loudly and quickly.

Riley froze.

"Lauren, we all agreed that you wouldn't say anything during this session, that you would let us handle this our way," Kaminski said.

"Fuck you! I didn't agree to shit!"

"Calm down, Lauren," Henry said quietly, "or we'll have to put you back in the restraints."

"I want to see my son! I have a right!"

McGann's lips thinned angrily. "Lauren, had you only waited, if you'd just *talked* to us before you did all this—"

"What difference would it make?"

"It would have made every difference, Lauren! Because by the time you pulled this stunt it was already too—"

He caught himself and bit off the last word.

But everyone in the room knew the word was *late*.

Lauren paled. "What're you saying?" She looked to Kaminski. "What is he saying?"

"An hour before your attempted escape, we received word about your son," Kaminski said, then paused, as if trying to figure out how to say what he wanted to say. Then he gave up and just said it. "I'm sorry, Lauren . . . he's gone."

Lauren's knees buckled, and Henry had to keep her from falling to the floor as she started screaming, a full-body cry of grief and sorrow that Riley knew all too well.

Then Lauren's eyes locked on Kaminski with the light of madness, and she lunged at him. "This is your fault, you son of a bitch!"

"Okay, I think we need to get her out of here," Kaminski said.

The orderlies started to lead her out when suddenly she yanked hard and the orderly lost his grip, tripped, and fell. Henry tried to grab the other arm, but she pulled free and ran out.

The room emptied, following as she raced into the cafeteria.

"Close the door!" Henry yelled to an orderly behind them. It slammed shut, cutting off her escape.

Kaminski approached slowly, hands raised and open. "Lauren, you have to try and calm down. You're only making the situation worse."

"Worse? *Worse?* How the fuck can this get worse? My son is dead! He's all I had!"

"There's nothing you can do for him now. All you're doing is hurting yourself."

"Yeah? You want to see hurt?"

Lauren picked up one of the chairs, but instead of throwing it at Kaminski she slammed it into the window, shattering the glass into shards and revealing the chicken wire within.

"Stop it!" McGann yelled. "You can't get out that way!"

"No?" She picked up a jagged piece of glass. "Watch me."

Riley lunged for her, but Danny held her back. "Lauren, no!" she yelled.

"Take a good look, you sadistic motherfucker," Lauren screamed, fist clenched tight around the glass, blood leaking between her fingers. "I'm going home to see my son! *I'm going home!*"

And she dragged the glass across her throat.

SECONDHAND CRAZY

The day after Lauren's death, Riley and the other ARC patients were only allowed out for meals, seated one to a table to discourage conversation, before being returned immediately to their rooms. The following morning, plainclothes police showed up and asked everyone to describe what they saw. Their answers must have lined up correctly, because no further interviews were conducted.

On the morning of the third day, the door to Riley's room buzzed and Henry entered. "Hey, Ready Riley," he said, but there was no joy in his voice. "How you doing?"

"I'm okay," she said, though her tired, red-rimmed eyes showed otherwise. "What's shakin'?"

He didn't finish the callback. "I'm making the rounds to let everyone know that the lockdown's over, at least for now. They also want me to tell everyone that trying to get out of the hospital like that can't ever happen again, okay? Folks are just gonna get hurt if they try. There's no way out and no point to even trying."

"I'm guessing the others didn't much like hearing that."

He shook his head. "That's why they sent me to do the telling instead of Biedermann."

"So how are *you* holding up?"

He shoved his hands in his pockets and looked away. "I dunno, Riley. Never saw something that bad happen right in front of me. I mean, yeah, we've had some suicide attempts here before, goes with the territory when you've got all kinds of patients with all kinds of problems, but never like that. Sets you back on your heels a little, you know?"

His eyes went soft as he looked back at her. "I thought I had her, Riley, swear to God, I thought I had her good and tight, but—"

"It's not your fault."

"Ain't what it feels like. Even worse—and I don't know if I should even be telling you this, but honestly, at this stage, what the fuck—they're using this against Dr. Munroe."

"What? How? He had nothing to do with it! He wasn't even there!"

"He instituted a policy last year that physical restraints can only be used on patients while in their rooms, for their own safety, so no straitjackets. Most every hospital has the same rule, but that didn't stop McGann from saying it was Munroe's fault because Lauren never could've done what she did if she'd been in restraints. They're also saying he exceeded his authority by countermanding the treatment plan Kaminski had all of you on, saying none of this would've happened if he'd been allowed to stick to the program. Julian's fighting it best he can, but a patient committed suicide while in custody, and the state board's gonna want someone's skin for it."

Riley bit back a string of profanity, enraged at the idea of McGann and Kaminski using Julian as a shield to cover their mistakes. "Do they know anything more about what happened when she tried to escape?"

He chewed at the inside of his cheek, then nodded. "There's a lot I can't say because there's still an inquiry going on. What I can say is that she found a way out she thought was safe, but it only looked that way from the inside. Ever since the ARC program moved in, McGann's been reinforcing the building to close up any holes. Some places need more work and more money than others. So while the contractors locked down the easy areas, he had them put in motion sensors to cover the rest of the exterior. Hardest part was putting in the sensors around the air conditioning building because there are all kinds of ledges and nooks and crannies. Last of the sensors went in around the same time you got here. They picked up Lauren the second she rounded the corner, and the security guards were out in force before she even hit the ground. She never had a chance. She just didn't know it.

"So yeah, it's been a hard few days," he said, heading out. "*Damned* hard days."

She was still sitting on her bed when the other ARC patients passed by on their way to breakfast.

"You coming?" Danny asked.

"In a second," she said, and smiled him away. She needed a moment alone because three data points she had previously failed to connect were suddenly lining up in her head.

Data Point One: The first time she'd seen Frankenstein, restrained in his room, she had been drawn by the sound of his voice, which she'd initially thought was coming from the air conditioning building just outside.

Data Point Two: When the nurse came in to shoo her off, she said *There's been a lot of construction work going on outside and all the noise upset him. Strangers also upset him.*

And now, Data Point Three: *Hardest part was putting in the sensors around the air conditioning building because there are all kinds of ledges and nooks and crannies. Last of 'em went in about the time you got here.*

She imagined Frankenstein peering out the window of his room, furious at the noise and disruption, watching through angry eyes as workmen installed and tested the motion sensors positioned right around the corner from where Lauren would later step out onto the ledge.

She never had a chance. She just didn't know it.

But *he* knew. Because he'd seen the sensors going in.

With a sharp pang, Riley realized that he hadn't pulled her back because he was being selfish or because he was mad at her for leaving.

He was trying to *save* her.

She'd screamed at him and cursed him and hit him and kept on hitting him, and the whole time, the most dangerous patient in the entire hospital, someone who could have snapped her neck without even trying, just stood there and took her anger and her fists until she wore herself out, then walked away, his eyes showing no rage, only sadness.

I have to make this right, she told herself. *I have to fix this.*

Though the ARC patients were finally free to leave their rooms whenever they wanted, all the usual counseling sessions had been canceled, leaving only a grief counseling session with Dr. Nakamura that no one wanted to attend. So Riley spent her time going from the solarium to Frankenstein's room on this ward, hoping to talk to him. But he had once again gone to ground in whatever hidey-hole he'd made for himself.

At four, their usual meeting time, she returned to the solarium to find him sitting on the bench, hunched over, hands folded in his lap.

Not sure how he would respond to seeing her, she stepped quietly forward. When she got closer, she saw that his hands weren't folded; they were moving ever so slightly. As she came around to the front of the bench, she saw that he was again shoving the tip of an unfolded paper clip under the fingernails of his left hand. His eyes were dark and distant, as if looking on from somewhere outside his body as the thin line of blood ran from his fingers to the floor. There was no sign of pain, only a dull resolve as he repeated the action, finger to finger, thumb to pinky and back again.

She sat beside him. If he was aware of her presence, he gave no sign as he continued to drive the tip deep beneath his scarred and blackened nails.

"Please stop," she whispered.

He didn't. The tip slid beneath the nail of his index finger.

"Please . . ."

Middle finger.

"Is that what your parents used to do to you? To punish you?"

Ring finger.

"Because sometimes we learn to hurt ourselves in the same way we get hurt. We do it when we've done something wrong because we think we deserve it, and we know how to punish ourselves better than anyone else because we know where it'll hurt the most."

Little finger.

"You didn't do anything wrong. I hit you and I called you names, and you didn't deserve any of it. You were trying to help. *I'm* the one who was wrong, and I'm sorry for the way I acted. If anyone here should be punished, it's me, not you."

Then she covered his hand with her own, shielding his wounded fingers. He could only keep doing what he was doing by driving the metal pin through her skin first. And as he silently studied her hand, it occurred to her that this might actually be an option.

She kept it there anyway.

"I know you *think* you can't feel pain, that you've *convinced* yourself you can't feel it, but deep inside, you still do. Please stop hurting the part of you that can't tell you to stop."

He slowly looked up, and as his eyes met hers, allowed the paper clip to fall from his fingers. Then he took her wrist and gently pressed the back of her hand against his forehead for what felt like a long time before returning it to its place.

In return, she took his hand, the skin cool to the touch, and pressed it to her own forehead. "Friend," she said, tears filling her eyes.

"Friend," he whispered, and as she again covered his hand with her own, she felt the wetness of his falling tears, and the weight of his silent, broken sadness.

They remained like that for over an hour, side by side, hands interwoven amid the lengthening shadows.

The next day, in need of some quiet time to process everything that had happened, Riley found a seat in the back of the cafeteria between meals where she could be alone with her thoughts. *I just need to try and let it all go, figure out my next steps and—*

"Hey, Riley."

She looked up to see Steve approaching. *So much for meditation.*

"Thought you might be in here," he said, sitting across from her at the table. "I heard about what happened with Lauren, wanted to see how you were doing. Are you okay?"

"It's either, 'Yeah, I'm fine,' or it's an hour-long conversation. So, yeah, I'm fine. Getting there, anyway."

"Translation: pushing it all down to where nobody else can see it so they won't be hurt by your shit until you get it all in hand?"

"Basically, yeah."

"Just had pretty much that same conversation with my sister," he said, pulling back his sleeve to show the scars that ran from elbow to wrist. "She said I can have these tattooed over so nobody else has to see them, and after a while maybe I'll forget they were ever there. Even suggested I get musical bar lines going up the arm, because they'd line up with the cuts and I could put the notes of my favorite song on it. Turn it into something beautiful."

"Ohmygod . . . a suicide sonata?"

"Yep."

"So are you gonna do it?"

He rolled the sleeve back down. "No. I want the scars where I can see them, because I think that'll make it harder for them to ambush me. When they were on the inside, like your scars, they were always trying to sneak out so the rest of the world could see them. That's when they're the most dangerous, because the only way out is to cut their way through. If I have them tattooed over, she's right, I might forget they're there, and that'll just piss them off, make them want to tear their way back out again to get my attention. Better for me if they're out here, where I can keep an eye on them, in case they decide to start trouble."

"I've come to a decision," Riley said.

"What's that?"

"I like you," she said, extending a hand. "You're okay."

He laughed and shook it. "Only took, what, two months? Three?"

"I'm what people call a slow burn."

"Yeah, I get that," he said. Then he glanced at the open door and waved. "Yo, Theresa, in here."

A woman Riley hadn't seen before started toward them: early forties at a guess, with auburn hair and the kind of skin that showed way too much time in the sun.

"This is the one I was telling you about, Riley Diaz."

"Oh, sure."

"Riley, meet my new friend, Theresa Connolly. She's a newbie, just got in this morning."

"Hey, Theresa."

"Good to meet you," Theresa said, joining them at the table. "What are you here for?"

"Protesting."

"Me too," she said. "And that's just so unfair. Neither of us should be here."

"I know," Riley said, "but for now, the system is what it is."

"Oh, you've got that right. Like I told the doctors, I don't belong here. This won't do any good, because I'm not crazy. There's nothing mentally or emotionally wrong with me, I just get a little excited is all."

"Totally get that," Riley said.

"You ask me, they want to turn the whole world into a prison so they're the only ones who are free."

"Yep."

"They say we're crazy or criminal so that when we say *they're* the ones who're the criminals, they can say we're just projecting."

"Hadn't thought about that, but it makes sense."

"They even have signs they use between them so they can identify each other and do things to us, and nobody else knows what they mean," Theresa said. "Sometimes it's, you know, the way they touch their face, it's a signal, and you have to watch them all the time, real careful, because you know, some of them can kill at a distance."

Waaaaaaaaaiiitasecond. "Sorry?"

"It just *happens*, they look at you a certain way, and it's all over for you. I can feel it when they're looking at me, like they're thinking about killing me but they're not sure if this is the right time, but I can still feel it, like I'm being choked or someone's squeezing my heart. Do you know what I mean? I can tell you do."

Uh, huh. "So Theresa, what did you do before you got involved with protesting?"

"Oh, I don't like the protesters," she said, as if she hadn't actually said what she'd just said. "They're trouble. I like having a regular job. I was a lawyer for ten years, but I could feel them watching me all the way back then, so I thought I should go into something more private, so I became an airplane pilot. Flew all over the world. I was in Mexico on layover, and my phone was turned off, but I could still hear people talking inside it, and that's when I found out they were following me, because they can talk to you through cell phones even when you think they're turned off. So I became a doctor to try and stop them, but they figured that out too, and that's when they put me here, so I can't tell anyone the truth, because people will think I'm crazy. I have to go pee. Be right back."

As she moved off, Riley turned to find Steve grinning at her.

"You're such a dick," she said. "I take back everything nice I said about you."

"Couldn't help myself," he laughed. "The paranoid delusional ones are amazing, you can never pin them down on anything, because they just jump to the next thing. It's like watching someone build a skyscraper out of words."

"You could've said something."

"Object lesson about this place. I always wait a while before agreeing with a newbie about anything. The secondhand crazy can be strong if you're not careful."

"Thing is, she was actually making sense there for a second."

"Sometimes sanity is the first sign of madness. And sometimes madness is the first sign of sanity. Maybe I'll put that on a T-shirt."

"Do you have *any* friends in the outside world? Like, at all?"

"Nope."

"Explains a lot," Riley said. The knowledge that she was stuck here for however long it would take to find another way out had gone down hard, but she was finally coming out the other side. *Being Irish means laughing in the face of whatever's trying to hurt you,* her mother once said. *And being Cuban means getting drunk in the face of whatever's trying to hurt you. So you are either going to be completely fucking invulnerable or a really funny drunk.*

Steve leaned in closer. "The reason I was looking for you, beyond wanting to make sure you were okay, is that I wanted you to be the first—well, *among* the first—to know that I'm getting out of here on Monday."

"You're checking out!"

"My sister turned twenty-one yesterday, and she signed the papers to get the trust fund transferred to her as sole signatory. There's nothing my family can do now to hurt her or hold over her head. Only reason I'm leaving Monday instead of today is that the lawyer is taking his time turning around the docs allowing me to un-commit."

Annnd there goes my last connection to the outside world.

"That's great, Steve! Congratulations! I won't lie, I'll miss seeing you around."

"Maybe I'll come by and visit once in a while."

"Don't," she said, and the firmness in her voice surprised both of them. "Either I won't be here by then, so there'd be no point in making the trip, or I *will* be here, and seeing you would just depress the shit out of me."

"I get that," he said, then stood, pushing his chair under the table. "At least we have a few days before I go. Catch you later."

As he turned away, he dropped a folded piece of paper onto the seat of his chair. Riley glanced around to make sure no one was watching, then slid the paper off the chair and unfolded it.

It read, art room. three o'clock. you had a call.

Two-thirty.

Riley was about to head for the art room when Henry knocked on her door. "Hey, Riley. How goes?"

"Goes good," she said, then she noticed he wasn't smiling. And he hadn't called her *Ready* Riley. "What's up?"

"Got to bring you to a meeting downstairs."

She glanced at the clock. "Could we do this later?"

"You got somewhere else to go?"

"No. Why?"

He shifted uncomfortably. "Let's just go, okay?"

Something's wrong, she decided as they took the elevator down to the first floor. *He's never like this.*

They stopped at the door to Kaminski's office. "I'll be right outside," he said pointedly, then opened the door to let her in. Kaminski was at his desk, flipping through papers. Biedermann stood behind him, silhouetted against the window.

What am I doing here, and what the hell is she *doing here?*

"Ms. Diaz," he said without looking up. "Take a seat."

"Thanks, I'll stand. Didn't much like the view last time."

"As you wish."

As he finished writing out his notes, Riley turned her attention to the desktop tower on the floor, remembering the text she'd received. *I've seen metadata from emails between K&M & Homeland Security but can't get past the headers. Might be nothing, but may be important. Need to get hard access. Any chance you can get in? I can send you a link to a keylogger.*

So near and yet so far. *Hey, doc, mind if I borrow your computer for like ten minutes? I need to order a few things online.*

Kaminski clicked the pen closed and leaned back, his attitude disturbingly self-satisfied. "Every month, we do a full review of all the ARC patients to assess their progress, or lack thereof, in order to fine-tune our treatment modalities. As you know, we began treating you with haloperidol to try to curb your violent tendencies."

"Is that why she's here?" Riley cut in, nodding to Biedermann.

"Nurse Biedermann is here because the presence of a matching-gender nurse is required under the terms of the treatment program you will shortly begin. May I continue?"

I was right, this is bad. Let's find out how bad. "Sure."

"The haloperidol initially had a positive effect, but as Dr. Munroe pointed out in his guidance, it's not intended for indefinite use. But as I predicted in my response to his guidance, once you were taken off the haloperidol you began to revert back to your past behaviors. You walked out on or refused to attend therapy sessions and incited the other patients to act against hospital policies, undoing weeks of treatment. And while we do not yet have sufficient evidence to confirm our suspicions, I'm not alone in believing that you helped coordinate the escape attempt that ultimately led to Lauren's suicide. Which brings me to this."

He picked up a sheaf of papers. "These are signed witness statements by staff members who were present when Lauren took her life. They confirm that you were so desperate to get to her that you attacked a fellow patient—"

"I didn't attack Danny, he was holding me back—"

He continued over her. "—descriptions that confirm my own written assessment of the events of that day, which led me to the opinion that you were trying to reach Lauren so you could take your lives together rather than continue to receive treatment. I believe that the two of you shared a suicide pact in the event that the escape misfired."

"That's bullshit!"

"Nonetheless, in my professional opinion, the self-destructive actions that have been evident in your behavior since your arrival—refusing to eat, your attempt to join Lauren in her suicide attempt, and your subsequent refusal to receive treatment necessary for your survival—are clear indications that you are still at risk of taking your own life."

The room turned very cold as Riley remembered his threat. *I am going to fuck with you in ways you can't even imagine. I am going to hurt you in ways that are disgusting.*

"So for your own safety, we are putting you on suicide watch, effective immediately. You will be moved to another part of the hospital for observation to ensure that we don't have another unfortunate incident."

"I want to see Dr. Munroe," Riley said.

"I'm afraid that's not an option," Kaminski said, pressing the button to call Henry back into the room.

"She's all yours," he said to Biedermann.

When Henry put his hand on Riley's arm, she yanked away hard. "Let go! I want to see Dr. Munroe!"

"The patient violently resists being moved for treatment," Kaminski said, noting it in her profile. "Understand that any acts of violence committed by you during your period of treatment, large or small, will be recorded in your file and used to determine how long you remain on suicide watch. This is your only warning."

She looked to Henry, whose eyes said, *Don't fight this, you'll only make it worse*, and when he took her arm again, she allowed the touch, her heart full of rage.

Biedermann led them to a locked ward on the third floor and into a narrow hallway containing four numbered rooms with heavy green metal doors and narrow viewing slots. She unlocked the door marked number 3 to reveal heavily padded interior walls in tones of cream and brown, with a single bed and an exposed sink and toilet.

"That's all for now, Henry," Biedermann said.

Henry nodded, glanced worriedly in Riley's direction, then headed out.

"There's a paper gown on the bed. Change into it."

"Can I have some privacy?"

"There is no privacy under suicide watch. You will be under observation at all times by a female nurse, either in person or via camera." She pointed up at a lens visible inside a plexiglass cage in a corner of the room. "You are not permitted to possess shoes, belts, or anything else that can be used for self-harm. Once each day you will be interviewed by Dr. Kaminski or another staff member to determine your state of mind."

"How long will I have to stay here?"

"The room has been made as safe as possible. Paper towels and toilet paper can be found beneath the sink. The bedsheets and blankets have been locked to the frame so they cannot be removed.

Your hands must be in view of the camera and staff at all times, even when sleeping."

"Nurse Biedermann, how long—"

"If your period begins, you can ask the on-duty nurse for Maxi Pads on an as-needed basis, but tampons are not allowed as they represent a choking threat."

"This is how you hide, isn't it? Repeating the rules over and over saves you from thinking about what you're doing."

Biedermann met her gaze levelly. "How long you remain under observation depends entirely upon your actions. Now please change into the paper gown, or I will have to call for assistance."

Riley began to unbutton her blouse.

There was no clock in the room, no television, and nowhere to sit other than the narrow bed that was bolted to a wall opposite the camera. They even took her watch because the glass could be broken and used to cut herself. The only way to know the time was to peer out the slot in the door to a clock down the hall. That was how she figured out that the nurses were coming in to check on her and run vitals at fifteen-minute intervals—"How are you feeling? Are you having any suicidal thoughts?"

Fifteen minutes later: "How are you feeling? Are you having any suicidal thoughts?"

Fifteen minutes later: "How are you feeling? Are you having any suicidal thoughts?"

She wanted to say *I wasn't when I got here, but I sure as hell am now*, but opted for discretion, knowing that every word was being recorded, logged, and dissected in search of anything that could be used to keep her here indefinitely.

"I'm cold," she said to the camera.

"The temperature is seventy-two degrees, the hospital standard," replied the voice behind the lens.

"Yeah, well, I feel a draft," she said, tucking the paper gown beneath her thighs to try to warm up.

The camera said nothing.

Dinner was a carton of milk served alongside a sandwich and food that could be eaten without a fork and knife.

I wonder if Steve knows what's happened to me. When I didn't show up, he probably started asking questions, but who knows what they told him, and it's not like he could tell them why he was looking for me.

Steve would be leaving on Monday. This was Thursday. That gave her four days to get out of confinement before she lost her lifeline to the outside world. *Tomorrow is Friday, Friday means grand rounds, grand rounds means seeing Julian, and seeing Julian means I could get out of here by the weekend.*

Riley tugged at the thin blanket anchored to the bedframe, trying for maximum coverage. Curling her legs into a fetal position only succeeded in pushing her knees outside the cover. To warm her hands, she tucked them between her thighs.

"Hands," said the voice behind the camera. "Please keep your hands where they can be seen."

She clasped them in front of her face, but every time she started to fall asleep, they drifted back beneath the blanket.

"Hands," the voice said repeatedly through the night, startling her awake. "Hands."

By morning she was exhausted, desperate for sleep, but a check of the clock down the hall showed that Julian would be along at any time. Despite the lack of a mirror, she did her best to look presentable and not at all suicidal, then sat primly on the bed, awaiting his knock.

Half an hour passed.

Any time now, she reassured herself. *He'll be here any time now.*

Thirty minutes became an hour.

Then two.

"Excuse me," Riley called to the camera. "When do grand rounds start in this part of the hospital?"

For a long moment the camera said nothing. Then: "Grand rounds have been postponed."

"Well, can I at least see Dr. Munroe?"

Another long pause. "Dr. Munroe is no longer on staff, pending administrative review of recent events."

Riley closed her eyes, suddenly dizzy, her hands flat on the bed for support. *That must be what Kaminski meant when he said seeing Julian wasn't an option. I'll bet he waited a whole five minutes after Julian was gone to send Henry to fetch my ass.*

Locked down on suicide watch, without anyone to help her or look for her, she felt as if she had been swallowed whole by some massive animal.

I'm in here, she thought at the universe. *I'm in here. Can anyone see me? Can anyone hear me? Anyone?*

Anyone?

THREE LETTERS,
ONE WORD

Biedermann returned shortly after breakfast. "Doctor Kaminski will see you now."

Riley plucked at the paper hospital gown. "Can I have my clothes back? Just so my ass isn't hanging out?"

"I'm afraid not," she said, then disappeared down the hall for a moment before returning with a thin robe. "This is all that's allowed."

Five minutes later she was standing in Kaminski's office, while Biedermann took her usual place by the window.

"Please sit," he said, indicating the chair at the other side of his desk.

"No thanks," she said, determined not to risk giving him a peek at the good china.

"Riley, you need to understand that this isn't a zero-sum game. We had no reports of violence or suicide attempts overnight, but a brief absence of unhealthy behavior doesn't provide evidence of healthy behavior. If you want to get out of there, we need to see real signs of progress."

"Like what?"

"Anything that shows forward momentum. It doesn't have to be big or difficult. It can be something simple, that any sensible person would be willing to do."

He leaned forward, enjoying the moment. "You could, for instance, apologize for attacking me in this office."

"Even if I don't mean it?"

"That's between you and your conscience. I just want to hear you say the words."

She thought about it for a tenth of a second before saying, "No," a pause born not out of doubt but from debating between *no* and *fuck no*.

"Then that will be all," he said to Biedermann, his voice frosty. "Please escort the patient back to the observation room."

A minute later, Riley was back in the elevator as Biedermann pushed the button for the third floor.

Halfway up, she pushed Stop.

Riley looked from the controls to Biedermann. "Umm . . . why are we stopping?"

Biedermann hesitated, as if coming to an inner decision, then said, "Several weeks ago, Nurse Sanchez told me what you said when you thanked her for lowering the dose."

Riley stiffened. *Is she really going to use Sanchez against me?*

"She didn't know what you were talking about, because she wasn't the one adjusting the medication levels."

Riley was about to ask, *Then who was it?* when she caught the inflection behind *she*.

Holy shit!

"That was *you*?"

"The doctors have their purview, and I have mine. I comply with their instructions to the extent that they will not lead to infractions that can harm me or my career. I moderated the dosage and made the appropriate notations in the medications log to ensure that we stayed within AMA, APA, and FDA guidelines for extended haloperidol usage."

"But . . . didn't Kaminski see the entries?"

"The doctors never check the logs, because they believe their word is final. Even if he did check, I was on the right side of the regulations concerning the administration of medication, and there's nothing he could do that wouldn't draw attention to his agenda. I also made it a point to intrude when I saw him enter your room and close the door, because anything that happens on my floor while I am on duty is my responsibility."

"So why are you telling me this *now*?"

Biedermann waited.

Riley sighed. *Are we still doing this?* "Why are you telling me this now, *Nurse Biedermann*?"

"This deal is getting worse by the minute."

What the fuck? Riley thought, then suddenly it hit. "Lando Calrissian—*Star Wars*."

"Yes."

"Julian!"

"*Doctor* Munroe, yes. Whatever you may think of me, Ms. Diaz, I took this position because I genuinely believed I could do some good. Lately, as I began to see where things were going with the ARC program, I asked Dr. Munroe if I could be assigned back to the regular ward. He declined, saying he needed me on this side of the hospital to keep an eye on things. He mentioned *you* in particular," she said, with just a flicker of resentment in her voice.

Stay close to Biedermann, Julian had told her. Now it made sense!

"I'm telling you this because there's only so much I can do while you're under observation. Every time you refuse to cooperate, you get farther from whatever safe harbor I can discreetly provide. So the next time he asks if you're sorry for attacking him, just say yes, don't give him an excuse to take this to the next level."

"Can't do it."

"Why?"

"Because I'm *not* sorry!" Riley said, her frustration finally boiling over. "Because I'd do it again if I had the chance! Because when I say no, *I'm* in control, not him! Look at me! *No is all I have left!* Take that away and you might as well leave me in here forever! Can I win in the long run? Don't know, don't care. All I know is that he loses every time I say no."

"Ms. Diaz, if putting you on suicide watch doesn't achieve the desired effect, and if Dr. Kaminski can document a continued predilection toward violence and disruption, that leaves ECT as the only remaining therapeutic."

"ECT?"

"Electroconvulsive therapy."

"You're just trying to scare me. Nobody does shock therapy anymore."

"Actually, it's still quite common. The voltage is lower than it was in the past, the patient is anesthetized, and we take every precaution against seizures, but yes, ECT is still practiced for violent patients, which is how you've been categorized. And while it's not as bad as it used to be, nobody comes out the other side of it the same as they went in, because that's the whole point of ECT."

"Shit."

Pause.

"Shit, *Nurse Biedermann*. Seriously, what's his deal with me? I mean, beyond the fact that I punched him in the dick?"

"He doesn't like the effect you have on the other patients. He had them more or less where he wanted them until you showed up. From what I've gathered from his conversations with Mr. McGann, demonstrating that their methods reduce opposition and instill complacency are crucial to achieving the long-term goals of the ARC program."

"What long-term goals?"

"I don't know. All I *do* know is that you are in a very precarious position. By now I know that I can't make you do anything you don't want to do, so you can refuse to follow my advice. But if you're half as smart as Dr. Munroe thinks you are, then you'll know when to pick your battles. Saying yes when Kaminski asks if you're sorry won't kill you, and it could save you a lot of trouble."

But Biedermann's expression, however, showed that she knew exactly what Riley was going to say even before she said it.

"No," came the reply, firmly, defiantly, and with finality. "*No.*"

Biedermann pushed the button, and the elevator continued its upward trajectory.

"So now that Dr. Munroe is gone, will you be staying or leaving?" Riley asked.

The elevator reached the third floor and the doors opened.

"This is where you get off," Biedermann said.

Day Two. Saturday.

Biedermann waited silently before the window as Riley stood before Kaminski.

"No."

Day Three. Sunday.

"No."

Day Four. Monday.

Riley was in anguish as Biedermann led her down the hall to Kaminski's office. This was the day Steve said he would be checking out of the hospital, and with him would go her last chance to get word out, call for help, or at least find out the reason behind the call he'd received.

A moment later, she was standing before Kaminski. "Do you acknowledge your inappropriate behavior, and apologize for your violent outburst?"

Just say yes, a part of her brain insisted. *You don't have to mean it. Just say yes. Three letters, one word. How hard can that be?*

Stop it, she fired back. *Doesn't matter what he says or does, we will not feed his ego or say that what he did to me or Lauren was right. If I do it, I'll regret it for the rest of my life.*

"No."

Only after Bidermann had escorted Riley back to her room and closed the door did she allow the tears to come. *It was the right choice*, she told herself. *It was the only choice.*

Yes, her brain thought back at her. *But what did it cost us?*

Day Five. Tuesday.

Riley took her usual place in front of Kaminski.

"No," she said, before the question could even be asked. *It's too late now anyway. What difference does it make?*

Kaminski didn't bother looking up from his paperwork. "Take her back to the room."

"I'm afraid I can't do that, Dr. Kaminski."

They both looked at her, as startled by what Biedermann had said as by the mere fact that she had spoken at all.

Kaminski's face flushed angrily. "Excuse me?"

"Under the most recent guidelines provided by the Washington State Medical Commission, inpatient residents can only be held in suicide watch for five days. If no further attempts at self-harm have been observed, the patient must be returned to the common ward."

"Nonetheless, it is my diagnosis that she remains suicidal."

"I understand that is your *opinion*," Biedermannn said, hands folded primly in front of her, "but more than that is required at the five-day mark. I must insist upon this because, while *your* position is secure, my license as head nurse is at risk if I continue this level of suicide watch without sufficient legal and medical grounds. If you can provide any evidence from the logs, recordings, or examinations that support your conclusion—any evidence at all—I will be more than happy to escort the patient to her secure room and continue the enforced isolation."

Lips thinned, Kaminski flipped through the observation reports on his desk, so furious that he barely registered anything he was looking at. "I don't have time to read all this right now."

"Then when you have had sufficient time to review the material, please forward any specific information I can use to reinstitute the psychiatric hold and I will do so at once."

"Fine. Get her out, then."

Riley waited until the elevator doors closed, then said, "Thank you for what you did back there."

"As I said, I can't afford to lose my license. I didn't do it for you, I did it for myself." But behind her eyes there was a glimmer of strength and resolve that hadn't been there before.

A little revolution is good for the soul, isn't it, Nurse Biedermann?

Just before the doors opened again, she turned to Riley and said with more than a hint of pride, "To answer your question: I'm staying. Someone has to bear witness. Just . . . please try to avoid making my task more difficult than it needs to be."

When Riley returned to the ARC ward, wearing the same clothes she'd been wearing when she was put on suicide watch, the others came out of their rooms to celebrate her return.

"Sonofabitch didn't know who he was fucking with, did he?" Danny said, then gave her a bear hug so tight she thought he'd break a rib.

As the hugs continued, she glanced down the hall in case Steve might have delayed his departure to wait for her.

"Sorry, he's gone," Callie said when Riley asked. "He shook everyone's hand, told me to say goodbye to you for him, then hit the road. Honestly, he couldn't get out of here quick enough."

"Yeah," Hector said. "He was moving so fast you couldn't even see him, just kinda heard him zoom as he went past."

When the impromptu party subsided, Riley returned to her room and found a Snickers bar on the bed beside a note from Henry: *Welcome Home.*

Yeah, maybe it is, she thought, *at least for the foreseeables, as Mom used to say.*

The celebration picked up again over lunch as Riley made up for five days of finger food and egg salad sandwiches by practically diving headfirst into the trays of tamales, guacamole, Spanish rice, carnitas, warm tortillas and green salad with apples, cranberries, and pepitas set out at the food counter. She didn't care that most of it had come out of cans; at that moment, it was the best meal ever.

"Enjoy the hot food while you can," one of the servers said as he dished out another helping of refried beans. "The Beast is acting up again—pilot lights keep going on and off. Got a guy coming in soon to scope it out for problems with the gas line, soap it up, crank it up, and see what bubbles out. They say it shouldn't take more than a couple of days, but we'll see. Sometimes you need a hunting dog and a Ouija board to find these leaks."

As Riley returned to sit with the others, she looked to Steve's usual seat, keenly feeling his absence. *I can't blame him for wanting to get out of here as fast as he could. For all he knew, I might have been in there for weeks. He was right to leave as soon as the door opened.*

But he wasn't the only one absent from the cafeteria.

"Where's Frankenstein?"

"Occupying the solarium," Jim said. "He's been there from doors-open to lights-out for days, just staring out the window. Wouldn't even come down for meals. Anytime one of us went in, he made it really fucking clear he didn't want us there."

"I've never actually been snarled at by someone before," Angela said. "Now that I know what it's like, I don't think I'll be doing *that* again, thankyouverymuch."

"I guess someone must have complained about him," Rebecca said, "because some of the orderlies went in to try and encourage him to leave. Came out looking like they'd just seen their own deaths."

After finishing lunch, Riley grabbed a packet of grapes and made her way to the solarium. She found him standing with his head pressed against the big window that looked out at the street. He didn't react as she came in, and for a moment she thought he might have fallen asleep standing up.

His eyes were the first to move, slowly turning in her direction and locking on. Then, as if the rest of his body had been given permission, he leaned away from the glass and turned toward her.

"Hi," she said. "Miss me?"

At first he didn't respond. Then a half smile curled his lips, and he loped across the room to her in a way that reminded her of videos she'd seen of massive dogs tackling their owners after they returned from duty overseas. He grabbed her around the shoulders and jumped up and down, making little sounds of happiness, like he wanted to laugh but had forgotten how.

How long has it been since he's laughed? she wondered. *Since he's had a* reason *to laugh?* Her eyes went moist at the thought, and when she looked up, saw the same tears in his as well.

"They say you haven't been eating," she said, "so I brought you some grapes."

His eyes stayed soft as he leveraged the gift into the oversized pocket of his shirt. Then tears surrendered to joy as he took her hand, looked outside to make sure no one was around, and pulled her out of the room and down the hall.

"Where are we going?" she asked.

He held his hand up in front of his face, fingers spread. *Don't ask, don't make noise, just follow.*

Halfway down the hall, they arrived at a locked storeroom door. After making sure no one was watching, he took the doorknob in both hands, pulling up and to the left, revealing that the hinges alongside the door were slightly off-kilter. Then there was an audible *click* as the lock popped free.

He opened the door and nodded for her to go inside.

She dashed past him, and he followed her into the room, reversing the process to ensure that the door was locked on the outside.

In the dim light that spilled in beneath the door, Riley saw stacks of boxes and suitcases along with clothes stuffed into bags, hung on racks, or stacked on shelves. *This must be where they keep the personal belongings of all the patients.*

He led her to the far end of the room, then pulled at a tall rack choked with clothes, shoes, and boxes to reveal a hidden space behind it, barely three feet across. She couldn't see his face but imagined him smiling a crooked grin as he waved her inside.

Well, at least now we know where his hidey-hole is, she thought. Crouching low, she picked her way through piles of clothing and boxes into the narrow space.

He pulled the rack back into place so they couldn't be seen from the other side, then slid to the floor beside her. Someone would have to poke through the rack of clothes with a stick to find the space behind, and she knew he would never react no matter how hard he got poked.

Something else we have in common, she decided.

He fumbled on the floor for a moment, then she heard another *click* as he switched on a flashlight.

Her heart rose in pain and beauty at what it revealed.

Small toys, most likely liberated from the closed pediatric ward, were scattered across the floor: horses and soldiers and clowns and dogs and figures of girls and boys at play. There were balls and alphabet blocks and a tiny baby stroller and action figures and a white duck on wheels and a toy xylophone.

Grinning broadly, he picked up the toys one at a time to show her his prized possessions, growing happier as she oohed and aahed and nodded her approval at each of them. Unguarded. Open. Not dangerous at all.

This is the child he never had a chance to be, and the toys he never had a chance to play with, she thought, but fought down her sadness so he wouldn't think she disapproved of whatever he was showing her next.

Then she remembered something Julian had said about his childhood. *He used to hide in a corner of the basement that was his special place, where he thought they could never find him or hurt him.*

As her eyes adjusted to the dim light, she noticed pictures taped to the wall behind her. Scooting around for a better look, her gaze fell on the nearest one: a magazine ad showing a picture-perfect family seated around a Thanksgiving table.

Seeing where she was looking, he tapped the picture excitedly, then tapped his chest.

Ohmygod, she thought, and again fought back tears. "Is this your family?" she asked, her voice soft in the darkness.

He nodded eagerly, then pointed to an image from another magazine ad that showed an African American family at the beach. He tapped it the same way.

"Your family?" she asked again.

He nodded even more excitedly.

He did this for five photos of five perfect families pulled from magazines, lovingly trimmed, and displayed on the wall.

The family he never had.

Taped to the wall beside the family pictures were ads and photos torn from articles about theme parks, vacation spots, cruises, beachfronts, and parks, where people playfully chased each other across the sand, threw snowballs, pulled big fish out of pristine lakes, went to prom, and—

The life he never had.

The tears came despite her resolve not to disappoint him, but he must have understood that *she* understood, because his fingertips grazed her face with surprising gentleness. Then the moment passed, and with sudden excitement he began searching the floor again. Whatever he was looking for, it wasn't where he thought he'd left it, and there was a moment of panic as he thrashed around, tossing the toys and figures until he pushed aside a shirt sleeve sticking out from the rack that had been covering the target of his search.

Riley's heart jumped when she saw what it was.

Steve's phone.

He held it out and nodded for her to take it. She flipped it over to the front, where Steve had left a Post-it note: *Going to try giving this to your pal. Hope he doesn't eat it. Or me. Don't say I never gave you anything. Just don't get me in trouble, okay? 317943.*

She toggled the power switch—not knowing how long she'd be gone, Steve had turned it off to conserve power rather than leave it on standby—and when the lock screen appeared, she typed in the code and was rewarded with the home screen, which showed a selfie of Steve in the woods, looking happier than she'd ever seen him before.

She checked the power level: 32 percent.

"Did he give you a charger?" she asked.

His smile diminished at her tone. Was something wrong? Had he done something to upset her?

"No, everything's fine. Everything's *perfect*, thank you, thank you *so* much . . . What I was asking is . . . Did he give you a thing that plugs into the wall?"

He cocked his head at her. *Aroo?*

"Never mind, it's okay. It's all great."

All right, she thought, *I have thirty-two percent—whoops, thirty-one percent—so I better figure out how to get the most out of this because I don't think I can ask Henry to let me borrow his charger without raising a whole lot of questions. So no voice or video calls, at least not for now. Chews up too much power. Stick with texts then sign off ASAP.*

The last incoming message on the encryption app, dated the previous Thursday, read, "Where's R? Need to connect."

She opened up a text screen.

> Hey. It's me.

Five minutes passed. She was about to turn off the phone to save power when a reply lit up the screen.

Where was the first place we
had dinner?

> McDonalds. And you still owe me
> a dollar.

Hey, R.

> Hey, C.

You okay? It's been a minute.

> I'm good. I was in lockup for a
> while. What's the 911?

Were you able to get into Kaminski's
computer? Or McGann?

Did you get the part about I was
in lockup?

Copy that. Sorry. Just really important
that you find a way inside.

Why? What's in there?

I think I may have worked out what
PL 92-98 85/Stat347 18/4001(c)
in their email headers stands for.
I figured if there's a PL 92-98 85/
Stat347 18/4001(c) there's probably an
18/4001(b) and (a). So I started poking
around and I found something, but
I need to be sure before I can bring
this to anyone who can do something
about it. I need more information, and
I need proof, and getting inside their
system is the only way to do that.

You need to be sure about what?

Long story. You got time?

She glanced up at Frankenstein, sitting cross-legged in front of
her, eating grapes, happy just to be there with her. *He'd be content
to sit here forever.*

Yeah, I'm good. Where'd you find

the info?

Congressional Records Dbase. What
do you know about the Emergency
Detention Act of 1950?

Nothing, why?

Buckle up.

TAKING CONTROL

Ten a.m., therapy room 1.

"I know we've all been through a lot during the last few weeks," Kaminski said, "but in the end, I believe these experiences will bring us together as we work toward our mutual goal of making sure that all of you get out of here when your periods of examination have expired. Wouldn't you agree, Ms. Diaz?"

"Absolutely," she said, hoping that her smile was broad enough to hide what she'd learned through the text exchange that she hadn't known before.

> The Emergency Detention Act of 1950 was passed by Congress at the height of the Red Scare. President Harry Truman was so horrified by what it represented and the ways it could be abused that he vetoed the whole thing. Congress overrode his veto, and it became the law of the land.

"I know there have been some misunderstandings along the way, but I want to assure you that I'm on your side."

The Detention Act gave Congress, the president, and the attorney general the authority to imprison dissidents without bail or evidence or adherence to the laws of Habeas Corpus. Those arrested didn't even have to be told what they were being charged with. There were to be no jurors, judges or attorneys; a hand-picked tribunal would decide their fate based almost entirely on what the government thought they might do in the future. Since you can't prove you're not planning to do something, they could keep people imprisoned for days, weeks, months, or years. This isn't a crazy conspiracy theory, this was an actual federal law.

"Being here is your *responsibility* but not necessarily your *fault*. That fault rests with the people who took advantage of your naiveté and hopes for the future to get you to do what they wanted you to do. The sooner you accept this and give us the information needed to find them and all the others who have fallen prey to such manipulation, the better it will be for them and for you."

The plan was to turn abandoned Japanese internment camps into makeshift prisons and start arresting people immediately. Truman was able to stop them, but the law stayed on the books for decades. When Nixon tried to use it against antiwar protesters, Congress passed a new act—filed under PL 92-98 85/Stat347 18/4001(b)—that said for now it was okay to ignore the other act, but they didn't repeal it. They left the Act alive and on the books in case it was ever needed in the future.

The email references to PL 92-98 85/Stat347 18/4001(c) indicate that there's been a revision of the original act. So it should be on file in the Congressional Record. But it's not, which means it's being held under a national security restriction.

"I want to help you, but there's only so much I can do on my own. It has to be a two-way street. Help me to help you. Work with me, and the other doctors. That's why the ARC program is here—so you can return to the world as constructive citizens. We don't want to keep you here forever. I sure don't."

We all know how this works. Rendition was illegal, but the government wanted to start using it after 9/11, so the Justice Department wrote a memo saying, "Oh, wait a minute, we looked under a desk and found a rationale that makes it legal, so let's start sending people to a hole in Pakistan!" But they didn't want to actually tell people what they'd done, so to cover their asses they classified the program. Enhanced interrogation? Torture? Guantanamo? Kids in cages? Same strategy: authorize it quietly, so nobody knows it's happening until after it's been going on for a while, then when they're caught, say, "Sorry, that thing we couldn't do before is our policy now, it's become an entrenched part of the system, so we can't just stop it, and besides, it's for the good of the country."

So with this new revision, it's possible that the president, Homeland Security, and his majority leaders in Congress put together an executive order reauthorizing the Emergency Detention Act so they can start putting away protesters without due process, and the ARC program is the first step in that process, the "proof of concept" you mentioned. Maybe that's why they're working so hard to get you and the rest to name names. Having those connections verified means they can

prove conspiracy, which as we saw with the Cop City Atlanta
arrests in '23, gives them all the ammo they need. Bonus round:
having protesters confess to being psychologically disturbed
gives the government legal grounds to start taking people off
the streets "for their own protection."

"That doesn't seem like a lot to ask, does it?"

If I'm right about this, we have to pull the fire alarm before the
"proof-of-concept" proves the concept, and the program goes
into full effect, or it'll be too late. So we need hard evidence:
names, documents, files, and emails—all the stuff that lives in
Kaminski's/McGann's computers.

You're the only one with a chance to get that information.
I know it's dangerous, but we need this, R. We need this
desperately.

"Riley?" Kaminski said. "Is that too much to ask? To work together
on a common goal?"

Riley smiled another manufactured smile. "No, not too much
at all."

"Then let's begin again, as if none of these recent events had
happened," Kaminski said. "So, who has something they'd like to
share with the group?"

Riley had committed the hospital's layout to memory to help her
find a way out. Now she would have to use that information to figure
out how to get deeper inside. She began by logging the schedule of
every nurse and orderly on the floor to memorize their routines,

noting who had key card access to the elevator, and where the cards were kept.

But even if she managed to get one of the access cards, and if the key code she'd memorized still worked, once she reached the first floor she'd have to get past dozens of staffers who would know who she was and that she wasn't supposed to be there unescorted. If by some miracle she somehow managed to pull off every inch of that, she'd *still* have to get into Kaminski's or McGann's office, access his computer without knowing the password, and back up all the needed information *on a flash drive she didn't have.*

She couldn't even risk bringing any of the other patients into this, because she didn't want to get them in trouble if this went badly, and besides, there was nothing they could do that she couldn't.

This is nuts, you're not Jason Bourne. Can't be done.

I agree. It can't be done. So let's figure out how to do it, starting with getting a keycard and a flash drive. Once we have that, all the other stuff will be easy.

No it won't.

No, it won't, but saying that keeps me from passing out.

Fair deal.

It would be impossible for Riley to walk unnoticed from the elevator to the first floor offices (*don't think about how we get there, just focus on what needs to be done once we're downstairs*) during the day, when everyone was at their desk. The only remaining option was to go at night, after the administrative staff left for the day, working in the dark because switching on any of the lights would give her away. That meant familiarizing herself in greater detail with the layout of the offices, the assistants' desks, the tables, all the twists and turns she'd have to navigate from the elevator to her objective. But she couldn't just go downstairs on her own to scope things out. She'd have to come up with a reason McGann and Kaminski would both want to see her in their offices, in person, rightdamnitnow.

She knew how to get the job done, but hated the idea of doing it.

Suck it up, buttercup. This isn't about us anymore, it's about everybody else. Sooner or later we all have to take one for the team.

The next morning, she asked Nurse Biedermann if she could be taken to see McGann and Kaminski.

"Why?"

"I've decided you're right. If apologizing for my behavior will get them off my back, then it's worth doing it, even if I don't mean it."

Biedermann looked almost disappointed. "It's the smart move," she said. "I'm glad you've decided to be sensible about this."

Kill me, kill me now.

Five minutes later Riley was standing in McGann's office. *Thirty-five paces from the elevator, then a right turn to the office. No blind spots to hide in between the door and the desk.*

"I realize that I've been a disruptive force, and I wanted to apologize and promise to do better going forward."

Tower computer, dead quiet, so probably air-cooled solid-state drives. Six speed screws on the outside of the tower to make it easier for the IT guys to access, mouse and keyboard hardwired to the console.

"And what brought you to this realization?"

"Seeing what happened to Lauren made me understand how short life is, and I don't want to spend that time fighting with people who are only trying to help me."

Bars on the windows, no personal bathroom to hide in, big-ass deadbolt on the door above the knob—he likes his privacy.

McGann frowned as if unsure of her truthfulness, then decided to at least acknowledge her words. "I'm glad you seem to be on the upward swing. But we'll still need to see action to go with the words."

One down.

Two minutes—and another twenty-seven paces straight, then right—brought her to Kaminski's office. In keeping with precedent, Biedermann stayed in the room with her, though Riley wasn't entirely sure if that was for her safety or Kaminski's.

"So you admit that attacking me was wrong," he said after she finished repeating what she'd told McGann.

Same office layout, same computer setup, speed screws, air-cooled, same barred window, but just a lockable doorknob, no deadbolt, and the mouse is wireless, so Bluetooth is switched on.

"Yes," she said, "it was wrong," inwardly finishing the sentence with, *because I should have punched you in the dick a third time before you went to the floor crying like a baby.*

"And you acknowledge that I have always behaved appropriately in your presence?"

"Yes, you have always behaved in an appropriate fashion." *Appropriate for a misogynistic piece of dogshit who, if I can pull this off, will maybe lose his license, you miserable little freak.*

"And you apologize."

HateYou HateYou

HateYou HateYou—

"Riley?"

"Yes, I apologize."

"That's a good start," he said, then turned to Biedermann. "You can escort her back to the ward now."

"There's something you're not telling me," Biedermann said once they were out in the hallway. It was a statement, not a question.

Don't tell her anything. The fact that she flipped your way means she could just as easily flip right back again.

"Nope. Just doing what you said: taking control of my life."

"Mmm," Biedermann said. Her tone made it clear she wasn't entirely sure if she believed any of this, but she didn't pursue it further.

Maybe she doesn't want to know what's in my head any more than I want to tell her.

And maybe she's going to start keeping a closer eye on me until she can figure out what I'm not telling her.

Ten minutes later Riley was back in her room. The first floor layout was as complex as she'd remembered, but seeing it with fresh eyes made it feel less daunting. *Just got to keep running it over and over until I can navigate it with my eyes closed. Because that's pretty much what I'll be doing once I'm out of the elevator.*

Yeah, but we still don't have what we need to make this work even if we do have a chance to get inside one of the computers. No key card, password, or flash drive—

I know, I know . . . lemme work on it, okay? These things take time.

Well, the way you're going, you'll have plenty of that in here.

_____

Riley had seen several flash drives on the first-floor desks, but there was no guarantee they'd still be sitting there at night, or that she'd be able to use them when the opportunity came. That meant getting hold of one ahead of time to confirm that it wasn't password locked. So for the next two days she watched the staff as they used their tablets to see if any of them had attached thumb drives she could liberate, but came up empty each time.

There has to be something *we can use*, she thought, increasingly frustrated. Then during lunch—cold sandwiches and a salad bar (the Beast was down again)—Riley was struck so hard by the solution that she had to stop herself from yelling out *yes!*

I do have *a flash drive! I've had it the whole time! I'm an idiot!*
Ten points for self-awareness and pattern recognition.
Will. You. SHUDDUP!

She scarfed down her food as fast as she could and ditched the plastic tray, driven by excitement and a need to get out before the other patients started crowding the halls. Moving quickly, she made her way to the hidey-hole. Being shorter than Frankenstein and not as crazy strong, she had a harder time lifting the door high enough to pop the lock, but with some effort it finally came free. She hurried inside, pushed her way into the tiny gap behind the rack, and turned the phone back on.

You there?

A minute later:

What's my favorite color?

You said you don't have a favorite
color, and for the record I still don't
believe you.

What've you got?

A cell phone with a memory card.
Can I use it to download from one
of the computers if Bluetooth is
enabled?

Should be doable. Can pair with an
app that will tell the computer to clone
itself to the card as a backup drive. Let
me check around to see what's small
and invisible enough to get it done,
and get back to you. Ten minutes?

Okay. Turning off the phone to
save juice.

How much do you have?

27 minutes and no charger
so don't even ask.

Copy that. Stand by.

Just as she switched off the phone and the room went dark, she
heard the door open then close again. She held her breath, afraid to

do anything that might give her away. Suddenly the rack shuddered as it was moved aside, and in the dim light from under the door she recognized Frankenstein's unmistakable silhouette.

"Hey," she whispered, relieved.

He slid the rack back into place and lowered himself to the floor. She'd been afraid that he might be annoyed to find her in his private space, but when he switched on the flashlight, his smile said that he was happy to see her there.

Secrets are always best when shared with someone you trust, she thought. *And I don't think there have been a lot of people in his life he could trust.*

With several minutes to kill, she turned back to the photos taped to the wall, each of them a happy thought in a desperately unhappy life. Catching her look, he tapped a picture showing a family coming out the end of a water slide, their hands raised in triumph.

What's this? his eyes asked her.

She raised her hands in the air, then dove down, going, "Shhhhhhhh," to simulate the sound of water, then up again, down and around and side to side, then with one last arc, she raised her hands high, just as they were in the picture. "Shhhhhooooom!"

He clapped his hands, eyes glittering with joy at the revelation, and parroted her actions back to her. "Shhhhhooooom!"

"Shhhhhooooom!" she echoed, laughing, and he applauded again.

She tapped the photo. "When you do the last big dive, they take a picture you can buy afterward, so you can remember where you were and what you looked like when you came out the other side."

He nodded but she wasn't sure he understood, so she edged over until they were side by side, then raised her arms to match the photo of the waterslide. "You too," she said, nudging him as she entered the passcode to unlock the phone.

He raised his arms, hollow eyes piercing the darkness, fingers crooked inward. For anyone else in the hospital, seeing this would be the worst kind of nightmare fuel, but she found it terribly cute.

"Say Shhhhooooom!" she said, flipping the camera on.

"Shhhhooooom!"

Click!

When she showed him the photo of the two of them faking a waterslide landing, his eyes grew wide then gentle and for a moment she thought that tears might follow, but then a text popped up on the screen, startling him.

"It's okay," she said. "It's a friend."

He nodded, spooked by the intrusion into their private moment, but if she said it was fine, that was good enough for him.

> Okay, I've configured an app that can download the contents of the hard drive to the phone's memory card using Bluetooth.
>
> Since we don't know the size of the drive, be sure to empty the memory card as much as you can because there's bound to be a ton of stuff to download and we don't want the app to run out of space and overwrite anything essential. The app will take about ten minutes to back up all the files, then another ten minutes

to download them to a server here.
That's 20 minutes total and you're
already getting close to that, so put
the phone in low-power mode to
conserve as much as you can.

> Any chance the app will set off
> a tripwire once I plug into the
> system?

Almost certainly no.

> You know that almost certainly
> no isn't actually no, right?

Worst-case scenario: if the system
figures out what's going on, it'll delete
all the files, send an encrypted alert to
everyone on the system, and log the
device ID, which would get your friend
Steve in trouble.

> Yeah, no shit.

Since they're using military-grade
encryption there are probably
safeguards against unrecognized
devices. Best I could do is configure
the app so it won't be interrogated by
the system. Once the app uploads the

transfer protocol it turns the phone
invisible by deleting the serial number
and switching off the enumeration
descriptors the computer uses to
identify new devises and find the
right drivers. That will limit slightly
what it can download, meaning it
won't detect hidden directories, but
it'll grab anything in open directories:
passwords, email, files, photos, etc.

> Roger dodger. Now all I need is
> find a key or a back door.

Okay. Sending the app. Chat soon.
Good luck.

While the app downloaded in the background, Riley switched
to low-power mode and began turning off location services and
deleting apps, anything that took up energy or space. The last items
to go were hundreds of photos of Steve with his friends, camping
or hanging out. *He looks so happy. I just hope he backed up these
pictures to the cloud, because otherwise he's going to be way pissed
off at me.*

She tagged all the photos for deletion, paused at the one she'd
taken of herself and Frankenstein, and sent it to an email address
she hadn't used in a long time, where nobody would be looking for
it, waiting for the download to complete as—

The storeroom door opened again, but this time the lights went on as someone entered and began going through the stacks in search of something.

Riley glanced back at the app.

Ninety-eight percent downloaded.

Ninety-nine percent downloaded.

Then the download hit 100 percent and *blooped* audibly.

Whoever was in the storeroom suddenly stopped in his search. Had he heard?

She turned off the phone.

The room remained silent. Then the lights went out.

He's looking for the light of anything electronic that might have been left on.

A minute passed. Then another.

It's nothing, let it go, you imagined it.

Finally the lights flicked back on as whoever it was turned back to the task at hand. He must have found whatever he'd come for, because the rustling stopped the door opened and closed, and his footsteps disappeared down the hall.

That was way too close, she thought as she set the phone down on the floor. "I should get back before someone realizes I'm not anyplace they can find me."

He stood and slid the rack aside, then raised a hand for her to wait as he pressed his ear to the door. When he was satisfied no one was around, he pulled upward on the knob until it popped free, waved for her to hurry out, then followed into the hall before slotting the door back into place.

As Riley walked back to her room, she felt a rush of excitement at the possibility that she might actually be able to pull this off. All she needed now was a key card for the elevator and a little luck.

Over the next two days, Riley intensified her scrutiny of the orderlies to make sure their schedules hadn't changed, and confirm where they kept their key cards in search of any who carried them in their jacket pockets instead of their pants. When she found her target, she waited until three o'clock when he usually mopped down the art room, then slipped in quietly while his back was turned. A quick check of his jacket, hanging over the back of a chair, revealed the key card in an inside pocket. She grabbed it, put the jacket back as she'd found it, and hurried quietly away.

Screw Jason Bourne, she thought excitedly, *I'm Beatrix Kiddo in* Kill Bill*! Somebody get me a katana and a yellow jumpsuit!*

You don't have *a future, Kaminski!*

She knew the orderly would eventually discover that his card was missing, but she also knew that it's a pain in the ass to recode an entire system, so the odds were good that they'd hold off taking that step unless it was absolutely necessary, which meant waiting until morning in case it turned up.

And that was fine. Tonight—*this* night—was all she needed.

Shortly before lights-out, she turned on the water in the bathroom sink and closed the door, so if anyone poked their head in before lockdown, they'd assume she was inside getting ready for bed. Then she worked her way back into the storeroom and closed the door behind her.

Okay, she thought. *Here we go.*

Riley slipped into the gap behind the rack and pulled it shut behind her. She would wait until after midnight to make her move, when most of the night staff went home and the cleaning crew came in. Most cleaners opened all the doors so they could come and go as needed and give any disinfectants or cleaning solutions a chance to air out. With luck, the door to McGann's or Kaminski's office would be open and she could do what needed to be done, then get the hell out before being discovered.

As she waited in the tight space, sitting for hours without moving, the room grew colder. *Guess they don't bother heating the storerooms after lights-out*, she decided, and wrapped herself in a sweater from one of the racks.

Until now there hadn't been time to think about what she was doing; she'd been too busy doing it. But now time was all she had, and her brain started crawling over all the ways this could go supremely bad. To distract herself she started flipping through memories of birthdays, road trips, Disneyland, and the impromptu living room film festivals they held every time her dad signed up for a new streaming service.

And of course *that* memory came swimming up at her as it always did when she let her brain pop into neutral for more than five minutes.

Why the hell is it that when we're standing at a stoplight or waiting for an order to come up at a coffee shop, it's always the painful memories that show up in full Imax? Never the happy memories, only and ever the ones where we've done something stupid or embarrassing, and by the time we finish shoving it back into the box, we've missed the walk sign or the pickup order and everyone's looking at us like, Who let that idiot in here?

She'd just turned seven and was halfway through watching a movie when her dad said it was late and she had to go to bed. She couldn't remember what movie it was, only her annoyance at being talked to like a child when she was in third grade and knew everything there was to know about maps and homophones and prefixes and why rivers were important, and she didn't *care* what time it was; she didn't want to go to her room, she wanted to watch the rest of the goddamned movie.

And that's exactly what she said. Out loud. Including the *goddamned*.

Unfazed, her father walked calmly past her, picked up the remote, and switched off the TV. "We'll talk about your vocabulary tomorrow. For now: Upstairs. Bedroom. Sleep."

Her fury was completely out of proportion to what she was being asked to do, but once uncoiled it stretched from her toes to the top of her head, and when she stood as requested, she turned to her father and spat on him before racing upstairs. Once she reached the other side of the slammed door, she instantly regretted what she'd done. She was sure that he would come up at any moment to yell at her about it, and lay beneath the sheets for hours, knees to chin, unable to sleep, awaiting the inevitable.

The inevitable never came.

When she went down to breakfast the next morning, he was smiling and happy and making waffles as if nothing had happened. Relieved not to be murdered, she cleaned her plate as he went upstairs to change for the quick drive to school while her mother cleared the table.

Once he was out of earshot, her mother put down the plates and sat beside Riley. "I've known your father for ten years," she said in that Irish lilt, her voice soft and low. "I've seen him get into accidents and fights; I even saw him fall off the roof of the garage when he was trying to find a leak, and he got right back up like nothing happened. I've never seen him truly, deeply hurt until last night.

He doesn't blame you, you're a young child, and young children do what young children do because they don't know any better, so you can't hold that against them. He blames himself, thinking he was a little too brusque, that maybe he should have at least waited for the commercial. Even asked me not to mention it. But you know how I am, tell me to say yes, and I say no every time.

"So all I'll say is this: your father loves you more than anything else in this good Earth, and I suspect that includes me. He would die for you, without even a second's hesitation. Frankly, I think he'd be honored, because he'd be doing it for you. I'm not telling you this to hurt you. I'm telling you because I want you to understand that if you ever spit on him again, I will burn your toys, disown you, change the locks, cover your clothes in the kind of sausage wolves like best, and put you out in the middle of the road at midnight. Do I make myself *absolutely* clear?"

Fighting tears, not of fear but of shame, Riley nodded.

"Then wipe your face so he won't know I broke my promise," her mother said, gathering up the plates as he came back downstairs, "and we'll never speak of it again."

And they never did.

But the shame of that moment, of acting like a child, never left. Many times over the years that followed she wanted to bring it up, to apologize, but at first she was too embarrassed, and then it became increasingly difficult to wedge it into the conversation. *You remember that thing I did five years ago? I'm sorry.* So the words were never spoken.

And now they never would be. But the memory of that moment would remain forever in her heart for the rest of her life, waiting to ambush her at unexpected moments.

Wrapped in the sweater, as she'd been wrapped in blankets that night, she wondered as she did then, what time it was and if anyone was going to come to the door. But as before, the door remained closed, the night quiet and undisturbed.

She stretched and unkinked her neck. *It has to be midnight by now*, she decided. *So yeah, here I am, just like Mom said: covered in the kind of sausage wolves like best, out in the middle of the road at midnight.*

Time to do this.

She shucked the sweater, picked up the cell phone, pressed the power button—

—and realized immediately that something was wrong.

The last time she'd been here, she'd switched the phone off as soon as the app finished downloading to save power, so it should have taken a moment to reboot. But the phone switched on immediately, meaning it was in sleep mode, which should have put her at the app screen, but instead she found herself looking at the photo she'd taken of herself and Frankenstein.

And the power indicator read 2 percent.

I'm gonna be sick, she thought, fighting the taste of bile at the back of her throat.

What the fuck happened?

Then in her mind's eye she saw Frankenstein coming back to the store room over the last two days, turning on the phone—the access code was right there on the Post-it, and he'd seen her use it at least once—and looking at the picture, hour after hour, just as he did with the photos on the wall, as the power slowly trickled away.

It's not his fault, she told herself, fighting tears, *he didn't know what I needed it for, didn't understand he was draining the battery, he was just happy to have that photo. He's a child inside, and he was just being that child. It might have made a difference if I'd explained it to him, but I didn't and he didn't know any better and godfuckingDAMNit!*

She opened the texting app.

> Have to abort. Phone is nearly
> dead. Nothing I can do now. So
> sorry.

A moment later:

> It's okay. I understand. Happens. It's
> on me now to figure out next steps.
> Try to get some sleep. Not your fault.
> Save what's left and check back when
> you can.

As the battery indicator hit 1 percent, she set a new passcode then switched it off. As an extra precaution, she slid the phone into a sock under a rack at the front of the room, where it would be nearly impossible to find, then balled up into a corner for warmth to wait out the night. *So much for Beatrix Kiddo,* she thought.

Hey, Bea?

Yes, Elle?

How does it feel to completely screw up the most important thing you've ever been asked to do?

Go to hell.

You first, sweetie. You first.

OFFENDED GODS
AND ANSWERED PRAYERS

After a sleepless, angry night, Riley made her way back from the storeroom to learn that, as she'd feared, the missing key card had been noticed and all the others were being recoded, rendering useless the one she had stolen. To cover her tracks, she dropped the stolen card behind the art room couch, where it would be found during the next cleaning.

The other ARC patients could see something was bothering her, but she couldn't bear to tell them how badly she'd failed. Danny did his best to cheer her up, starting with a detailed recitation of every fart joke he'd ever heard. She nodded and smiled and even laughed from time to time because she didn't want him to feel unappreciated, but everything behind her eyes was lost to rage and frustration. She wanted to dig a hole, jump in, pull the ground in after her, and never come out again.

Can someone please tell me—just for future reference, so I can understand why the universe keeps fucking with me like this—which god did I offend?

All of them, her brain whispered back at her.

Okay, well . . . that's fair.

"During our last session, we talked about how we were going to start over and earn back some of the trust that was lost due to recent events." Kaminski said. Once again he made it a point to glance at Riley when he said *recent events* but she didn't care enough to get annoyed about it. *Whatever. Can I go now? I need to throw up for about a day and a half.*

"So as a show of good faith, I'm going to make the first move in repairing that trust," he continued. "Let me start with a question. What's the difference between all of you, and the people who organized the protests that got you arrested?"

"They ran faster?" Jim said.

Kaminski put on his smiley face. "No, but you're close. The difference is that they're still *out there*, going on dates and dinners, hiking and swimming and making plans for more protests, while you're stuck in here, paying the price for their actions. And what have they done to help you since being arrested? Nothing. To them, you're just collateral damage. I don't see you that way. Yes, we disagree on many things. Yes, you made mistakes. But you're not ringleaders, you don't use other people; you're good, decent people who wanted to make the world better and ended up being exploited and abandoned."

"If we're such good people," Angela said, "then why not just let us go?"

"Good question," Kaminski said, then turned to Callie. "How much longer is left on your committal here?"

"Three weeks," Callie said, her voice rising at the end of the sentence like, *Is that about to change, in the wrong direction?*

"I mean, I've been doing everything I can to show, like you said, good faith—"

"And you've done a very good job, despite a lapse in judgment at the breakfast table a few weeks ago."

Riley straightened. Was he going to punish her for standing up to him during the hunger strike?

"We know who someone really is by what they do most of the time," Kaminski said. "When there's a break in that pattern, you can either define that person by the exception, or weigh it against how they live and who they are the rest of the time. So should we give that incident equal weight to everything you've done since coming here?"

"No," she said, fighting tears.

Where is this going?

"I agree, Callie. You've worked very hard to earn your way out. You've shown that you understand what you did wrong and why you did it. As a result, I feel you've become a better person. The rest of the staff concurs. So after consulting with Mr. McGann and going over the points you've earned toward rehabilitation, balanced against the relatively short time remaining on your commitment, we've decided that your behavior should be rewarded with an early release."

Her hand flew to her mouth, hardly believing what she was hearing. "How early?"

"Would today suffice?"

And the tears came in a rush as the other patients began applauding, high-fiving, and hugging her.

"The paperwork's already been drawn up, and is sitting on my desk awaiting signature. I should mention that it includes a nondisclosure agreement stating that you received the best available care, that you were always treated professionally, that you will not discuss the terms of your treatment, and that you absolve the hospital of any potential legal issues. I'm also required to let you know that violating the NDA will incur significant penalties that will almost certainly put you right back here. So I understand if you'd rather not sign it. You're welcome to hang on another few weeks until you're discharged through normal channels, which won't require signing an NDA."

Unless you decide to change your mind at the last minute and keep her for another six months, and you *know that* she *knows that's always an option.*

Callie hesitated, weighing her options, then nodded. "No, it's okay, I'll sign it."

"Excellent. Then there's just one last item, and then we're done. A gesture of good faith from you to match our own.

"We're still working out how the protests are organized, who does what, and who's in charge of which geographical areas. Understanding the situation on the ground will let us be more effective as we try to help others like yourself. One of the gaps in our knowledge concerns the identity of the organizer for the protest that landed you here."

And the room got very quiet.

"I can't do that," Callie said, her voice little more than a whisper, oblivious to the tears that were rolling down. "I can't give you that name."

"And I'm not asking you for it. I understand that you might feel a sense of loyalty to these people, despite them having turned their back on you. For what it's worth, we have a pretty good idea of who this person is because several other people have already confirmed it for us. So I'm not going to ask you to say this person's name if that would make you comfortable. You don't have to say anything at all. I'll simply say a name, and if it's the right name, all you have to do is nod. That's it. And you'll be out of here before dinner."

Riley thought back to the conversation about the Emergency Detention Act. *"Is that why they're working so hard to get names, so they can prove conspiracy?"*

"Don't do it," Riley said.

"This conversation doesn't concern you," Kaminski snapped. "This is between Callie and myself."

Callie stared at the ground, fist pressed to her lips, agonizing over her decision.

"What's the name you have?" she asked at last.

"Derek Winters."

She looked up, startled. "No," she said, relieved. "That's not him."

"I know. That was just a test of your sincerity. Derek Winters was my principal back in high school. If you'd said yes, it would show that you were still in need of further treatment. Only an honest answer will suffice. Do you understand?"

She nodded. Dreading what came next.

"Is his name Thomas Madigan?"

She closed her eyes tight, and even before she nodded, Riley knew that was the name.

"Then you're done," Kaminski said, rising. "There's an orderly waiting outside to help collect your things. I'll be along in a bit to see you off."

"Okay," she managed, and everyone was crying as they hugged her goodbye. She saved the biggest hug for Danny.

"I never meant any of the mean things I said to you," she said, holding him tight.

"That's okay, I meant all of mine."

She laughed through the tears, then turned to Riley. "Good luck."

"You too," Riley said, and hugged her.

"You could at least stay for Barbeque Day," Jim said.

"Not a chance," she said, then waved goodbye. "Be safe, everybody, okay?"

When she was gone, Kaminski turned back to the group. "I want you to remember this moment because despite what you might think, despite what you might have been *told*," he said, once again looking at Riley, "cooperation is not pointless. Cooperation has its benefits. We didn't have to release her early, but we did. *We*. Not your friends, or your organizers, we did this. So as we go forward, I urge you to remember who your friends are and who they are not."

An hour later, Riley and the others sat behind plates bearing ribs, fries, and corn on the cob from the outdoor grill—the Beast was on the fritz again—but very few of them were eating. Or talking.

Then Hector glanced outside. "There she goes," he said.

They crowded the window and watched as Callie put a small bag into the trunk of a taxi and looked back up at the hospital one last time. They couldn't tell if she could see them through the glare of the glass, but she waved anyway. They returned it. Then she climbed into the back seat, and the taxi drove off.

They watched until it disappeared from view, then returned to the table.

After what felt like a very long time, Hector pushed away his plate and leaned forward, his voice as sad as it was angry. "Does anyone here, and I mean anyone at *all*, really believe that somebody confirmed this Madigan guy's name before today?"

No one raised their hands.

"Yeah, same here," he said resignedly. "They probably suspected it was him, but didn't know for sure. Until now."

"Bitch of it is," Becca said, "I saw Callie's eyes when she nodded, and I don't think she believed his line. She just wanted out."

"Can you blame her?" Angela said. "Raise your hand if you know for sure you wouldn't do the same in her position, given a chance like this."

No one did.

He's wearing us down, and as of right now, everyone at this table knows we can't take much more.

"So what's the next move, Jim?" Danny said. "Where do we go from here? How do we push back?"

"I don't know," he said, and there was fatigue in his voice. "First Lauren, now this . . . I won't lie, I'm feeling a little lost right now. From day one I've been all about not pushing back. It's what I know best, what I trained for. 'Find consensus. Build alliances.' If there's another way forward, I can't see it."

Then he paused, and when he came out the other side of whatever thought he was chasing, Riley realized he was looking at her. "We need fresh eyes and a fresh approach. I've carried this as far as I can. I'm ready to step back if you want to step in."

Riley took a breath, then nodded, the move so slight it was almost imperceptible. "Okay."

And just that quickly, it was done.

Now earn it, she thought.

"Hector, you asked where we go from here," Riley said. "I think what we do is get up on our hind legs and say fuck you, we're not cooperating anymore. I'm not suggesting anything noisy, or public, where there can be witnesses, we keep this just about him and us.

"The only reason they let Callie go is so we'd start thinking about the cooperation carrot, that maybe it's not such a bad idea, and it sure as hell beats the stick. There are a hundred ways he could have made that point, but he did it in the most personal way possible to beat us down and get us to give up on ourselves and each other. Making everything personal is how he tries to drill into our brains. So I say we turn that around, and make it personal about *him*."

"How?" Angela asked.

"We freeze him out. We play nice with all the other doctors, the nurses and orderlies, even Nakamura, without giving them anything useful. But when we go into a session with Kaminski, we don't talk. That's all, just silence, nobody raises their voice or does anything he can use against us. We're not being violent or threatening, we're happy to talk to the staff, we're just not talking to *him*. If anybody asks, we say we love everybody else, we just have a personal conflict with him as our doctor. It happens."

"Won't he just bring in another doctor?"

"Maybe, but I doubt it. This is his Big Thing, and I don't think he wants to share that, or give us the satisfaction of forcing him to bring on someone else. That would be the worst kind of surrender."

"He'll call it another strike," Hector said.

"He can call it anything he wants as long as *we* don't call it that. We're not fighting, we're not resisting, we're just not going to play *his* game by *his* rules anymore. We make it personal, about him; we freeze him out, and we do it together."

"You know what he's like," Becca said. "All the things he did to you when you two were slugging it out, he can do just as easily to the rest of us, and then some. What if he comes after us?"

And for a moment, Riley felt her mother's blood in her veins. *Say something that would make her proud.*

"If he comes after us, then we'll face it—and we'll do *that* together too," she said, looking to each of them in turn. "We all know what it feels like to stand at the front of a march when the police line starts to move, that moment when we think, maybe today's the day I get beaten up or shot with a rubber bullet or lose an eye or get killed when somebody plows his car into the crowd. But we stayed put.

"Kaminski keeps asking, *Why are you here?* We're here because we didn't run. We were scared and outnumbered but we stayed when everybody else took off. We didn't stay because of a conspiracy or because we had orders from some faceless master on a distant mountaintop; we stayed because that's what we *do*, we look out for each other. We put our bodies in the cogs of the latest fucked-up machine the government built to chew up the world. Sometimes we stop it, and sometimes we slow it down long enough for someone else to take the fight to the courts, the boardrooms, to Congress or the White House. We stayed because we believe in something better and more important than ourselves. *That's* why we're here.

"If we were willing to put our bodies on the line out there, then we can do the same thing in here. Because trust me, this isn't just about us, it's about everyone else who's going to be put away after us if we don't slow down the machine."

The others shared a look, and for the first time since Lauren's death, Riley saw determination returning to their eyes.

"Okay," Danny said. "We're in."

Boots on the ground. Bodies in the way.

Bring it, motherfucker.

Riley slipped into the storeroom, made her way to the hidey-hole, and fumbled through the shirts in the bottom rack, hoping the phone would still be there. When her fingers closed around it, she breathed a sigh of relief and pushed the power button. The phone struggled to life, the power indicator hovering near 1 percent.

A second later the screen filled with text messages.

> Sending this to you in advance so there'll be a backlog when you log in. Makes more sense than going back and forth if you're almost out of juice and I don't have to worry about typing fast to beat lights-out.

> I gave the information about the ARC program to a couple of journalists I know, along with the little I was able to find in the other computers, but there's nothing they can do because there aren't any direct emails between K or Mc and anyone else, that confirm they've activated the Emergency Detention Act, just metadata and subject headers. They said the file number in the emails might refer to the EDA, but without verification it's still speculative and open to interpretation. They won't stick out their necks if there's a chance they could be wrong. They need solid evidence, otherwise it's just too risky, especially with everything already so

tense out here. So there's nothing we can do on that front.

But I do have one piece of good news. For the last few months there have been protests in front of ARC #1 in Chicago because we thought that was the hub for the program. They even leaked a bogus schedule for Kaminski to convince people he was working there. So when I told the group at our last meeting that he's been running the program out of #14 the whole time, holy crap were they pissed. They're telling everyone to shift their efforts to Seattle, to the belly of the beast. I don't know when the protests are gonna start, could be a couple of days, maybe more, but I expect it'll be even bigger than Chicago, given how everyone feels about the fake-out. It won't get you out of there, but maybe putting a spotlight on the place will shake things up. I guess we'll have to see what crawls out from under the rock when the light hits.

I wish I had better news, that lawyers are coming or we've got a plan or

> that this is all going to work out, but
> they still own your ass for the full year
> of your revised sentence. I spoke to
> a few lawyers about filing an appeal
> based on your not being told the risk
> of extension when you agreed to the
> commitment, but they say it won't do
> any good because it's hard to prove
> what you did or didn't know when
> you signed the papers.
>
> I'll send a key to delete this app when
> I finish sending this, so be—

Then the power died, and the screen went black. She tried turning it on again, in case there was even a smidge of reserve power, but the phone remained dark and dead.

She removed the SIM card and the memory card, then used the butt of the flashlight to smash it all to bits, hiding pieces in different parts of the room to reduce the odds of it being useable. To make sure the flashlight had survived the effort, she turned it on and off a few times, illuminating the magazine ads taped to the wall, each featuring a young boy smiling broadly as he looked out at a world full of promise. The boy Frankenstein could have been if things had been different.

If we are all the product of the soil in which we grow, what kind of tree would you have become if they hadn't poisoned the ground? If you had been allowed to grow straight and true and loved? Where would you be now? College? Maybe an artist? Someone creative and gentle, rather than the monster they made you into?

She shook her head, correcting herself. *No. Like you, Frankenstein's creation came into the world innocent. The real monster was his creator, the one who twisted him through neglect and hate, the one who should have known better, like your parents should have known better, but they did what they did anyway. And now here you are, trapped in a world you can only survive by forcing yourself to believe that you can't feel any of it. Maybe we all do that a little. And maybe some of that truth applies to me, a truth that I haven't been willing to confront. And maybe I should do that one of these days.*

But not tonight. Tonight we get ready for war.

There were no protests outside the center the next morning.

Or the next day.

Or the day after that, when the ARC patients were scheduled for their next session with Kaminski.

They were seated in their usual places as he came with his usual coffee in hand and nudged the door closed with his foot. "Okay," he said as he sat. "Where were we?"

No one said anything.

"Is something wrong?"

Silence.

He set his coffee down on the floor. "All right, so who wants to tell me what this is all about?"

Silence.

"Becca?"

Becca stared straight ahead.

"Jim? C'mon, tell me you're not playing the I-can't-hear-you game. Tell me you're not that immature."

Jim didn't even offer a shrug.

"And here I thought we were doing so much better after our last session. With Callie's release, I felt that we'd reached an accommodation, made a fresh start. I don't have to say you'll lose points for this, because you already know that, just as you know this can't go on forever. Sooner or later we'll have to restart our conversation. Better to do that now, don't you think?"

Not just silence. *Arctic* silence.

"Fine, then we'll just sit here for the hour."

And they did.

The cone of silence came down again when he approached them at lunch, while they were talking with the orderlies about the coming Superbowl.

And again, when he convened a special counseling session that evening.

And again, the next morning.

They seem fine with the rest of the staff, Riley overheard one of the orderlies telling Kaminski. The knowledge that other doctors *weren't* being shut out infuriated him almost as much as the fact that he *was*. So she wasn't surprised when a new schedule was delivered to the ARC ward at the 7:00 a.m. knock-knock announcing that *all* counseling sessions had been canceled, even those with the other doctors, like Nakamura—along with exercise periods.

"He's pissing off the staff," Jim told the group at lunch after making sure no one else was close enough to hear. "I heard some of the doctors saying they can't do their jobs as long as Kaminski keeps up the blockade. They're worried that their salaries might get docked for lost sessions if this drags on."

"He went personal to try and split us up," Hector said. "Well, now it's our turn."

The next morning, acting on Kaminski's instructions, Biedermann informed them that they were not allowed to leave their rooms, citing unspecified "safety reasons."

The morning after that, they were given a choice: stay in their rooms all day, or come to a session with Kaminski.

They stayed in their rooms.

We're getting under his skin, Riley decided as she lay in bed that night. *How do you like it, motherfucker?*

Then she closed her eyes.

And awoke at dawn to the sound of a drum line.

She ran to the window and craned her neck to look past the edge of the hospital to where a hundred protesters had commandeered an empty lot across the street. As a drum line pounded, they chanted, "Shut down ARC!" and waved signs that read "This Isn't What Noah Had in Mind," "Let Our People Go," and "End Medical Establishment Abuse!"

"Yes!" Riley yelled out the window. "Yeah! Welcome to the freaking party!"

SHUNK-POP!

The "stay in your room or see Kaminski" order did not come on the morning the protest began. The ARC patients were free to go and come as they chose.

But the staff were nowhere to be seen.

They're probably trying to figure out how word got out that this was their flagship operation, and what they can or should say about it when the press shows up. They've gotta be shitting their pants right now—Kaminski most of all, Riley thought, and smiled for the first time in what felt like a long, long, very long time.

When she reached the breakfast table, she found the same smile on the faces of the other patients.

"I've never been on the other side of a protest," Danny said, looking out the window and grinning. "I gotta say, it's kind of fun."

The reaction by the original patients at the other end of the cafeteria was considerably more variable. Some were excited at the growing number of bodies, drums, and voices outside the hospital, while others were clearly agitated, unable to understand what was going on.

When Frankenstein entered, everyone grew quiet, worried about how he would respond. He crossed to the window and stared silently out at the crowd in the street, arms hanging limply at his side, furrowed brows casting deep shadows over his eyes.

Then the corners of his lips turned ever so slightly upward in a fractured smile.

The next morning a thousand protesters filled the street, the volume growing exponentially as more people arrived throughout the day. Poised on tiptoes at her window, Riley strained to get a good look at the crowd, but all the good stuff was happening out front.

"Hey, Ready Riley."

She turned to find Henry in her doorway, wearing a worried expression. "Hey, Henry. Everything okay?"

"It's a long goddamned way from okay on the first floor. Everybody's super tense. Lots of closed-door meetings between McGann, Kaminski, and Dr. Kim. Some of it got pretty loud; you could hear it clear down the hall."

"Anything interesting?" Riley asked. She knew she was pushing her luck, but she needed information.

Henry chewed his lip for a moment, already pretty close to the limit of what he was prepared to talk about. "They came to an understanding. McGann said he'd take care of the protesters outside, while Kaminski would deal with you and the other ARC patients in here."

"Deal with us how?"

"He didn't say, but I got the sense it's something he was going to do anyway, just not yet. 'I don't like having to move up the schedule, but I can do it.'—those were his exact words. Then just a little while ago, I got this."

He unfolded a sheet of paper from his shirt pocket. "They're asking for a complete inventory of patient belongings. They'd only do that if they're planning on moving everyone. So I started checking around, just real casual, and I saw a requisition for a prison bus that's going to be here midnight Saturday."

"Did it say where they were taking us?"

He nodded.

"Where?"

He looked down at his shoes. Shook his head.

"Henry? Where are the taking us?"

"Look, I like you, okay? You're good people. I knew that about you the day you showed up, just like I know that you speak for the others now."

"No idea what you're talking about."

"Riley, c'mon. Dr. Munroe used to call this place a glass box because the staff sees everything that goes on, even more than the doctors. The silent treatment has your fingerprints all over it, and if I can see that, you can bet your ass that by now even Kaminski's figured it out. But the thing is . . . and maybe I'm stupid for saying this, but I trust you as much as I trust anyone in this place, which, okay, may not be saying much.

"I'm worried that I might be helping these people do something they shouldn't be doing. I don't want that on my soul, my conscience, and I sure as hell don't want it on my résumé, not if I can do something about it. But if I tell you what I know, and they find out it came from me, it's my job and then some. So I need you to look me in the eye and promise that no matter what happens, you won't tell anyone you heard this from me, okay? You don't tell the other patients, the staff, the doctors—you don't tell *anybody*. If you can do that, we're cool."

She held up a hand. "I promise. Scout's honor."

Henry allowed a slight smile. "You were a Girl Scout?"

"Depends. Does cosplay count?"

The smile faded as the noise from the protest outside rose with a new drum line. "What a goddamn mess," he said, his voice tired. "Fucking Kaminski."

Then he straightened, having decided to do what he knew he was going to do before he showed up at her door. "They're taking you to San Pedro, California."

"What's in San Pedro?"

"That's what I wondered. I assumed it was another hospital, but when I did a web search, I couldn't find any hospitals in San Pedro comparable to this one."

"So like I said, what's in San Pedro?"

He let out a long, slow breath. "The Fort MacArthur Army Base."

"They're moving us to a military base?"

He nodded gravely. "I was able to verify that by pretending I was in on the transfer. The base was decommissioned a while back, but the government held onto the barracks to use as needed, along with buildings that can house administration and support staff."

"Did a judge sign off on our being moved?"

"Apparently, under the rules of the ARC program they don't need it."

Riley was about to ask, "What rules?" then she remembered the texts she had received.

The Detention Act gave Congress, the president, and the attorney general the authority to imprison dissidents without bail or evidence or adherence to the laws of Habeas Corpus. Those arrested didn't even have to be told what they were being charged with. There were to be no jurors, judges or attorneys; a hand-picked tribunal would decide their fate based almost entirely on what the government thought they might do in the future. Since you can't prove you're not planning to do something, they could keep people imprisoned for days, weeks, months, or years. This isn't a crazy conspiracy theory, this was an actual federal law.

The plan was to turn abandoned Japanese internment camps into makeshift prisons and start arresting people immediately.

That had to be the endgame Munroe was worried about when he said Kaminski and McGann had sold their program to Homeland Security. Instead of using abandoned internment camps, they'd be using decommissioned military bases when the time was right.

Except the time's not right. They've had to move up the schedule because of all the attention, which means they're going before they're ready, when they're still trying to get all their pieces in place. Knowing that doesn't give us a huge advantage, but at least it's something.

"Anyway," Henry said, "I wanted you to know what's coming. I may take tomorrow and Saturday off so I'm not here when it all goes down."

"Probably smart. Thanks for telling me, Henry. It means a lot."

"Long as we have a deal."

"We do. I never heard any of this from you. Scout's honor."

He smiled thinly, then left the room.

After breakfast, Riley told Jim and the others to meet her in the art room. Once they were assembled, she moved them to a table by the window, where there was less chance of being overheard from the door and enough noise from the street to mask the conversation. Without mentioning names, she filled them in on everything she'd learned, and what was going to happen to them.

"Why didn't you tell us about this Detention Act stuff earlier?" Hector asked.

"Because there wasn't any proof, just a possibility. Even my source on the outside wasn't sure if this was really a thing or not. If we'd acted on it and been wrong, it would've just made things worse."

"And that line of communication is gone?" Jim asked.

"Completely."

"So what do we do about it?" Becca asked. "If we let them stick us in a military base and nobody knows where we're going, we're screwed."

"We have to try and get the word out," Danny said. "There's a huge crowd outside, there has to be some way to let them know what's going down. We could put up banners in the windows, or write Fort MacArthur on our bodies and pull up our shirts when they lead us out."

"They already thought of that," Jim said, "or they wouldn't be paying overtime for the bus to come for us at midnight, when it's dark and most of the crowd will have gone home for the night. And banners won't work, because none of our windows can be seen from the street."

"There may not even *be* a crowd when this goes down," Riley said. "My source says McGann is going to make a move to clear them out."

"Police?" Hector asked. "Regular or NPF?"

"Probably the latter, since that puts them under direct government control and they don't have to answer to local authorities."

"Shit."

"Yeah, no kidding."

———————

Nothing happened that night, and Friday morning began without incident.

Breakfast was fruit and cold cereal because the oven had been torn apart. "Beast's finally gonna get tamed," one of the servers said. "Opened up the wall six feet to dig out the gas line clear to the back of the stove. Gonna do one last soap-test on the pipe tomorrow, find out why we keep having trouble, then fix it once and for all. After that, every day is gonna be Barbeque Day!"

Except we're not going to be here to see it, Riley thought, eating in silence with the others as they tried to figure out how to stop what was coming, running through one possibility after another, going nowhere. The staff must have noticed the tension, because an order came from Kaminski that all ARC patients would be confined to their rooms except for meals. *Maybe they suspect we know something, or maybe they just want to tighten control over our movements before shipping us out tomorrow night. Either way, they're not taking any chances.*

When night fell and it was time for dinner, orderlies escorted them to the cafeteria, where the regular patients were already eating. Riley nodded a silent greeting as she passed Frankenstein, sitting alone at a table beside an untouched plate of food. He didn't respond, gaze fixed at a nowhere spot deep in his own head. *Probably thinks I've been avoiding him. Don't know if he understands that we've been under isolation.*

She'd barely settled in beside the others when she heard the sirens.

They ran to the windows as red and blue lights washed over the street. A bullhorn called out something they couldn't make out, but from the way the protesters yelled back, it was almost certainly an order to disperse. The drums got louder. So did the shouts, the bullhorn, and the sirens, as more NPF patrol cars and vans approached from both ends of the street.

Then they heard the familiar *shunk-POP!* of tear gas canisters being fired into the crowd and could taste its acrid smell in the back of their throats even from the second floor. The crowd started to break up, cutting across the parking lot and jumping fences as NPF in body armor and shields pulled them down.

Then Riley realized that Frankenstein was standing beside her, eyes wide as he watched the police beating the fleeing protesters. His chest rumbled, and he began moaning in rhythm to the cries of the people down below, as though feeling every blow.

It's bringing everything back, she realized. *All the beatings. All the pain.*

"You shouldn't be here," she said gently. "Don't look at it."

But he stayed, eyes widening in pain—

—and anguish—

—and anger—

—that snowballed into blind rage, and he began slamming his fists into the wall, blood splattering paint as he roared out in fury at the scene below.

"No, stop!" she said, and put her hand out to keep him from hurting himself.

Startled by her touch, he cried out and backhanded her hard enough to send her tumbling over a table, landing on the floor with the crash of shattered dishes.

Two orderlies came on the run.

"It's all right!" she called to them, "I'm okay! He's just scared! Don't hurt him!"

But they were past listening. "Grab the sonofabitch!"

"No!"

The orderlies dogpiled him, and for an instant he disappeared beneath them. Then there was another roar of rage as he fought his way out from under, throwing one of them across the room and smashing the face of the other into the floor. Breathing hard, fists clenched, he turned and looked at Riley, and for an instant she saw a last glimmer of humanity in his eyes. Then the wall came down behind them, shutting out the world.

It was on.

An orderly lunged at Frankenstein with a stun gun, but he arced out of the way, turned, and grabbed the orderly from behind, tearing at him like a wild animal.

Riley tried to get between them, but Danny pulled her back. "Are you crazy? He'll rip you to shreds!"

"No he won't! He knows me!"

"Not anymore he doesn't!"

The orderly freed one arm and tagged Frankenstein with the stun gun, but it didn't make full contact and the pain only enraged him further. With the strength of madness he hurled the orderly over the serving counter into the kitchen. Cooks and servers ran out as he stalked past them into the kitchen in pursuit of the orderly, hands covered in his own blood, continuing the battle to the crash and clatter of breaking glass. Through the door she saw one of the terrified servers grab a heavy cleaver and swing at him, but the blow went wild, cutting into a pipe at the back of the Beast.

Riley smelled it first. *Gas! He's ruptured the line!*

"Gas!" she yelled. "*Run!*"

If he uses that stun-gun again—

They were halfway to the door when the explosion came.

The floor lifted up beneath them and crashed back down again as the ceiling split, tearing away from beams and electrical wires as flames erupted from the kitchen.

Riley picked herself up off the floor, ears ringing from the blast, barely aware of the fire alarms screaming overhead. The sprinkler system clicked and rattled, but no water came out, the pipes crushed in the explosion.

Then she felt someone tugging at her, and she turned to see Jim leaning into her face, yelling over the noise. "—to go! Come on! We have to go!"

He helped her out of the cafeteria as doctors, nurses, and patients, desperate to get away, raced down hallways that were rapidly filling with smoke. Suddenly Biedermann was there, giving instructions and pulling orderlies back into the fray. "Get the patients outside; they're the first priority! Get everyone out! I'll make sure nobody's left behind! *Move*, goddamnit!"

More terrified of her than of the fire, they raced from room to room, pulling out patients and getting them to the fire stairs that led to the first floor.

Fire doors are open, Riley thought as if from a great distance. *That means they're clearing out the first floor . . .*

Dazed by the blast, head swimming, she pulled away from Jim. "I have to get something from my room! It's important!"

"Not a chance—"

"It'll just take a second! I'll be right behind you! Go on!"

He hesitated, then joined the exodus of patients and staff surging down the hall.

She waited until he turned the corner, then staggered back the other way, fighting to stay on her feet. There was nothing in her room that she needed. What she needed was on the first floor.

If this place burns down it'll destroy the evidence in Kaminski's computer. Not gonna let that happen.

If she went downstairs with the rest, the staff would make sure she was contained and controlled. Her only chance was to wait them out.

She made her way through the smoke-filled hall to the storage room. The door popped open more easily than before, knocked further off its hinges by the explosion. She slipped inside and went to the hidey-hole.

This is insane, a part of her brain screamed at the rest of her. *You need to get your ass out of here right now!*

We wait five minutes, that's all! Just until they've cleared the building!

She counted the seconds, hands shaking as smoke seeped in through the bottom of the door. *One one thousand, two one thousand, three one thousand—*

Biedermann's voice echoed down the hall. "Is anyone still here? Hello? If you need help, call out! I'll find you!"

In here! her brain yelled.

Shutup! the rest of her yelled back.

Then: departing footsteps, followed by silence.

Riley waited another few seconds, then threw open the door. Thick gray smoke curled through the hall as alarms screamed overhead. She covered her face with a T-shirt from one of the racks and started toward the fire stairs. She stayed low, but the smoke was growing thicker by the second, tearing at her throat and lungs.

Just keep moving. It's not that far.

Her hand brushed the open fire door, and she lunged through. The smoke in the stairwell wasn't as bad, rising past her to the third floor.

She raced downstairs, hit the first floor, and found herself again engulfed in smoke. *If the fire's this bad down here, then the whole second floor must be collapsing!*

Bent low, unable to see more than a few feet ahead, she forced herself to keep moving.

Coughing up smoke, fighting for each breath, she reached McGann's office, but the double locks were shut tight.

She staggered down the narrow hall, heat and smoke rising around her, then turned right, feeling her way along the hall until she came to Kaminski's office. Whispering a prayer under her breath, she tried the knob.

Unlocked!

She hurried to the computer and fumbled for the speed screws. When they refused to turn, she pulled the cloth from her face and used it to get a better grip. *Come on, you son of a bitch! Turn!*

She twisted harder, and the first one began to move, spiraling out of the hole until it fell to the ground. *Three more! We've got this!*

Yeah? Even if we grab the drive, we still have to get it and us out of here without being caught!

We'll burn that bridge when we come to it! Two down!

Fire trucks will be here any second!

I know! Shut up so I can do this!

The last screw came loose and she tore at the case, shredding nails until the side panel popped loose, revealing two solid-state drives.

She pulled until they popped free, then shoved them into the waistband of her pants. *Okay! We're clear! Let's go!*

She covered her face and stepped through the door as—

something smashed into her face.

and suddenly she was on the floor, the world spinning around her.

"Looks like we had the same thought."

Kaminski.

No . . . no, no, no, no . . .

He glanced at the driveless computer. "Given how quiet you all got the last few days, I had a hunch you knew more about what was going on than you let on." His voice was calm despite the chaos, actually triumphant, savoring the moment, even as the fire got nearer the office. "You were probably afraid the drives wouldn't survive. I came back because I was afraid they *might*."

He stooped down over her and began patting her down. She struggled to get away, but another fist drove her head hard into the floor.

"Been wanting to do that for a long time," he said.

Fight back, she thought through the haze, trying not to pass out. *Fight!*

She clawed at his face, drawing blood, and this time when he hit her, she felt her jaw pop loose. The world kicked slantwise and she spun toward the dark.

Hold on . . . goddamnit hold on . . .

He cocked back his fist for another blow.

Here it comes.

Then a shape rose up behind Kaminski, silhouetted against the flames.

Frankenstein.

Bleeding badly, his face burned by blast and blackened by smoke, he fell on Kaminski, arms and legs wrapped around his body.

Kaminski kicked and screamed and clawed at the figure behind him, desperate to get free as a burning chunk of ceiling collapsed into the room.

Riley struggled to her knees, fighting to stay conscious.

"We have to get out of here," she said. "Let him go, he's not worth it."

But he only tightened his grip further, and as flames licked up the back of his neck and snaked into his hair, she saw pain in his eyes for the first time.

"Please!" she said, pulling at his arm. "Come with me!"

He shook his head as the fire pooled around them, forcing her back.

"Go," he whispered. "We—"

And before he said it, she knew exactly what was coming next.

"We . . . *belong* . . . dead."

Then his eyes reached out to her, where his seared and ruined body could not, and with a roar of pain and triumph he yanked Kaminski backward and they disappeared into the flames.

Riley tried to stand, but the smoke was too thick. She bent low and pressed her lips to the floor for air, crawling toward where she thought the front door was.

Then, in the distance: the sound of sirens.

Keep going, she thought as acrid smoke seared her lungs, pulling herself across the floor by her fingernails, inch by agonizing inch.

What if we're going the wrong way?

We're not. I think.

We're going to die, aren't we?

No.

Her nails tore out of her fingers as she clawed her way forward. Then the last inch of breathable air became choked with smoke and she couldn't see, couldn't breathe. The hallway swirled around her.

Okay, so . . . maybe we're going to die after all.

Then for just a second she felt cool air on her right cheek.

The door . . . it's that way . . . has to be.

She crawled to the right as another hint of air touched her face.

There! There it is!

The door!

She reached up as a firefighter almost stepped on her. "We got another!" he yelled, grabbing her by the arms and pulling her outside.

The parking lot was awash in red lights, and she fell to her knees, coughing out smoke. A paramedic ran toward her with an oxygen mask. "Breathe slow," he said. "Go easy!"

She sucked at the respirator, distantly aware of fire trucks and paramedics on this side of a police barricade, while protesters were held back on the other.

Police, she thought.

Have to get out of here, fast.

She pulled off the mask.

"No, you have to leave it on—"

"I'm okay," she said, and started to rise.

Then there was a hand on her arm.

Cop.

"You okay?"

"Yes, I'm—"

"We were told to separate staff and patients. I need to see some ID."

Near tears, she said, "I don't . . . I left it upstairs—"

He took her by the arm. "Then you'll have to come with me."

It's over, she thought.

"It's okay, officer, I can vouch for her."

She turned as Julian came toward them. "Debbie, are you all right?"

She nodded, not sure of the play.

"This is my assistant, Deborah Arwen," he said, then turned back to Riley. "I told you not to go back inside, there's nothing in there that can't be replaced."

The officer hesitated. "We were told to see some identification."

"Fine, here's mine," he said, and handed over his hospital ID. "I'm the Director of Inpatient Services, and Deborah has worked for me for five years. Good enough?"

The officer checked the ID, then looked to where some of the protesters were struggling with police. "Okay, fine," he said hurriedly, then rushed off to help push back the crowd.

"Thank you," Riley said when he was gone.

"Unnecessary. As I said, you don't belong here. I'm just setting the universe back on its proper trajectory." He nudged her face upward, examining the damage. "Your jaw looks like it's been dislocated. You need to get this fixed."

"I know, believe me," she said through the pain, then looked up at him. "*Arwen?* As in *Lord of the Rings*?"

"She reforged the sword that took down Sauron," he said. "I'm guessing that's Narsil sticking out of your waistband. Best if nobody else sees that."

She shoved the drives in deep. "Are the others okay?"

"As far as I know. I got here as fast as I could, I only live a few blocks down, but they were all in custody by the time I arrived. Now I suggest you clear out before the police come back with more questions."

"Thank you," she said again, and as she hugged him, she realized she was crying.

"You're welcome. Now get going."

Walking slowly to avoid attracting attention, she made her way past the fire trucks toward the crowd. The police were more focused on keeping everyone away than stopping anyone from leaving, so she was able to walk past them and disappear into the crowd until she reached a group of three women in protest garb watching the hospital come down.

"I need to get out of here," she said to the nearest one. "Fast and quiet."

They exchanged a glance that went from confusion to determination when they saw the bruises on her face. "Yeah, okay," the nearest said, "come on."

Fighting shock and nausea, Riley climbed into the back of their car and felt the world sliding away. *I hope they're not serial killers*, she thought as she passed out, *that would be ba—*

BOOTS ON THE GROUND

The next morning, after Riley explained her situation, Claire—the owner of the car Riley had passed out in and moments later, in a completely unremembered incident, threw up all over—said that she could sleep on the couch as long as necessary. She also explained that she was a second-year nursing student and volunteered to reset Riley's jaw.

"It's easy, it literally takes two minutes."

By minute twenty-seven, Riley was trying to figure out a way to casually slip off the chair so she could beat Claire to death with it, but just as she worked out the problem, her jaw abruptly popped back into place.

"There," Claire said, sweating and breathing heavily, "that wasn't so bad."

Riley nodded, too sore to talk. *You have no idea how close you came to being buried in the backyard.*

Using Claire's three-generations-back iPad, Riley checked in with worried friends, arranged for the drives to be picked up, then did a web search on the hospital fire to see what was being reported.

The first hit was a headline:

EDWARD KAMINSKI,
BELOVED AREA DOCTOR,
KILLED IN TRAGIC FIRE.

Beloved my ass, she thought, scrolling through the article until she reached the part she'd been searching for.

> As of this morning, police and firefighters were still searching the burned ruins of the hospital in search of an unidentified female patient who is still missing. Also killed in the blaze was Gerald Kane Jr., 26, institutionalized a decade earlier after murdering his parents.

The police booking photo showed the patient she'd known as Frankenstein, taken while he was still a teenager.

Gerald, she thought, trying to associate the name with the young man she'd come to care about. *Gerald. I wonder if he went by Gerry?*

Then she noticed the *Jr.* behind his name. *Jesus Christ. Bad enough he was tortured his whole young life, but to have to bear the same name as the man who did the torturing? No wonder he was desperate to become someone else. Better to be that monster than the one that shared his name.*

When a courier came by the next day, Riley hesitated at handing off the drives without doing a backup. She'd gone through too much to risk anything happening to them but she lacked the finesse and equipment needed to access the encrypted files without hitting a tripwire that might erase everything. But that didn't stop her from *saying* she'd backed it all up, just to be safe.

A week passed with no further word about the drives, but there was plenty on the news about *her*. By now the authorities were able to confirm that she'd escaped in the confusion, and her face was on every NPF website in the state.

"I can leave if you're worried about me staying here," she told Claire. "I don't want to get you in trouble."

"It's fine. Don't worry. Worst-case scenario, I'll say I never saw the photos, and you lied to me about the whole thing. I'll turn on you in a hot second, if you're cool with it."

"Yeah, I'm good. Go for it."

Two more days passed in silence.

What if there was nothing useful on the drives? What if all that was for nothing?

Another two days.

Then all hell broke loose.

It started before dawn, when her borrowed iPad began blowing up with text notifications.

> OMG RILEY HAVE YOU SEEN THIS?

> HOLY SHIT!

> IS THIS WHAT YOU WERE TALKING ABOUT?

> FUCK THESE FUCKING FUCKERS!

She clicked on the first link, and the screen filled with text.
Oh. My. God.

J. MICHAEL STRACZYNSKI

EMERGENCY DETENTION ACT
COVERTLY REACTIVATED

*Email Dump Reveals Administration Plans
for Dissident Internment Camps*

By Jasmine Visconti

New York Times Exclusive Report

In a series of emails and documents obtained by The New York Times and confirmed by sources inside the covert program who prefer to remain anonymous, President William Jacobs signed an undisclosed executive order in late February reauthorizing the Emergency Detention Act of 1950 with the assent of Senate Majority Leader Roger McInnis, Speaker of the House Elaine Trent, Attorney General Fred Forsythe and the Office of Homeland Security.

Conceived at the height of the Cold War, the Emergency Detention Act was passed into law on September 23, 1950, by a bipartisan vote of 286 to 48 in the House and 57 to 10 in the Senate. It gave the executive branch and the attorney general's office the authority to arrest and indefinitely detain dissidents without access to appeal, formal charges or attorneys in a system that operated independently of the judicial system.

These provisions allowed for the establishment of guilt by association, enabled administrators to decide on their own authority whether the protections granted by the First and 14th Amendments applied to the defendants, gave officials the right to designate defendants and their associates untrustworthy based on publicly expressed ideas or suspicions about future conduct, denied the right of cross-examination while allowing the participation of military officials in decisions of guilt and permitted the use of secret testimony by anonymous witnesses. Individuals convicted through this process would be held at military bases outside the jurisdiction of the penal code system and could only be released by an act of Congress or intervention by the office of the attorney general.

While the Emergency Detention Act was not utilized during the Cold War, provisions of the act have been cited more than once as grounds for the indefinite detention of United States citizens designated "enemy combatants" in the aftermath of the 9/11 attacks, a list that included José Padilla and Yaser Esam Hamdi.

Once the bill supporting the new executive order had been passed in a joint confidential session of the House and Senate Judiciary Committees, Attorney General Forsythe signed off on the program only after lawyers at the Department of Justice drafted a legal opinion justifying its implementation. The document drew heavily on the work of Mr. Thomas McGann, a consultant with Homeland Security, and clinical psychiatrist Dr. Edward Kaminski, who was quoted by sources as saying that the structure of the psychiatric community could be used to justify institutionalizing individuals determined to be mentally unstable and a danger to themselves and others, a subjective evaluative process that would operate entirely outside judicial review.

Clinical interviews with detainees could also be used to gather information about other dissidents that could be developed into charges against these individuals in violation of Miranda rights, the laws of evidence and Fifth Amendment protections against self-incrimination.

According to classified documents obtained by The Times, the Office of Homeland Security provided funding to Dr. Kaminski and Mr. McGann to create a pilot program that would provide proof of concept while eliciting information needed for further prosecutions. The Times has also confirmed that 37 abandoned military bases were being set aside as holding facilities, with more than a dozen already fitted out for occupancy.

Responding to these revelations, the American Civil Liberties Union and other civil rights organizations vowed to file legal challenges in federal court demanding an immediate injunction against the program's implementation. The ACLU also called for congressional hearings and the immediate release of all individuals currently being held under the umbrella of Mr. McGann's American Renewal Centers.

"This is the kind of thing we'd expect to see in the old Soviet Union or, currently, with the North Korean Sunshine Camps," said ACLU Executive Director Harrison Thorne. "The only good thing is that we found out about their plans before the final trigger could be pulled on these detainment camps. As we've seen in prior administrations, it's hard to reverse repressive policies once they become institutionalized in the name of national security."

In preparation for this article, The Times reached out to Mr. McGann for comment, but a spokesperson for his office declined to reply, citing the tragic death of Dr. Kaminski, who perished in a fire at the Seattle ARC facility Saturday evening. However, others who worked at the hospital, including Director of Inpatient Psychiatric Facilities Julian Munroe, Chief Nursing Officer Elizabeth Biedermann, and General Administrator Dr. Lee Kim expressed willingness to testify about alleged abuses committed under the authority of this classified program.

Elizabeth. Her first name's Elizabeth.

Nice to meet you, Elizabeth. Looks like you finally found a match and some oil.

Riley closed the article and flipped to Twitter as reactions to the news spiraled exponentially up the trend line, watching an entire country become enraged in real time.

Then, more incoming texts:

WE HAVE TO STOP THIS

DO WHATEVER'S NECESSARY TO KILL
THE PROGRAM

CAN'T LET THEM GET THIS GOING
OR WE'LL NEVER STOP IT

GET THE WORD OUT: MARCHES
PLANNED IN NY, CHICAGO, MIAMI

YOU IN?

Riley glanced at the trend line as the numbers grew, then back at the text.

YOU IN?

She put her fingers on the touchscreen keyboard.

I don't have to do this, she thought. *I've done plenty. Wouldn't it be nice to stay home for a change, watch it all on TV, let someone else carry the weight? After everything that's gone down lately, I've earned a break.*

You're right, she thought back. *Absolutely.*

"I'M IN," she typed back. "WHERE AND WHEN?"

You're such an asshole, the back of her brain said.

Yeah, I get that a lot.

The crowd rolled down Sixth Avenue toward Times Square in what the TV Talking Heads said was the biggest protest they'd seen in years; fifteen thousand voices raised in peaceful defiance of the rules of repression. Patrol cars and vans lined the street, surrounded by NPF squads in body armor, clutching shields, batons, tear gas launchers, and guns loaded with rubber bullets. And maybe the other kind.

But nobody turned away.

That was the last rule she'd been taught, in the days before her parents were taken.

Once you open the book on these people, you don't stop, you don't turn back, you keep going until you win. Doesn't matter how long it takes. That's what united our family across the years back in Ireland. You stood on the same corner as your father and mother, which was the same corner where their parents and their parents' parents stood, demonstrating for the same things: decency and fair dealing and humanity. It took four hundred years of families, united in hope, to push the English out of Ireland. That's twice the life of this country, spent in a single struggle. A lot of us fell in the process, but in the end we won.

You stay and you wear them down until the job is done, until there's peace, until the bully boys learn that using force against people doesn't work anymore, because it requires fear on the other side. The fear is always bigger than the actual threat. Once you stop being afraid, the threat falls apart.

Never stop. Never give up. Never despair. Never.

The burner phone in her pocket buzzed at her. She flicked it on.

> More police coming up 47th Street.
> Pass the word.

"Copy that," she typed back.

She closed the text window, pausing to look at the home-screen photo she'd taken in the storeroom that showed Frankenstein sitting beside her and smiling. *Thank you*, she thought at him, not for the first time, and certainly not for the last. *Thank you for being there when the lights went out.*

"Here they come!" someone yelled.

She slipped the phone into her pocket as the police line advanced toward them, shields raised, batons in hand.

Then she closed her eyes and took a long, low breath, feeling her parents standing beside her.

Riley Diaz opened her eyes and threw a fist in the air. "Boots on the ground! Bodies in the way!"

And fifteen thousand voices called back, "Boots on the ground! Bodies in the way!"

"Boots on the ground! Bodies in the way!"

"Boots on the ground!"

"Bodies in the way!"

Bring it!

ABOUT THE AUTHOR

J. Michael Straczynski is an award-winning producer and writer for television and film as well as graphic novels that have topped the *New York Times* bestseller list. His writing credits include hundreds of TV episodes, including *Babylon 5* and *Sense8*, and five major films including the Oscar-nominated *Changeling* (directed by Clint Eastwood) which earned him a British Academy Award (BAFTA) nomination for Best Screenplay. His extensive list of awards includes two Emmy's, the GLAAD Media Award, the Eisner, two Hugos, and the E Pluribus Unum Award from the American Cinema Foundation.

For more fantastic fiction, author events,
exclusive excerpts, competitions, limited editions and more

VISIT OUR WEBSITE
titanbooks.com

LIKE US ON FACEBOOK
facebook.com/titanbooks

FOLLOW US ON TWITTER AND INSTAGRAM
@TitanBooks

EMAIL US
readerfeedback@titanemail.com